PAINT ON THE SMILES

GRACE THOMPSON

ISIS

LARGE PRINT

Oxford

First published in Great Britain 2011
by
Robert Hale Limited

Published in Large Print 2012 by ISIS Publishing Ltd.,
7 Centremead, Osney Mead, Oxford OX2 0ES
by arrangement with
Johnson & Alcock Ltd.

British Library Cataloguing in Publication Data
Thompson, Grace.
  Paint on the smiles.
  1. World War, 1939–1945 - - Great Britain - -
  Fiction.
  2. Large type books.
  I. Title
  823.9'2–dc23

ISBN 978–0–7531–9058–6 (hb)
ISBN 978–0–7531–9059–3 (pb)

Printed and bound in Great Britain by
T. J. International Ltd., Padstow, Cornwall

CHAPTER
ONE

Summer visitors were beginning to come to the town, its beaches and shops and fairground a draw for families inland. The children gripping new, shiny tin buckets and spades heading for the beach seen only once a year, the youngest not quite sure what to expect, being given confusing descriptions by parents that made eyes shine with excitement.

Parents were already looking weary as they carried heavy cases and baskets, looking up addresses on pieces of paper as they searched for their rooms. Some had dogs on leads and a few carried birds in cages as well as the luggage.

Cecily and Ada had already been stopped twice by anxious fathers flagging down the car and asking for directions.

"We'll never get to the beach at this rate," Ada chuckled, driving around the corner and on to the road leading to the Pleasure Beach.

Cecily and Ada ran a shop selling green groceries and fresh fish and in recent summers had increased their business by serving the shops and tea stalls on the popular holiday destination. It was Wednesday and a half day. When the shop closed at one o'clock, they headed for the beach to visit customers, some of whom had become friends.

They parked the car then headed to find the green-painted stall to find Peter Marshall. He had seen them approaching and was pouring teas for them as they arrived. The sun had brought the crowds, locals as well as visitors, and Peter and his young assistant were kept busy. The sisters didn't stay long. Promising to see him soon, they left to wander around to talk to other stall holders, take a few orders and leave lists of all they could supply.

As they were leaving, Ada saw a dark, angry-looking man watching them and guided her sister in a different direction. Danny Preston was the last person Cecily needed to see.

"Cecily!" Danny shouted. His voice was powerful but the noise of children laughing, people on the fairground rides screaming and the loudspeaker warning people to behave drowned his voice. Ada hurried Cecily away. Danny had caused enough trouble with his jealous, possessive, tainted love for Cecily.

Since their father had died and they had been able to run the shop as they chose, they had been helped by two friends. Waldo Watkins ran a large and successful grocery store on the main road; Bertie Richards was a successful businessman buying properties, some of which he rented, some he resold. Bertie and Beryl and Waldo and Melanie came every week to examine the accounts and order books to make sure everything was running smoothly.

The following evening the four of them were due to visit once the shops closed and Cecily's daughter Myfanwy waited impatiently for them to arrive. She watched as her mother and aunt dragged the boxes of meal and seed in from the porch, squeezing past them and looking up the hill for the first glimpse of Edwin.

"Uncle Bertie and Auntie Beryl will bring Edwin, won't they?" she asked.

"Of course they will. They wouldn't miss a chance of you two spending an hour together."

"Can we go into the stables and play on the swing?"

"No, dear. It's better that you stay away until the building work is finished."

"That means forever! Why don't you ask Willie to get on with it?"

"There are other things to spend our money on. It's sound enough for the shop van and the car to be garaged there, so there's no hurry." The stable had suffered a fire, which although not serious had left the walls soot covered and made it an unsuitable place to use.

When the five visitors had arrived and settled in the small room behind the shop, Myfanwy asked again, "Uncle Bertie, when will Mam repair the stable?"

"No hurry, lovely girl. It isn't needed now there are no more horses."

"But it's a mess and I like to go there and play with the empty boxes, like I used to do when Grampa was here."

"Van," Ada said with a laugh, "that's silly. It's 1938 and you are fourteen years old! Grampa left us a long time ago."

"You do silly things sometimes. And I still miss Grampa, even if you don't!"

Cecily glanced at her daughter's expression and could see that another argument was brewing.

Ada gave a sigh. Everybody leaves us, she thought as Van left the room, banging the door behind her, Edwin following. "I don't think our Van will stay once she's old enough to move away."

"Of course she won't leave. She's difficult, I know, but she'll grow out of it."

Ada ignored the interruption. "Our Mam running away with the coal man, Dadda dying in an accident, Gareth frightened away from marrying you by his mam, and my Phil in prison for burglaries . . ."

"Oh, for heaven's sake, cheer up," Cecily said with a laugh. "We've still got Van and lots of good friends, especially dear Waldo and Melanie and Bertie and Beryl."

The men examined the accounts and the order book and nodded approval. "You are increasing your stock well," Bertie said, "but a lot of the things you hold are slow sellers. Are you sure you want to continue to sell these odd spices and things used only by one or two local cafes and boarding houses?"

Ada nodded. "We believe that if they ask and we can't help them, they'll go somewhere else and probably buy other things there too. So we try not to say no."

Cecily added, "If it's something we don't have, we promise it for later that day and Willie, our wonderful

4

stable boy, goes to get some. The time he spends isn't wasted if it keeps a customer we might otherwise lose."

The two men nodded approval.

"About the stable," Bertie said as they were collecting their coats. "It might be a good idea to get the place repaired properly and perhaps use it for storage. The fire didn't cause great damage — the shelves are gone and the floor between the stable and the loft above is gone but the rest is no worse than smoke-blackened wood."

"But we don't need more storage. We have the back room next to the kitchen and that's plenty."

"For the moment," Waldo added, looking seriously at Bertie.

"We're thinking that if there's a war, you might be glad of extra space — perhaps bulk buying so you have a start if things get scarce."

"But there's a risk of mice and rats if we store food, and also burglaries, if food gets scarce."

Ada's face stiffened with distress. "It's all right, my Phil is in prison — he won't be a danger."

"Oh, Ada, we weren't talking about Phil! He'll never do anything like that again."

"And Myfanwy has learnt her lesson about allowing strangers to sleep there," Cecily said hastily, to overcome the embarrassment.

Van had taken pity on two homeless people. They sang on the streets and had been thrown out of room after room. She had found them in the lane cuddled up together under a piece of tarpaulin surrounded by the bags and blankets that were all they owned. The skinny, crippled old man called Horse and his wife — named Honoria but simply called Wife — had to resort to sleeping in barns and even shop doorways, so Van had unlocked the stable door each night and allowed them to sleep there. One night, feeling confident that they wouldn't be discovered, they lit a small fire, luxuriating in the glow and the warmth. Then, becoming more brave, they cooked some sausages on a small paraffin stove. Full, warm and sleepy, they dozed off and as they slept the stove was kicked over and set fire to the boxes and papers that were carelessly stored there.

Gareth Price-Jones, who had once been engaged to marry Cecily, had been out on a midnight stroll to avoid another confrontation with his difficult mother when he saw the smoke. He and Willie, the sisters' delivery man, got the old couple out, shocked but unharmed, before the firemen arrived.

They spent a few days in hospital where they were cleaned up and fed, then a room had been found for them. Two weeks later they had vacated the room, scared of not earning enough to pay the rent, and were now back on the streets holding out a tin for coins.

Edwin and Van were sad that their idea of helping had ended so badly, wishing Horse and his wife hadn't been discovered and had enjoyed the shelter for many months more. For Edwin the plan had been kindly meant but for Van it was the pleasure of outwitting her mother that gave the plan its appeal.

Since she had learned that her Auntie Cecily was in fact her mother, her anger against Cecily hadn't eased. She dreamed of a revenge that was at that moment vague, knowing that one day an idea would come and her mother would know she had been the instigator. Sitting in the kitchen playing with the two cats, she and Edwin moaned as usual when told it was time for the visitors to leave.

Goodbyes were said, promises to meet were arranged and the visitors departed.

It was Saturday evening and the shop was closed for the day. Cecily and Ada were scrubbing the counters and putting the rubbish ready for Willie to take away. The fresh fish that hadn't sold they would cook for their supper, the few less than perfect apples and pears and bananas put in a box for children to help themselves. They didn't talk much, both wrapped up in thoughts of their future.

Ada wondered if today might be the day Phil changed his mind and allowed her to visit him. She desperately wanted to see him and assure him she would be waiting when his sentence ended. So far only his mother had seen him and she brought back little news of him. There was a letter on the shop counter, one of the many Ada had written but to which she received no reply. She would post it and hope it would be the one that finally broke down his resolve.

Even though it was mid-summer, the day was dark with rain threatening, making the shop, with its door blind down, seem even more gloomy.

Cecily became aware of voices and saw that outside there was a group of people talking in subdued voices. That the people outside were talking about them was in no doubt as they glanced frequently in their direction and at times spoke behind their hands.

"I wonder whether it's your affair with Danny or my criminal husband Phil?" Ada whispered with a sigh. "We certainly give them plenty to talk about, don't we? You seeing Danny Preston, even though he's married to Jessie, and my Phil convicted of burglaries."

There was a quiet tap on the door as the rest of the group walked away. It was Gareth's mother, Mrs Price-Jones. Cecily opened the door and the woman pushed her way in.

"Mrs Price-Jones. Sorry but we're closed," Cecily said, beginning to guide the woman back out of the shop.

"I just called to say I'm sorry about your Phil attacking a prison guard," she said, addressing the words to Ada, who stared in shock at the news she was hearing for the first time. "Lose any chance of getting out early now, won't he?"

"Phil, yes, he's so unhappy and I think anger against himself flares sometimes and he loses his temper." She prevaricated a bit more, hoping the information matched the story Mrs Price-Jones was so gleefully passing on. Why hadn't her mother-in-law told her what had happened?

She learned very little after Mrs Spencer visited Phil; she seemed to pretend he was ill and she had visited him in hospital, not the prison where he was serving a sentence for burglaries and assault. Anger towards her mother-in-law flashed and was gone. She couldn't blame the poor lady for the way she dealt with the disgrace and anxiety of her son's imprisonment.

Mrs Price-Jones obviously wanted to say more but Cecily firmly led her to the door. "How is Gareth?" she asked politely. "We don't see him so much these days."

"Gareth is fine. Happy and content with his business and meeting friends now and then."

"Yes, a barber is a steady job, isn't it?"

"More than a job! My Gareth has a high-class business."

Cecily smiled as she closed the door behind her. "I was sorry when my wedding to her son was stopped but imagine having her for a mother-in-law. We'd have had to leave the country or kill her!" She chattered for a while, giving time for Ada to recover from what had been a shock, then asked, "Did you know about this?" Then, as Ada didn't reply, she saw the look on her face and said, "You hadn't been told, had you? If Mrs Price-Jones and her cronies know, your mother in-law must. So why hasn't she told you?"

"She hardly says a word about Phil. When she's been to see him, she answers questions vaguely telling me nothing except that he's well and hopes I'll be there when he comes home. Assures me that he loves me."

"You must ask her about this. What if *she* doesn't know? Is there any way others could find out? Do we know anyone with a relative in the same prison?"

Myfanwy burst into the shop and nodded to her Aunt Ada and ignored her mother and went straight upstairs to her bedroom to change out of her tennis clothes.

The sisters finished cleaning and went to check on the casserole simmering in the oven. When the food was on the table, Cecily called her daughter, who came down and at once said, "What were you talking about that I can't hear? The minute I come in you two go quiet. I'm not a child and I don't like being treated like one!"

Cecily sighed. Van only opened her mouth to complain these days.

"Nothing to interest you, Van, lovey."

Ada disagreed. "We've just heard that your Uncle Phil is in trouble again. I don't know the details but if the gossip is correct, he was fighting and hurt a prison guard."

"Delaying his release, is he? He must dread coming home, to face you and all the disapproval."

"Van! What rubbish you talk! Of course he wants to get home. Longing to be back with your Auntie Ada where he belongs."

Van shrugged. "Auntie Dorothy thinks that he'll do something every time he gets close to . . . parole is it called? Early release he dreads and he'll do something to stop it."

"Dorothy told you? You knew about this and didn't tell me?" Ada was upset.

Van shrugged. "You never talk to me. How could I know you hadn't been told?"

"Your Auntie Dorothy is a wicked and very unkind person and I wish you wouldn't listen to her lies. She makes up facts and persuades others she knows more than everyone else."

10

"She doesn't stop talking when I appear," Van said defiantly, "and secrets are no better than lying. My own mother knows about that! Pretending to be a friend of my mother all these years."

Cecily tried to interrupt but Van went on, "And Auntie Dorothy wasn't lying, it's true. Uncle Phil is a criminal and he did hurt one of the guards."

Cecily rarely lost her temper with her difficult daughter, hoping that with tolerance on her part Van would outgrow her anger towards her, but now she stood up, dragged Van from her chair and pushed her to the door. "Go to your room and don't come down until you're ready to apologize to Auntie Ada. She doesn't deserve your wicked, ill-informed opinions." She hadn't raised her voice but her handling of Van was rough as she pushed her towards the stairs. She went back into the room, covered her face with her hands and fought against the sobs that threatened to tear her apart.

"You shouldn't have treated her like that," Ada said sadly. "These are my battles and it doesn't help me if they cause other battles between you and Van."

"Go and see Mrs Spencer. If it's true we'll deal with it, both of us, but if it's lies, I'll make sure everyone knows the lies were created by Mrs Price-Jones — encouraged, no doubt, by our sister-in-law Dorothy."

Ada shook her head. "I can't face her now. I need to calm myself or I might upset her by insisting she tells me what's going on. Wednesday, I'll go Wednesday." She picked up the evening paper lying unread and turning to the relevant page said, "Let's go to the pictures. Better than sitting here waiting for that stubborn daughter of yours to apologize."

"You're right, we'll be waiting forever."

Ada called up the stairs and Van came down after a lot of coaxing, red-eyed and subdued, and held a hand of each sister as they walked to the picture house.

Wednesday was half-day closing but Cecily and Ada had nothing planned. Nothing more had been said about Ada talking to her mother-in-law about Phil's attack on a guard. She had visited each lunchtime as usual, hoping to be told, but Mrs Spencer said nothing. So after closing the shop and eating a simple meal they went together to the cottage where Ada had lived with Phil and his mother until his imprisonment, after which Mrs Spencer had asked her to return to the shop and leave her alone. It was how she coped best, she assured a disappointed Ada.

Cecily didn't go into the cottage but walked a little further to call on Willie's wife and children. Willie had worked for them since he was fourteen years old and was an invaluable help. He had married Annette, the daughter of Cecily and Ada's widowed sister-in-law Dorothy, and worked for them in any capacity in which he was needed. He was also building a reputation for making quality furniture. He was partnered by Danny, once Cecily's fiancé but a man whose jealousy had ruined their lives. Danny lived near Willie and Annette but Cecily avoided looking in the direction of his house.

While Ada went into the Spencers' cottage, Cecily stayed with Annette, admired the children, drank tea, then wandered back. Ada was still inside, the door was firmly closed and, unwilling to interrupt what she hoped was a valuable, open discussion, she wandered around the small, colourful garden.

Almost hidden by climbing flowers and shrubs, she saw the workshop where Phil had carried out his printing business. The door was locked but the key hung outside and, idly curious, she went inside. Everything was neatly arrayed even though the police had searched the place for stolen items he hadn't yet managed to sell. Mrs Spencer's work no doubt. She was a person who loved to have everything neat and tidy, straightening things, even when there was no real need. The tools and machines were clean and there were no oddments of paper, no cleaning cloths as there would have been when Phil worked there. The windows were shining; any cobwebs had been brushed away. Cecily felt sad looking at the abandoned room and wondered if it would ever resound to the noise of the machines again.

She went out into the garden but there was still no sign of Ada and the door remained closed. After overnight rain, the clouds were still low and the air was chilly. She stepped back into the workshop and picked up one of Phil's order books. She saw their name in there, Owen's Grocery and Fresh Fish Shop. It was an order for letterheads and leaflets to distribute around the stall holders and cafes near the Pleasure Beach.

There was a page in the book she was idly examining and it was smudged and difficult to read. She put on the electric light and noticed that the bulb cable didn't hang straight. Mrs Spencer couldn't have noticed that, she smiled to herself, or it would have been straightened. Or perhaps she couldn't reach and had no one to ask for help. She knew nothing about electricity, the cottage was still lit by gas light, but it wouldn't hurt to take a look in case it was just something in the way.

She climbed up onto the bench and stared at the ceiling rose, afraid to touch, then she saw something glinting between the rose and the ceiling. She moved the light bulb holder on its cable a little to one side and the object became clearly visible. It was a small earring. With a pencil she eased it out and then realized there was more.

She stepped down, frightened by the implications of what she had seen and waited for Ada. When her sister came out with her tearful mother-in-law, Cecily refused tea and pulled her sister away. "What's the hurry?" Ada demanded. "And don't you want to hear about Phil?"

"Of course I want to hear about Phil, but Ada, I've found some jewellery. Remember there were two offences to which Phil refused to plead guilty? Two robberies that he insisted he didn't do?"

"Yes, one of them our friends, Bertie and Beryl. I knew he wouldn't have stolen from them."

"The other was Waldo and Melanie."

"So?"

"I sheltered from the cold in Phil's workroom and, I'm so sorry, Ada, love, but I think I've found the items that were stolen."

"Nonsense! Phil wouldn't have taken anything from our friends. And the police searched the place. If they were there they would have been found. Someone must have put them there! Someone wanting to add to his sentence."

When Ada had calmed down, they went back to the garden and, making sure Mrs Spencer was in the kitchen at the back of the house, slipped into the workshop. Together they eased out the jewellery that had been carefully and successfully hidden in a cavity in the ceiling behind the light fitting and spread it on the work table. There was no doubt who the pieces belonged to; they each recognized several.

"What do we do now?" Ada whispered. "I can't give it to the police. It would mean another trial and another sentence. I couldn't cope with any more. I want him home."

"Hide it again, but not in here. Then we'll think carefully about the best way of helping Phil."

"Thank you," Ada sobbed.

They took the jewellery home and found a place for it in the heavy old wardrobe in the room that had once been their parents' and sat in silence, each wondering about the best way of dealing with the discovery. Days passed and the problem seemed insoluble. They couldn't give it back to Beryl and Melanie without an explanation that they didn't want to give, and it seemed that every time they passed the bedroom door there were vibrations of disapproval coming from the large, old wardrobe.

The following Sunday, they went to the beach to try to forget the situation, even if it was only for a short time. The weather had improved and the sun shone bright and strong as they set off.

The smell of hot, damp sand met their nostrils as they stepped from the car. They chose to ignore the whispered comments and mumblings from people who recognized them but were well aware of the latest gossip they had engendered. The summer of 1938 had been good so far, rainy days and dark clouds quickly forgotten, rumours of imminent war ignored, as memories were being made of this wonderful summer.

Cecily smiled as she took off her lightweight coat. "It's a hot one. There'll be more in the sea than on the prom today." She picked up the basket, which contained Van's bathing costume, their sun hats and an inflatable beach ball.

"I wish we'd brought our bathers," Ada sighed. "Lovely it would be to sink into the waves."

"Buy one," said Van. "It's years since you two went into the tide."

Above the sound of cars pulling into the car park, they could hear the whirring and clacking and whistling of the dozens of rides in the amusement park. Above the trees shielding the cars from the road, the top of the figure eight could be seen, the carriages pausing at the highest point before swooping down leaving the screams of its passengers in its wake.

"Remember how we used to love that?" Cecily said.

"Yes, but the fun was not the ride but the excuse to cling to the boys," Ada said with a laugh.

"I think that sort of thing is childish," Van said, slamming the car boot for emphasis. "I can't understand how people can go on it and make such an exhibition of themselves."

Ada shrugged. "That's young people for you. Fourteen and already too old for fun."

"Nineteen thirty-eight isn't fun though, is it?" Cecily said as they walked towards the sand. "Everyone's anxious about the future. Things were more relaxed when we were your age, Van."

"D'you realize how old we sound?" Ada exclaimed when they were waiting to cross the road. "Talking like two old women we are and us not far past thirty."

"Most are married and settled with children an' all," Van said critically. "Missed the boat you two did, for sure, and that's why the past sounds so good — there was still hope for you then."

The sisters stared at her in surprise.

"I was talking to Edwin about it yesterday," Van went on. "He thinks that only unhappy people look back and say everything was better then."

"Oh, he does, does he?" Cecily looked at her daughter, an eyebrow quirked questioningly. "And what else did he say about us?"

"He says he loves you both but you aren't fun any more."

Crossing the busy road a reply was delayed, then, as they reached the wide pavement and the start of the stalls and shops, Peter Marshall called and waved. He had been waiting for them.

Peter had been a friend since they had first visited the traders to persuade them to buy from their shop, promising good prices and reliable service. He had been one of the first to become a customer and remained a friend.

"Peter, love." Cecily smiled a greeting and asked, "Where can we buy bathers? Ada and I want to go into the sea."

They chose simple identical costumes in red and bought white head-hugging caps to protect their hair. Walking through the established groups on the hot sand, they found a place where they could spread out their belongings and take possession for a few hours.

"You'll need this." Peter handed them a large towel and looked studiously at his book while the three of them took turns doing contortions under the towel, to emerge ready for the sea. He slipped off his shirt and trousers to reveal his woollen bathers of dark blue tied with a white cord.

Seeing him as an elderly man possibly a little overweight, Cecily was surprised to see how lean and fit he looked. His body was nothing like his rather fleshy face but strong and surprisingly youthful. She felt shy taking his hand as they ran between the scattering of people towards the distant sea. Peter looked back and offered his other hand to Van.

"Come on, Ada," he called. "Last one in is a cissy!" He laughed and the mood was set for a happy afternoon.

Used to seeing Peter either in overalls as he worked in his garage or in a neat suit with a shirt and tie, Cecily hadn't thought of him as anything else but a middle-aged man who spent most of his time in an office chair. A lovely, kindly man, a devoted friend but older than the rest of their friends. Now she saw a man who, although in his early fifties, was still young enough to enjoy a day out. She laughed then, beginning to see the day as one they would remember with pleasure.

They ran, stumbling on occasions as they wove in and out of families and their clutter. Strings of donkeys strolled across and barred their way, old men wandered aimlessly, selling balloons and flags, young men played football and were being shouted at by pot-bellied sunbathers. Then they were on the wet sand chasing the tide, which was as far out as it would go.

The air was cooler and they were glad to increase their speed to stay warm. The sand was a complicated pattern of ripples, hard ridges where water, warmed by the sun, was trapped, a treat for their feet. The subdued roar of people behind them faded to a hum as their feet touched the foaming surf. All this Cecily noticed as though for the first time. It was so long since they had enjoyed a day of simple pleasures like this.

Peter released their hands and, after running as far as he could, he threw himself into the frothy white waves. He surfaced and looked back for them. Van was the next to swim out to where he was treading water and jeering at the sisters' hesitation. He and Van coaxed and teased and laughed together until Cecily and Ada sank with gasps of shock under the clear water.

Then they swam and raced, disappearing underwater to appear alongside unexpectedly, splashing each other like children.

"Why haven't we done this before?" Ada gasped. "I'd forgotten what fun it is."

"Make sure you do it again, soon," Peter advised.

Peter took charge of that afternoon in July 1938. He organized a ball game after the swim, insisting it was important to get thoroughly warmed before getting dressed. They took turns to squirm about under the large towel to dress themselves, then, while they were combing their hair, he said, "I own part shares in the Golden Schooner. We'll eat there."

Van was right about Ada and me, Cecily thought as they packed the wet clothes. Since the court appearance, she and Ada had built a wall around themselves and were crouching behind it, afraid of allowing anyone inside for fear of being hurt. Fun had been firmly locked out.

Such troubled lives they had led. First their mother leaving them, then their father being killed in an accident on a grain ship, then her planned marriage to Gareth Price-Jones cancelled when Dorothy had revealed that she was in fact Myfanwy's mother. She knew the fault was hers in that instance. She should have told Van long before but she had been afraid of upsetting her — although finding out like she had was far, far worse.

And Ada's marriage to Phil, which had been so happy until he had been caught with the proceeds of a robbery, and through it all there was Danny Preston and their on-off love affair ruined by his unreasonable jealousy.

Peter had come into their lives soon after the death of their father when they were just starting to build up the business and coping with their grief and the troubles that followed. He was the understanding, uncritical, reliable friend they had needed.

Phil's arrest was a humiliation for both Ada and Cecily, less so for herself but an extra agony all the same, to be endured while people gleefully spoke of them as the ugly sisters — the ugliness not a factual description, more an opinion of their unsavoury characters.

During Phil's trial, Cecily and Ada had seen him shrink from the lively, optimistic, lighthearted man into a shell of skin and bone. The colour went from his cheeks and the laughter drained from his eyes. His appearance altered as the trial continued until, at the end, where he was given a custodial sentence, he was an old man without a sign of the fun-loving, cheeky character Ada had married.

He had remained unmoved and apparently unaware as his counsel asked that ninety-eight cases be taken into account. It had been explained to him that it was wiser to face them all now, rather than come out of prison and face another trial and sentence if further evidence had come to light. Two charges he had denied.

Ada had comforted her mother-in-law, who refused to believe it, even when Phil himself told her it was true. She was particularly shocked at the stories of violence against three people who had caught him on their premises and had suffered injuries as he made his escape.

Bringing her mind back to the present on the summer beach, feeling the warmth of the sun, hearing the laughter of children, she smiled at her sister encouragingly as though she had shared her melancholy thoughts.

Van was in front walking with Peter as they made their way up to the restaurant on a rocky headland where windows looked out over the sea. They ate crab salad and fresh fruit and drank a bottle of wine, which, as they rarely drank, made both girls a little sleepy. Van, to her chagrin, was given lemonade.

"I feel as if we've had a holiday," Ada said, lazily stretching. "Thank you, Peter, for a lovely day."

"Perfect," Cecily agreed. She looked at her daughter. "Don't you agree, Van, lovey?"

"Yes. It's the sort of day my friends have often." The censure in her voice was the only cloud.

Peter walked them back to the car as families were packing up to go home. The donkeys were gathered ready to be taken back to their field and an evening meal. Shutters were going up on stalls on the sand and the balloon seller had fallen asleep against a wall. The midget cars were still doing a good trade and the shops selling fish and chips had queues outside as hunger drove the people from the beach.

Cecily looked back as she drove away from the car park to see Peter still waving. He appeared to her then to be a lonely figure, standing in the lengthening shadow of the trees. She turned the car in a circle and called to him, "Come for lunch on Sunday?" He happily agreed.

"He loves you too," Van sulked. "There's Danny, Gareth, Peter *and* my father. They all love you and you still aren't married."

"Hush, girl," Ada admonished.

Since parting from his wife in 1935, Danny Preston had continued to live in the house next to Gladys Davies, near Willie and Annette. Although he hadn't wanted a child, knowing he had a daughter, now almost three, distressed him dreadfully. He had tried repeatedly to see her but Jessie's mother refused to let him in.

"The divorce agreement doesn't include you seeing little Danielle," the sharp-faced woman insisted. "Go away or I'll call the police."

"But she's my daughter."

"You've never behaved like a husband so how can you know how to be a father?"

"I pay for her, don't I? And generously too. More than the courts decided was fair." He often resorted to anger in the hope he could bully her into letting him spend some time with his child but it never worked.

"In fact," he admitted to Willie, "I think it only makes her more determined to keep me away."

"Give it time, Danny. Jessie might relent as Danielle grows up. At least paying as you promised you'll keep some sort of contact."

"Unless Jessie marries again."

"Plenty of time to worry about that when there's cause. No hint of another man so far." Willie put down the heavy plane he was using and patted Danny's shoulder. "Come and have a cup of tea with Annette, then we'll try this new window for size."

Danny was a postman and Willie still worked at Owen's shop, but with Annette dealing with the office work, their own business was flourishing. Both men worked well with their hands and could tackle every aspect of house repairs. When they weren't working on the pieces of furniture for which they had a steady list of customers, they were kept busy with small repairs. They filled every moment and apart from the hours spent in his room, where he felt the loneliness of his bachelor existence, Danny was as content as Willie.

He put down his tools and followed Willie to where Annette was making bread. She put it to rise near the fireplace and smiled a welcome. Her plump arms were floury and there were smears of flour on her rosy cheeks. Willie felt a lump in his throat as he looked at her from the doorway. She made him so utterly happy. He still marvelled at his good fortune.

Her eyes and nose wrinkled as she blew him a kiss. "Ready for a cuppa, are you, boys?" She gestured to the black, highly polished oven range, where a white tea towel covered some freshly baked Welsh cakes. "Saw you coming so the tea's ready to pour — help yourselves."

"Thanks, love," Willie said, reaching for the plate.

"Welsh cake for Victor?" a small voice asked.

"Hello, Niblo." Danny smiled as Willie picked up his son, asked if he'd been good and rewarded him with a cake.

24

When tea was poured and the two men were sitting one on each side of the oven range — "Like Toby jugs," Annette often said — Willie made an announcement.

"We are all going on holiday," he said. He picked up Victor and, ignoring the butter which transferred itself from the boy's hands to his own face and hair, went on, "All of us, Danny as well. What d'you think of that, then?"

"A holiday?" Annette frowned.

"Yes, we're all going to a place in west Wales, for a whole week. It's a proper hotel near the beach where Victor can bathe every day and learn to swim."

"But are you sure? Will the sisters give you the time off? And will it be all right to leave the house for a week?"

"Can I please have another Welsh cake?" Victor asked.

He was given another cake by Willie, who explained, "We've all worked hard these past years and I think it's time we had a reward. Danny, you will come, won't you? We'll have a great time. I've already asked the sisters and they've agreed. All we have to do is pack the car and go."

"When?" Annette asked. She looked around her urgently as if already deciding what to pack and what she must do before they left. "How soon will we be back home?"

Willie and Danny laughed so loudly that Victor ran to his mother, startled by the sudden noise. "We'll stay a whole week and the house will be here when we get back."

"Things are looking bleak," Willie said when he and Danny were back working on the replacement window. "All this talk of war. Damn me, we ought to get away and have some fun while we still can."

All through 1938 there had been regular war scares and the town was preparing for the worst. From lectures by the St John's Ambulance and gas mask drill to discussions about insurance in case of bombing, all the talk was about the imminence of war against Germany.

Back in May, war manoeuvres had taken place, with the army, navy and air force testing the strength of the town's defences. Searchlights lit up the night skies, a hundred planes flew over, Avro Anson and Hawker fighters displaying their ability to defend the country from attack. And a thousand new planes had been ordered for the RAF.

There were appeals for volunteers for the fire brigade, air raid wardens and ambulance drivers. Both men and women over forty were asked to come forward for training.

"They say Hitler will attack as soon as he's got the harvests in and that's why I decided we should have a holiday; it might be our last chance for a year, or longer. The last one went on for four years, remember."

"I think you're right," Danny said. "Who knows where we'll all be this time next year."

That evening when Victor was sleeping, Annette began to write out a shopping list for the following day.

"I'll need a few more clothes for Victor," she said to Willie, "in case I can't get any washed."

"Buy whatever you need." He leaned over the table, the first thing he had made, and squeezed her arm. "Annette, my lovely girl. We can afford it. Go on, treat yourself to something nice as well. Right?"

She blushed, her eyes glowing in the low light in a way that made Willie's heart lurch with happiness. "I'd better not buy a dress, Willie. It might not fit me for long." she added shyly. "We're going to have another child. Isn't that wonderful?"

For an answer he picked her up and ran around the room with her in his arms. "My lovely, clever Annette," he said, then kissed her soundly.

The following morning when her daily tasks were done and a stew was cooking on the hob, Annette set off, with Victor in his pushchair, to the shops. In the department store where her mother worked, she met Beryl and Bertie Richards. She had known them all her life and called them auntie and uncle.

She knew how much Bertie had helped Willie when, as a young man without family to back him up, he had been in danger of drifting into a life without prospects or hope of making a place for himself. She had often tried to thank them and now, filled with the excitement of a new baby and the prospect of a first holiday away from home, she stopped them.

"Hello, Auntie Beryl, Uncle Bertie. Are you busy for half an hour? Could you come and have a cup of tea with Victor and me?"

Bertie frowned. "Nothing wrong, is there? You look a bit worried."

"I'm so happy I could burst!" Annette laughed. "I would just like a chat, if you have time."

Annette waited until they were seated in a cafe and had been served with teacakes toasted and liberally spread with butter, and a pot of tea. She told them first about the new baby and the holiday then she became more serious.

"I just wanted to tell you how much I appreciate the way you helped Willie, Uncle Bertie. He was only an errand boy for the sisters, not related in any way. Yet you helped, advised and set him on his way, showed him he could make something of himself. I'm so grateful and, well, I love you both." She smiled, feeling self-conscious now she had said her piece. It had sounded wrong, too formal. She was surprised to see how touched Bertie was by her words.

"My dear girl," he said. "Helping Willie was the most worthwhile thing I ever did. And, d'you know, I didn't do that much. He'd have grown up and away from the limitations of his childhood without any help from me, you can be sure of that. I can't have you thinking I'm responsible for his success — it was all his own effort. Remarkable man, your William Morgan." He patted her head and Victor's as though they were both children. "He's a lucky one too."

"Why did you help him? What could you see in him that made you believe he was worth the helping?"

"My dear, he was alone. His family had left him to shift for himself. I wanted to be sure he had a reason to get up in the mornings. And another thing. I've been very fortunate in this life. Very lucky. It isn't a bad thing to pass on your luck, share it by helping someone else who needs a bit of a bunk up the ladder. And, before you say it, I'm not religious, trying to make my place in heaven! I just think it isn't a bad thing to say thank you to life."

When they left the cafe, Annette kissed them both and went on her way, looking very thoughtful. She was carrying a parcel of new baby clothes which Beryl had insisted on buying. She was thinking about Bertie's words and wondered whether his philosophy of helping someone to say thank you would work for her, too.

She caught the bus but didn't go home. Instead she headed for the beach. It was a pleasant day; a gentle breeze cooled the warmth of the sun and made walking from the bus to Foxhole Street a pleasure.

Victor, having eaten more cake than the adults, dozed in the folding chair. Annette hummed as she walked, slightly nervously, to her intended encounter, with Bertie's words running through her head. Repaying life for her good fortune. It was more sensible every time she repeated it.

She knew where Jessie Preston lived, with her mother just a few doors away from where she had lived with Danny. Leaving the pushchair with its sleeping passenger at the gate, within sight, she knocked on the door.

"Jessie," she said. "I want to talk to you. It's about a holiday Willie is planning," she added hurriedly as the red-haired girl began to close the door. "It's all paid, a little treat for you and Danielle. A week in west Wales, it's near the beach. It sounds lovely. Will you come? I've taken the liberty of booking a room for you. It won't cost you anything; accommodation and food, all paid. You can get there by train easily."

So far Jessie hadn't said a word and Annette felt her words drying up.

Still wearing a suspicious frown, Jessie opened the door wider and invited Annette in. Collecting the pushchair with its sleeping passenger, she stepped inside. Jessie's daughter was sitting at a small desk, chalking on a framed slate. Annette smiled and was rewarded with a wave.

"I can imagine what it's like, back to sharing everything with your mam, no real home of your own, living through and through, with your mother making the decisions. I just thought you'd enjoy a week away, just you and Danielle. Here's the address." She took out the card and waited while Jessie copied out the details.

"You're sure this isn't some scheme of Danny's?"

"Danny knows nothing about this," Annette assured her, fingers crossed against the part truth.

"All right. I'd be a fool not to, wouldn't I?" She sat on the edge of the table. She hadn't invited Annette to sit. "You're right, I do need to get away, be my own person for a little while. Thank you. Can I ask why? Sorry for me, are you?"

"How could I be sorry for someone with such a beautiful daughter?" She smiled at the dark-haired girl watching them solemnly. "I just think that when life is good to you — as it's been to me — it's nice to pass on some of your good fortune. But you won't tell anyone, will you?" She spoke earnestly. "I mean, passing on good luck isn't so people will tell me how generous I am. People knowing would spoil it." She handed her a ten shilling note, part of the money Willie had given her to buy what she needed for the holiday. "This is for the train fare."

Victor began to rouse and Annette wanted him out of there. She promised him an ice cream if he stayed in the chair a little longer. She hurried him away, hoping he wouldn't mention the visit to Willie, or worse, to Danny.

They called to see Peter Marshall but he wasn't there so she caught the bus home. There were letters to write, and postal orders to send. She didn't know what she'd do if the hotel had no other vacancies!

Phil Spencer looked an old man. His hair, always thin, was cut very short and was a yellowish grey. The yellow was caused by the cigarettes he now smoked. He spent most of his day, apart from work and exercise, in the small cell shared with another burglar and, although the man wanted to compare notes and share knowledge and past errors, Phil refused to discuss his criminal "career". All he wanted was to get out and see if Ada meant her promise to be there waiting for him.

Yet as the time approached, he was frightened. Prison had been a completely new world and he'd had to learn its rules and esoteric laws.

Returning to the old world, facing people who had been friends, noticing changes that had happened while he'd been away, would again be entering a strange world, its rules needing to be relearned. The prospect kept him awake at night. When he had hit the guard, he'd felt shame but also a relief that the day he went out had been delayed.

There was a letter on his bunk from Ada and as usual he stared at it without opening it for a long time. Afraid to read that she was leaving him, saying goodbye. As his fingers touched the envelope flap, his eyes blurred with panic and he couldn't read the words for several minutes. It was only when he had skimmed through it, and found nothing but concern and love, that he would settle and absorb every precious word.

The routine of each day was a torment. They would see an eye through the peephole, then the key would turn in the heavy lock and they were allowed the artificial freedom of walking down the catwalk with the night soil, all in a line, trying not to look at the filth they carried. They shuffled along at a regimented speed between the cell wall and the wire mesh covering the open area between the cells and those opposite. The walls were brick, painted with so many coats of paint over the years the joins hardly showed.

Even in the exercise yard there was nothing to see but bricks, and his mind often wandered to pretend he could see people on the other side, going about their normal, perhaps boring, lives. Passers-by were so used to the gaunt buildings with the high, windowless walls they hardly noticed them and certainly never gave much thought to the men inside.

He knew he would never forget the smell. It permeated his clothes and oozed from his skin, a part of him forever. How could he go back to Ada, his sweet-scented wife, and share a bed with her, touch her, kiss her, make love, smelling like this? There were times when, if the wire hadn't prevented it, he would have jumped, hoping to end the painful sojourn in death. The railway line wasn't far away; perhaps, when he was released, he could end his life there?

He fiddled with the most recent letter, thinking of Willie and his family going on holiday. If he got out with his mind intact he would never want to go away. He was lost in the agony of his situation, staring at the wall, behind which was that other world. His thoughts became distorted, with fact and imagination becoming confused.

Ada was huge and he was small, then Willie was shouting at him for upsetting the sisters, then he was down in a well, the water rising and Cecily looking over the top and laughing. Voices all around him were chanting "worthless, worthless" and he was agreeing with them when the man sharing the cell shook him awake and he hit out at him, just as he had when the guard had done something similar. His companion sat him on the edge of the bunk and, wiping blood from his face, urged him to calm down.

When he heard the small metallic sound that told him the eye was there, he watched and waited for the rattle of the key and jerked his troubled mind back to the present to eat yet another prison meal.

CHAPTER
TWO

Cecily and Ada had asked their cousin Johnny Fowler to help them while Willie was on holiday. He was unemployed apart from an occasional evening on the taxi and was delighted to be asked. He still looked the same gangling youth who, eight years before, had helped carry their father's coffin and walked ahead of the funeral cortege, Cecily thought. His thin brown hair was still plastered down and sticking out in a stiff fringe over his ears, refusing to follow the contours of his bony dome.

"It's stuck there like a piece of badly woven cloth," she whispered to her sister. "Poor dab, you'd think someone would tell him."

"Best if he goes to Gareth for a decent haircut. He'd give him a bit of style if anyone can," Ada suggested. "Gareth is good with difficult hair."

Cecily felt the remnants of regret at the mention of Gareth Price-Jones. If she had been honest and told him that Van was her daughter, they might be together now. They had been happy days: building the business, dancing and planning her wedding. She stopped then, remembering Van's unkind remark that only unhappy people looked back and said the past was good. Nonsense, of course, but . . .

"I said we should suggest it," Ada said, obviously not for the first time.

"Suggest what?"

"Suggest that Johnny goes to Gareth for a decent haircut."

"Yes, that's a good idea, but how do we tell him he looks a sight?"

Johnny came in from the beach deliveries, having called into the fish market on the way home. He smelled strongly of fish although he had only carried the wooden boxes.

"We'll make you a cup of tea before you go out again, while you wash your hands."

"It's not my hands that stink of fish," he groaned. "It's leaked all over my coat, and there's me going out this evening straight from work!" His Adam's apple wobbled in indignation.

"Where are you going?" Ada asked.

"To Cardiff to see a show. Taking a girl I am and now I'll have to meet her stinking of fish!"

"Tell you what, Johnny, there's an old coat of Dadda's in the wardrobe and we'll treat you to a smart haircut at Gareth's."

"It was as easy as that," she told Cecily later.

They persuaded him to leave before the shop closed, insisting they could manage for the last hour, and watched him stride up the hill to the main road, his long skinny legs looking more spider-like than ever in the too-tight trousers and the too-large coat.

It was raining and they were glad to close the shop. The rain darkened the buildings, bringing them closer and making the night oppressive, and they were glad to block out the dull, chilly evening.

"Imagine those people still working at the beach." Cecily shuddered. "They stay open for as long as there's a chance of a customer. Lucky we went last week with Peter, there might not be many more days left for bathing this summer."

Waldo arrived at 7.30. He'd been asked to call by the sisters, who had a plan to put to him. He looked ill. Waxy faced, but with spots of high colour on his cheeks that made the pale skin even more alarming. Fatigue showed in his eyes but he seemed cheerful and full of enthusiasm, as always.

"We want to buy the shop next door," Cecily told him. "We can't carry the stock we're selling in large enough quantities to get the best price. Everything goes so fast we even have to collect from the wholesalers on the way to make deliveries sometimes."

"An extra few rooms would make it easier, specially as you advise us to carry greater stock," Ada added. "What d'you think?"

Waldo looked doubtful. "I can see the sense in what you're saying, but there are other points to consider. Everything goes up. Rates, heating, insurance, and why pay to hold stock that the wholesalers will hold for you for nothing? Use the stable, leave the van outside if necessary; that will cost nothing extra."

"We thought of renting out the top floor to cover the extra expenses," Cecily explained.

36

"More responsibility, and you two have enough already. Phil will be home soon, Ada, and he'll need more of your time, not less. And you, Cecily, will be on your own, with Van. No, I think you should expand but not like this. If you open another, separate, shop, get someone to run it as a business, then if there's a war you'll be in a stronger position."

"You really think we'll fight against Germany again?"

"Hitler became chancellor as far back as 1933. He announced the intention of destroying or driving away all the Jewish people and developing a one-party system and no one attempted to stop him when he became dictator in 1934. Earlier this year he took control of the army and still no one tried to hold him back. He's all set to take on the rest of Europe and his country is behind him. His promises are impressive and his people look upon him almost as the finest leader they had ever had. I can't see anything less than full-scale war stopping him now."

It was a long speech for Waldo, and Cecily found it distressing, not because of the contents but for the way Waldo had to keep stopping to take a breath. She hardly heard what he actually said.

"Won't Chamberlain talk him round?" Ada asked.

"Maybe, for a time, but don't underestimate the danger. Yes, I think you should invest in a second shop, diversify if you can. This business is bound to suffer."

The sisters were gloomy as they made tea and offered Waldo some of his favourite cakes. Then Waldo seemed to cheer up and asked, "And how is young Van? Where does she fit into your plans?"

"Van is fine. She and Edwin planned to play tennis this evening but the weather changed that to table tennis," Ada told him.

"She doesn't want to stay on at school," Cecily said. "We've tried to persuade her. She was wrong to take a place at the grammar school if she had no intention of staying. There were others wanting her place, girls who'd make better use of it."

"She's talking about working with Dorothy and learning about fashion. Such a waste of her qualities."

Waldo shook his head. "Not necessarily. She'll succeed at whatever she does. Perhaps the world of fashion will interest her even if she does stay on."

"If you're right about there being a war," Cecily said gloomily, "how much fashion will there be in khaki uniforms?"

They were both waiting for Johnny the next morning to see his haircut. Ada saw him first and she groaned. "It's like a smaller piece of badly woven cloth," she reported. "Poor dab. There's one who'll benefit from premature baldness!"

Johnny had something on his mind. He wanted to tell the sisters but was afraid of putting it badly and upsetting them. He compromised by telling Van.

"I saw your gran last night," he told her.

"Where? Have you found out where she lives?" Van was excited. "Oh, I'd love to see her. D'you think she wants to see me? If I went without telling Mam and Auntie Ada?"

"I know where she's living but I can't decide whether or not to tell the sisters."

"Not!" Van was emphatic. "Please, Johnny, tell me and let me see her on my own before the others find out. Please, Johnny."

"That boyfriend of hers was with her," he said, giving himself time to think, "and his son."

"Happy is she? Without us?"

"She seems different. The son, Paul Gregory, was about twenty and looks a bit of a handful. Tough as a mad gorilla he was, with sinews like steel hawsers. He's been in the army since a young boy, so Auntie Kitty — your nan — told me. They asked us to go back for supper, me and my girlfriend, Cleo."

"Cleo? Cleo Robbins? Is she your girlfriend, Johnny?" Van chuckled at the thought of her cousin courting. He'd always been a source of amusement and it was hard to imagine him taking a girl out, especially one she knew.

"We've been going out for a couple of months, until last night. Now she's going out with a big, bull-necked bloke called Paul Gregory!"

"You let this Paul Gregory steal your girl?"

"Glad I was really. She started looking at furniture shops and jewellery." His Adam's apple went into top gear and a faint blush drifted across his angular features. "Hey, what am I telling you all this for? Not old enough yet, you aren't, Myfanwy Owen."

"Neither are you by the sound of it!"

After a great deal of pleading, Johnny agreed to take Van into Cardiff to see her grandmother and also not to tell the sisters. Johnny was not completely happy about this but Van was hard to argue with when she wanted something really badly.

When they reached the small house in a road near the canal, Johnny knocked and insisted Van waited around the corner while he asked Auntie Kitty if she would see her. When she knew her granddaughter was near, Kitty ran to greet her and almost lifted her off her feet in a wild hug of joy, although Van was taller than her.

Johnny walked along the canal bank, looking down into the greenish, glutinous water while they talked. When they caught the bus with their story of a visit to the museum well rehearsed, Van sat silently gloating over the secret which she intended to keep from her mother and aunt. Finding Gran was her secret, something to be cherished, a private possession safe from interference, Johnny her unwilling accomplice.

"It's Gran's wish that they aren't told," Van told him several times on that bus journey. "You've got to promise not to tell." So he promised and the secret remained intact, and Van kept in touch with her grandmother without anyone else finding out.

Outside the holiday cottage in the little village in west Wales, Danny was checking on the fishing. He had driven most of the way to the hotel where Willie had booked a week's stay and, leaving Willie and Annette to unpack and settle Victor in, he'd taken his rod and set off to explore the river running alongside the delightful property.

There was no one else staying at the hotel, although the manager had told him another booking had been made but not yet filled. He wondered idly if there would be another child for Victor to play with.

He walked slowly, looking around him, enjoying the peace and quiet, listening to birdsong and the occasional slap as a fish jumped out of the water after a fly. At thirty-five he was still a handsome man, and he kept that carefree gypsy look that women found so fascinating. His figure had thickened a little but the dark hair was as black and curly as ever. The earring with which he showed defiance of convention glinted in the sun.

This week had been a good idea on Willie's part and already he felt the tension easing from him. The shock of Jessie's divorce and her initial refusal to keep Cecily out of the notoriety had been a nightmare. This week was the perfect opportunity to forget it and refresh himself. Willie's family were good company even if they were a constant reminder of his solitary state. They made him aware that he was alone, with no one who cared a pig's bristle for him.

He walked for several miles along the bank of the river, noting the deep pools where large fish might lie and seeing from the pattern of worn grass where feet had walked and fishermen had stood, casting hopefully into the dark waters. Further up, where the river ran through woodland, the river was deep and wide. In a small clearing he came across several coracles lying upside-down, the smell of tar evidence of their recent maintenance. There was a smell of rotting bait too. He could see where unused worms had been thrown carelessly towards the water, some getting caught on the branches.

A water rat scuttled through the grass and stopped to chew at a freshly discarded morsel. The water ran swiftly past, sleek and smooth, its surface hardly showing a ripple as the rat slipped in and headed for its home in the bank.

Danny left the coracle station, having decided to return in the early morning to watch them set off. He would love to try and manage one of the fragile craft but thought it unlikely they'd agree.

"Caught any fish, then?" Willie called as he walked back into the hotel.

"No. Nice walk though. I think I'll go down early tomorrow and see if one of the fishermen will let me try one of the coracles."

"My brother is one of the coracle men," the landlord told them. "In fact, he caught the lovely Sewin you're having for dinner tonight. Shall I have a word with him?"

So it was arranged for Danny to have an early call, an early breakfast and maybe a trip on the river.

He went to bed but didn't sleep straightaway, allowing the sounds of the strange house and the nearby river to settle around him. Muffled voices from the room next door gave him moments of self-pity, in which he felt envious of Willie, his plump wife and small son.

Cecily should be here with him. Cecily with whom he shared a love neither would accept. She was independent and he couldn't help wishing her father had left the shop to that brat Owen, the son of the unpleasant Dorothy. There would never be a time when Cecily would settle for a quiet life; she would always want a new challenge, a goal to achieve. He believed he could learn to cope with all that, though. It was the easy way she had with men, flirting and driving him to anger, that he found so difficult.

Perhaps he should have settled for Jessie. She was the antithesis of Cecily: quiet, submissive and patient. But she was so irritating he found himself wanting to hurt her deliberately by being sarcastic — something she couldn't cope with — and treating her unkindly when she didn't deserve it. Best he stayed away from her, but now, lying all alone, he wished she were with him. Darkness is a large space to fill when you're lonely.

The friends ate separately, Danny rising early to meet the coracle men and leaving before Willie and Annette came down, although he heard the lively chatter from their room, reminding him of how early three-year-olds awoke. A stab of jealousy trapped in his thoughts from the previous night jolted him as he passed their room with his rods and the box of tackle. He sighed it away. A good day stretched out before him.

He was welcomed by a young man who earned a precarious living from the river and after a lot of wobbling, and two soakings, he managed to sit in one of the wildly bobbing boats and find the point of balance. He was glad he was attached to the bank by a strong rope. There was no possibility of fishing!

"Spent five years at sea I did," he told the young man. "But I never tried anything like this. It's like sitting in a bowl of jelly!"

"Let her take you, don't fight her," he was advised. "Sit tight, relax and you'll soon get the feel of her."

"Sit still? Man, I daren't move! How do I paddle without going arse over tip?" But the men had moved off. They were willing to give him a ride but not generous enough to miss the tide which raised and lowered the river so dramatically. He watched them until they disappeared, marvelling at how easy it looked to manage the unstable craft, then hauled himself back to the bank. Although he was a strong man, the struggle with the unwieldy boat had exhausted him. He sat for a while before finding the strength to walk back to the hotel. He was too tired to fish, or to think about Jessie and Cecily. He'd thought of nothing but the boat during the busy and enjoyable hour.

The others were in the garden when he reached the gate. "Hello, young Niblo," he called to Victor, who came running to greet him.

"Poo, Uncle Danny, you smell of fish!" Victor laughed as he was swung in the air. "I bet you didn't catch one though."

"Damn me, you should have seen the giant salmon I wrestled with. Never seen a bigger one, not even on the fishmonger's slab!"

He talked to them for a while then went into the hotel to change. As he was about to open his door, the door next to Annette and Willie's snapped shut and a gasp made him turn.

"Jessie!" he said in disbelief.

It was Jessie who recovered first from the appearance of her ex-husband. "So, it was you behind all this!"

"All what? What are you doing here?" He stepped towards her. "Where's Danielle?"

"I've just put her down to rest. She's tired after travelling. It was a long journey and tomorrow we'll have another one! Straight back home! Don't think you can trick me like this, Danny Preston!"

Her face, usually so calm, was bright with anger and he felt a wave of deep sympathy and affection for her. "But, Jessie, what are you doing here? Did you know I'd be here? Is that why you've come? Who told you? What d'you want? I've tried time and again to talk to you at home and your guardian dragon wouldn't let me in. Is that why? So we can talk about us and Danielle without interference?"

She didn't answer any of his questions, just staying quiet until he fell silent, then said, "I'm going back home at once. If there was a train to take me I'd leave now but as I have to wait until the morning, I'll stay in my room until then. Please, Danny, go away."

He was shocked at the vehemence of her words. "It was at my instruction that Mam wouldn't let you near me or my daughter." She turned and fumbled with the key, trying to unlock the door, and Danny took the key and turned it. As she went in, he followed.

"Please go," she said. "I don't know what you hoped to achieve by this trick but it won't work."

"It's no trick," he said. "I'm as surprised as you." He was alarmed now at the harshness of her expression, the tightness around the once-generous mouth. He had done that. He was responsible for the change in her. He went to the single bed, needing to get away from the reproachful stare in her eyes, away from the inimical accusations showing in their depths. Danielle was sleeping peacefully, unaware of the anger that filled the air in the small room.

Pain showed on his face as he watched the dark-haired sleeping child. His child. "Jessie, I don't want to hurt you any more than I already have. I've done enough damage to this little sleeping beauty. I won't stay or cause a fuss but please explain why you're here. Don't tell me this is a coincidence that you arrived at this hotel this particular week."

Jessie hesitated, her mind grappling with the confusion his appearance had caused. When she had arrived she had hoped her fears of some unexplained and unwelcome reason for the invitation were groundless and she was simply going to enjoy a pleasant week. Then, just as she began to relax in the luxury of the unexpected holiday with Willie and Annette, Danny had appeared, wild, untidy and smelling of the clean, fresh country air, like some demon king shot up onto a stage.

She thought of Annette and guessed the idea had been her attempt to help, a genuine belief that confrontation far from home would give them a chance to sort out their differences. Kindly meant but misguided.

"I think someone meant to be kind," she said at last, in a voice nearer to normal. "Kind but misguided," she added, repeating her thought.

"But who?"

"I don't know for certain, but I was offered a free holiday. I think whoever did it thought we might be glad to talk privately and far from any interference." The harshness was back in her voice as she added, "They were wrong, I'm sure you'll agree."

Danny had been standing, looking down at the sleeping child. He sank into a chair and stared at her. The curtains were drawn across the window and she stood very still in the shadowy room.

"I'll go," he muttered. "I don't see why you and little Danielle should be deprived of a holiday. If someone 'kind but misguided' arranged it, you shouldn't turn down the generous offer. I only wish I'd thought of it myself," he added quietly.

"And you didn't?"

"No, Jessie, I didn't."

Even in the poor light he saw a slight pain cloud her eyes as she asked obliquely, "Are you alone?"

"Yes, and no." He smiled for the first time and leaned over to look again at Danielle. "I'm with Annette and Willie and little Victor. So, alone and not alone, depending how you mean it."

"I — I don't want to see them. I'll stay here until the morning, in my room. Will you take a note down for the manager? I'll ask for a car to take me to the station for the early train. Until then I'll stay out of sight."

"No, Jessie. Don't do that, please." He stood up and looked down at her and a flood of tenderness engulfed him. She was so vulnerable. Small, defiant and surprisingly fierce. "Stay, come down and have a cup of tea with us all. I won't bother you. You have my word on that. Just stay and enjoy the week. Annette is good company and Danielle will have Victor for company." He hesitated, watching her face to see if his persuasions had any chance of success. "I'll go if you prefer, but if you allow me to stay I'll be off fishing most of the time so I won't embarrass you. Don't say anything to the others about how you got here, just put it down to one of life's remarkable coincidences. Please, Jessie," he coaxed when he saw she was wavering. "Better than going back to your mam, isn't it?"

"I do need a break," she said, and before she could reconsider Danny went to the door.

"We'll go and tell the others. So pleased they'll be."

"Danny," she said firmly as the door opened wide, "this isn't a change of mind."

Danny nodded, lowering his head in case she saw the gleam of hope in his eyes. Jessie and Danielle! Someone of his own. With Cecily far away and with little hope of her ever coming back to him, he'd settle for second best — if he could persuade Jessie to do the same. Lifting the sleepy little girl, they went down to meet the others. Willie greeted Jessie with a surprise that Danny thought was genuine.

For the rest of the day they stayed together, Annette and Jessie formal and rather ill-at-ease, Danny showing nothing but pleasure at the unexpected arrival of his daughter and ex-wife. When the two children began playing together, it seemed the week would be a success.

"How did you work it?" Willie asked Danny suspiciously but Danny assured him the idea had not been his.

The following day, Danny went to wander along the river and fish as he had promised Jessie, but he found no pleasure in the solitary activity and returned early to the hotel. There was no sign of the others and he sat in the garden under a tree and waited for them to return.

"Hello, Danielle, hello, young Victor," he called as the children ran through the gate, barefoot, dusty and sun-kissed. "Been to the beach, have you?"

"No, Uncle Danny," Victor called, running to hug him. "We've had a picnic in the woods."

Danny sat with a child either side of him and listened as they told him of the small brook where they had paddled and splashed, and the birds they had seen, which Jessie had identified for them.

"Why don't you come with us tomorrow?" Victor asked.

"Yes," Annette agreed, "it's good fun watching the antics of these lively characters discovering things we've known and half forgotten."

"Well, I . . ."

"Yes, Danny. Why don't you?" Jessie said, relieving him of his promise.

So he agreed and the rest of the week was one of the happiest times he had known.

On the morning they were leaving, Danny suggested he travelled back with Jessie and Danielle to help with their luggage.

"No, Danny." Jessie's voice was firm and he saw the cold look was back in her eyes. "Nothing has changed. It was a lovely interlude and I'm grateful to whoever arranged it for me, but it's over and I'm going back to Mam's."

"But Jessie, it's been so good."

"It was a holiday. Today we return to reality with all its problems. Please don't make a fuss, Danny, you promised."

Her small hands packed away their days together, closing the lid on their brief reunion with a firm click. His sense of failure drenched him in melancholy. Why couldn't he make a success of love like Willie?

First there had been Cecily, who loved him but whom he tried to change from the person he'd been attracted to, now Jessie, who he had deliberately driven away in the hope that he and Cecily could begin again. Wrong decision all the way; now this. Someone had given him a week to play happy families and he'd failed again, failed to impress Jessie with his willingness to work at their marriage. His acute unhappiness gave a need for honesty.

"Jessie," he asked as he took the case from the bed and dropped it near the door, "tell me the truth. What is wrong with me?"

"Truthfully?" She looked up at him, her blue eyes bright, clear and tempting him to bend his head the short distance to look into them while his lips found hers. Sensing the desire, she stepped away. "You,

Danny, have a love-hate relationship with Cecily Owen. You can't make up your mind which is the stronger."

"But here, this week with you and Danielle, it's been wonderful and —"

She raised a small hand to interrupt, moving towards the door as if to escape, he thought sadly.

"If we tried again," she said, her face closed against his pleading, "Cecily would only have to call for help, or plead for you to come back and I'd be left all over again."

Since Phil's imprisonment, and Ada's return to the shop, Cecily had kept her very busy. She determinedly filled as many hours of the day as possible. Besides the hectic hours when the shop was open, every week they went to the pictures, sometimes twice. They also went to many of the summer entertainments during the two months of the holiday season, when the town was host to thousands of visitors.

On their half day, instead of staying in and dealing with the bookkeeping, they went to the beach or the park when the weather was suitable and Van went with them. Peter, too, when his business allowed.

There were tea dances and at several of these they met Gareth, with their sister-in-law, Rhonwen, and her daughter Marged too. Marged was now a pretty twenty-year-old, still giggling constantly as Gareth patiently showed her the steps of the popular dances.

They watched as Rhonwen and her daughter tried to master the simplest steps but unlike Cecily and Ada, they had no skill and were content to watch.

On evenings when they didn't go out, and when Van and Edwin joined them, they often pushed the furniture back in the big room above the shop and danced to records or the wireless. Cecily shared with Ada the dances of sentimental songs like Hoagy Carmichael's *Stardust*. Also *I Get Along Without You Very Well*, particularly poignant at that time.

They went on picnics too and one day they began as a party of four and ended up with fourteen. Ada had risen early that Sunday morning and had already packed their wicker hamper with food and drinks when Cecily and Van rose.

"Come on," Ada said, smiling, "it's going to be a lovely day and we're going to the rock pools." That was a stretch of beach on the far side of town.

"Can Edwin come too?" Van asked.

She didn't add that if he didn't she wouldn't go either, but Ada recognized from the scowl that a confrontation would spoil the day.

"Of course, lovey, you ring and invite him and we'll pick him up on the way."

Van phoned, then ran out. She returned an hour later with Edwin and his parents.

"I phoned Melanie and Waldo," Beryl said. "They're coming too."

"Might as well invite Dorothy and Owen," Ada said. And then Annette and Willie were brought by Waldo and soon there was a procession of cars containing thirteen people heading for the chosen spot.

"Damn me, there are thirteen of us," Bertie said.

"I'll get Danny," Willie said at once. "There'll be plenty of food."

"Good," Bertie agreed. "I don't fancy starting the day with thirteen."

Amid teasing, he turned the car. Cecily crossed her fingers, hoping he would be out. Danny's company for the day was something she did not want.

No one had bothered to make sandwiches; they had packed loaves, butter, cheese and jars of fish paste and jam into their baskets. Ada had packed cakes and biscuits and a supply of bottles to fetch water from the tap for the necessary cups of tea. They would make a bonfire from driftwood gathered on the beach. There were two kettles plus teapots and twists of paper holding sugar, tea and salt. Dorothy had brought a tablecloth and some salad wrapped in a tea towel. Annette had packed extra cups and plates.

It was a breathless, rosy-faced party that eventually clambered down the rocks to their chosen spot with all the paraphernalia of the day out.

Danny — who much to Cecily's dismay had come with them — and Willie chose a place for the fire. The tide was on its way in and below the place they had chosen to sit. The children helped to gather wood from the irregular line of the tide's ending. Van and Edwin helped Victor build a sandcastle before the incoming tide drove them back up to the rocky plateau where they would eat.

With the fire burning satisfactorily, even if clouds of smoke had caused several of the party to change their position, Danny and Willie filled the kettles at the tap high about them on the cliff path and set them to boil. Ada filled extra bottles to replenish their supply. Some splashing occurred, causing riotous enjoyment for Victor who was shrieking and laughing at Ada's attempt to keep her feet dry.

Annette and Willie stared at their son with amusement and wondered why children felt the need to shout when they were out of doors.

Cecily knew she couldn't ignore Danny for the whole day, but was angry with Willie for inviting him. She tried to behave with him the same as she did with the others, and helped him build a cairn of stones to protect their food from the sun. As usual it failed to stop the butter melting but they always tried.

They were some distance from the others when Danny said, "Cecily, I want to talk to you."

"Let's enjoy the day out. Can't we pretend for a few hours that we're nothing more than casual acquaintances? Look at them all, expecting a happy relaxed day. Don't spoil it for them."

"Did you arrange for Jessie to be at the same hotel when I went with Willie and Annette? Was it you who planned a grand reunion for me?"

"What are you talking about?"

"Someone booked a room for Jessie and Danielle at the same time we were there. Was it you?"

"Don't be ridiculous. Why would I do anything for Jessie after what she did to me?"

"Someone did. They must have hoped that spending a week together, without her mother interfering, we might have come together again."

"And did you?"

"I felt happy seeing Danielle every day and knowing she's mine. I was tempted to try again, just for the pleasure of being a family, like Willie and Annette, but no, it didn't change anything. I'm a fool, and I hate knowing my foolishness has ruined three lives — four with Danielle, growing up without a father in her life. What can I do? It's you I love and —"

Cecily stood up, pushed him away and moved towards the others. "No, Danny. You want too much of me. You can never be happy with me unless you tie me in chains and I'm not the woman to enjoy that!"

Willie was walking up the narrow path to refill the water bottles again and as Cecily ran off to sit with Ada, he had overheard the last exchanges. Danny was still sitting by the food cairn when he came back down with the filled bottles.

"Why can't I be happy with a woman like you are with Annette?"

"Cecily's right, man. You ask too much."

"Annette is different."

"So am I!" Willie sat beside Danny, one each side of the cairn of stones. "Look at us, like two Toby jugs again."

He tried to laugh Danny out of his solemn mood but Danny replied, "I can imagine me in twenty years, sitting beside a fireplace like a Toby jug, but it won't be my fireplace and there won't be another Toby jug opposite me."

"Come on, face facts. How can you expect a successful woman like Cecily to become the dull little housewife to please you?" He didn't expect a reply and gestured to where Owen was sitting beside his mother, munching a fish paste and lettuce sandwich. "Look at Dorothy — she wouldn't be pleased if you and Cecily married. She thinks her Owen will inherit the shop as long as neither of the sisters have a child. She discounts Van as an illegitimate daughter with no claim on what their father left them."

"Too much time has passed. Cecily is thirty-seven and I'm older. Little chance of a child if we did marry. Dorothy can forget that particular worry."

The beach party divided itself up into couples, Danny and Willie sitting away from the rest as if they were guardians of the food belonging to a shipwrecked crew on a desert island. Cecily and Ada were sorting wood into sizes for the fire. Bertie and Waldo watched the simmering kettles and arranged teapots ready to be filled. Beryl and Melanie chatted like the good friends they were and Van climbed down the rocks towards the lapping waves with Edwin, searching for limpets to use as bait when the tide filled.

Van threw the last limpet into the bucket and, after depositing them with Willie and Danny, climbed up to the tower of rock that, from a distance, looked like the crumbling ruin of a castle keep. Thrift, wild spinach, samphire and grasses grew in the crevasse and droppings from thousands of sea birds decorated the ledges. Edwin followed her and sat beside her.

They stared out over the sea, a darker patch here and there as small clouds threw shadows on the surface. There was little to disturb the tranquillity. What surf there was was hidden by the rocks which over-hung, cut away by a million storms.

There was a companionable air around them, a comfortable ease and a sense of belonging that might have given the impression they were brother and sister if it weren't for the complete contrast in appearance. Edwin was heavily built and already showing his father's tendency to loose-fleshed features, but it didn't suggest weakness or lack of fitness. He looked self-assured. His calm stillness and size belied the fact that when necessary Edwin could move fast, and think with a speed that impressed.

To Van, he was the reliable and constant anchor in her life. Edwin was completely trustworthy and someone who, unlike her mother, had never let her down.

Van was graceful, her slim, tanned figure turning many an eye. Although topping her mother by an inch or two, she had small hands and feet and her features were delicate. Her blue eyes lacked the calmness of Edwin's dark ones, and now her gaze moved nervously around, resting first on her mother, then on her aunt, wondering if she would ever forgive them for their deceit in denying she was Cecily's child, and thinking she would not.

"Shall we swim, later?" Edwin suggested. "We might as well get the most out of the occasion. The sea's calm and warm and with food to greet us when we come out, perfect."

"Uncle Waldo brought potatoes to cook in the ashes. Just think, Edwin, most children have days like this all through the summer, while for me it's an occasion."

"Aw, poor you!" he teased, then added, "Your family have the shop to manage and summer is their busiest time, remember."

"I resent my mother," Van said quietly. "I didn't have a normal childhood. I was cheated out of it by my mother pretending she was no relation for all those years. And I still don't know who my father is. Can you imagine what that's like? Not knowing who I am? It gives me nightmares sometimes, wondering if I've inherited traits that will make me a criminal, or send me crazy before I'm thirty."

"Look in a mirror, Van. That's who you are. Whether your father swept roads or worked in a slaughter house or was a professor in some fine university doesn't matter — unless you allow it to!"

Van continued as if she hadn't heard him. "Being passed from pillar to post, never going on picnics except when your mam and dad or Uncle Waldo and Auntie Melanie took me. Never going to the beach for a day of fun."

Edwin was laughing, trying to disperse her mood of self-pity. "You can't say you never go to the beach!"

"All right, I can't say never, but look at those over there." She pointed to where a group of about thirty people were sitting, the sound of a mouth organ floating across to them with the smoke from their fire. "Not like them. Belonging. Having a proper place."

More seriously, Edwin said, "There's a lot in your life people would envy, Van."

"Whenever I went out I was dressed up like a fancy cake without a plate to sit on."

Edwin laughed loudly then. "Van, you are an idiot."

"Frills and ribbons like those over there would never believe. And fancy white ankle socks and ankle-strap shoes in black shiny leather." She was trying not to laugh. "Not daps I could run around in without making a sound, but shoes that clacked all the summer through so everyone knew it was me coming. I did envy my friends their freedom from socks and their daps."

"Shame. Pity. Poor you." Edwin was still laughing.

"I hate my mother," she said, sobering him up immediately.

"Van, you mustn't say that — or think it."

"No father, no gran, a mother who doesn't care. One day I'll pay her back and make her sorry for what she's done to me."

Deciding it was safer to treat it as a joke, Edwin laughed again. "Oh, Van, stop it or you'll make me fall from this rock." He was relieved to see a smile beginning to curl her lips, but her eyes didn't soften. One day she would have the means to punish her mother for the way she'd treated her.

"Do you miss your gran?" he asked.

"Yes, and I miss Grandpa. He listened to me and read to me and told me stories about the big ships that come from all over the world to our docks."

"It was sad that he died."

"I miss seeing his boots. Every night he'd take them off to climb the stairs and leave them on the fender. I sometimes expect them to be there, with some spilt ash near them from his old pipe."

"Come on, let's have that swim."

Several of the party swam, diving off the rocks, and when they were back, with their towels spread to dry in the hot son, they ate. Food was shared, everyone accepting hungrily everything that came their way.

"My potatoes aren't cooked," Waldo said sadly. "We'll have to have them later."

"Can I try one?" Owen asked, holding out a hand.

Dorothy slapped his hand down. "No, Owen. You've eaten plenty already!"

"Pig," Van hissed, just loud enough for Owen to hear.

Danny ate very little and sat apart from the rest. He wandered off to a part of the beach where few went. The surface was uneven, not the levels of flat rock as on the rest, but rough and difficult for walking. Out of sight of the others he took off his clothes and swam naked in the cool refreshing water. He swam strongly and then when he grew weary, trod water and looked back, unable to see a soul. He swam back lazily and climbed out and sat, ignoring his nakedness, for an hour.

His thoughts were sombre. The sea stretched to infinity, almost silent now and empty, like his life. He imagined rather than heard the shouting and laughter from family gatherings like the one he'd left. He had no one who cared about how he felt, or spent the slightest effort to please him. And it was his own fault.

His body longed for Cecily yet his head knew they were incapable of creating a warm, loving atmosphere to keep them safe from whatever life threw at them. He forced his mind to create a picture of her that was less than desirable, trying to quell the aching void within him. They were incompatible and he must accept that if he were to move on. He stood, deciding that he would make his excuses and leave, even though it meant a long walk back.

He was stiff with the effect of the sun, which was stronger than he'd realized, with the sea breeze caressing his skin. He strolled back and saw Cecily standing apart from the others, shading her eyes and watching him approach. His resolution fell from him like the water as he had climbed out of the sea.

"Danny," she called, "we were getting worried."

"Cecily, I hate being alone. Come back to me, please, love. When this divorce is finally settled, we'll get married."

"Danny, this is stupid."

"I won't want you to change a thing. Dance if you want to, flirt if you want to, just stay with me."

"I don't —" Cecily began to protest but he hushed her with a finger on her lips, playing with them, watching her face with such intensity in his dark eyes that she felt her breath flow suddenly inward, like a cry.

"Do anything you want, be anything you want, Cecily, my love, my only love. Just come home with me. We've wasted so many years. Will you?"

She took his arm and they walked back to where Waldo was proudly handing out baked potatoes with blackened hands. Owen was already eating his but the others were jiggling them about, laughing and pretending to be burnt by the hot food.

"Hot potato, that's what you are, Danny Preston," Cecily said smiling. "But equally as irresistible. Yes, we'll give it another try to be *friends*," she emphasized. "Only friends, nothing more. Right?"

He kissed her lightly then, in sight of the others. Van looked away, disgust distorting her young face. Others oohed in a teasing way but Dorothy stood and said, loudly, "Cecily this week, is it, Danny? How did you enjoy your week with your wife? Not enough for you to have one woman, is it?"

Annette reached for Willie's hand. "Mam!" she said in distress. "How could you?"

Danny kept a hand on Cecily's shoulder, his fingers gripping her firmly to stop her moving away. "Was it you who arranged that meeting, Dorothy?" he asked angrily. "Well, it didn't work. And Cecily knows about it, so your attempt to bugger things up this afternoon won't work either!"

"No? Not when the solicitor knows how you and Jessie spent the week together? The divorce will still go through, will it?"

Everyone was silent. The shouting and laughter from nearby families seemed like an echo of the happiness they'd enjoyed and which was now shattered.

Waldo touched Dorothy's arm and whispered something. The potato she had been holding fell, and Owen, apparently unaware of the tension around him, picked it up and began eating it.

A cloud appeared over the sea and raced towards them, a crowning finish to the day that had started so well. They all began gathering their things, refilling baskets with the untidy remnants of the picnic. Waldo and Bertie threw sand over the fire, which smoked and spluttered as it died.

"Well, Dorothy," Waldo said quietly, "that's another beautiful thing you've ruined with your vicious tongue. Aren't you ever going to learn to be quiet?"

"Not when I can harm the sisters! They stole that business from my son."

"Who? Old get-up-and-go there?" Melanie looked towards the overweight, podgy faced boy who was eating the last of the potatoes, which he'd rescued from the ashes of the once-glorious fire. "And what would he do with it if he had it? After he'd eaten the contents, that is!"

"He's as capable as those two of managing a shop," Dorothy retorted. "He's been with your husband long enough to learn to run it properly. Sharp he is, my Owen. Your husband will tell you."

"Oh, yes. He tells me how sharp he is. Sharp at getting out of any real work!"

Cecily didn't speak to Danny again. She pushed him away every time he tried. She watched him carry Victor up the rocky path and get into Willie's car. Why did she punish herself by dreaming, if only for a moment, that she and Danny could ever be anything but a disaster?

Danny told stories to Victor on the way home, making them all laugh as he dragged humour from everything and anything to hide his inner torment. He knew he'd made the wrong decision again and it had blown up in his face. If he hadn't been persuaded to join the picnic he'd intended to go to Foxhole Street and try again to arrange to see Danielle. No chance now with Dorothy reporting his every move.

Perhaps it would be better if he did what Jessie had advised and went away, leaving them both in peace. Peace was something he seemed unable to find for himself.

Cecily and Ada were artificially cheerful as they went back to the shop. Van didn't speak, her disapproval showing on her face, and when they got back to the shop she went straight to her room. Ada pleaded a headache and went to bed early. Cecily unpacked the sad remains of the lovely day that had been ruined by Dorothy. Although, she admitted to herself, the day was really spoilt by Danny. Always Danny. Whenever he appeared he ruined everything.

She wished then that they had thought to invite Peter. Danny was synonymous with disaster but Peter was her shield against all her stupidity. The one uncomplicated person who made everything all right. It would all have been different if Peter had been with her. The significance of that thought kept her awake for a long time.

CHAPTER
THREE

Van told her mother she was going shopping with friends but instead of walking up to the main road, she went down to the railway station and caught the train for Cardiff. They wouldn't expect her back before late afternoon. She went past the house where Willie's mother and sisters lived and on to the house she was now visiting regularly, to see her gran. The fact that she had found her was a secret from her mother and Auntie Ada and that alone was a delight. What was also very pleasing was the way she had convinced Gran that the sisters wouldn't welcome her if she tried to make up the long-lasting rift in their relationship.

"I've tried," she would tell her gran with what looked like sincere regret, "but they get upset if I suggest looking for you, and insist they wouldn't speak to you if you met." Then she would comfort the old lady and promise she would never stop coming and bringing news of them.

When Kitty left their father, Owen, she had written many times but each letter had been intercepted by Owen and destroyed. Birthday cards and gifts had been thrown into the ash bin; Christmas gifts treated in the same way. He had convinced the sisters that their mother simply didn't care.

The fire was burning brightly in the neat, well-furnished room where Gran waited for her. It smelled of polish and the welcome was as bright as everything else.

"Darling girl, lovely to see you. I've made some of your favourite cakes and Mr Gregory has made you a little gift." She handed Van a package, which when opened surprised her with a cleverly carved kitten. Van hugged her in delight. "He knows how you love cats," Gran said proudly.

When Mr Gregory came home, Van told him how pleased she was with the gift.

"Perhaps I should make a second as you have two cats," he said.

"I wish I had a father to make me things," Van said sadly. "Gran, you must know who he is. Why won't you tell me?"

"I don't know, lovey, so I can't tell you."

"Am I like him?"

There was a brief pause. "How can I know? I haven't met him." She frowned. Was Van sharp enough to try and trick her? she wondered. "You're like your mother," she added.

"No. Don't say that. I'm not like her and I hate it when you say I am. She lied; said I was a daughter of a friend."

"Having a baby was considered a shameful thing and everyone tried to persuade her to go away, have you adopted so no one would know."

"Why didn't she?"

"Because from the moment she knew, she wanted you."

"She still pretended."

"People could be so unkind."

Changing the subject, unsatisfied with the responses, Van asked, "Why didn't you go to Grampa's funeral?"

"I did go. I sat at the back of the church and no one recognized me."

They sat and ate the meal her grandmother had prepared, and the three of them talked more freely and laughed a lot, and Van was smiling when she left to get the train home.

Gran smiled sadly as they waved her goodbye. "We have these conversations so often and I don't know what to say to help her to understand."

"Growing up, more experience of life, that's probably the only way she'll understand. Something will happen to disperse the bitterness in her heart," Mr Gregory said. "It might have been easier if Cecily had told her earlier perhaps. Children usually accept what is their life without question."

"Maybe. It's certain that Dorothy blurting it out as she did was the worst possible way for her to learn."

In the shop, Ada was sorting through the post. There was a letter from her mother-in-law and she opened it in haste. "Something's happened to Phil," she muttered, panic making her fingers struggle with the envelope. She read the brief letter and then read it again more slowly before handing it to Cecily. "Phil's coming home next week," she sobbed.

Later, when Ada had calmed down, Cecily asked, "What shall we do about the jewellery and money we found?"

"I don't know. She doesn't even tell me the exact time that he will be home. He won't even let me be there to greet him. I seem to have lost my marriage completely. He's gone back to his mother. What an unbelievable situation. How do I get out of this? Why doesn't he want me to be the person waiting for him? To be the first person he sees when he steps through that door?"

"Go and see her. She must see that it's important for you to be there. Tell her you want to know the exact time of his release. She can't forbid you to be there."

Ada went down to the cottage where his mother lived and an hour later she returned, hurt and tearful. "Phil was released from prison two days ago and tomorrow he will be coming home at four o'clock. He's been staying at a boarding house, giving himself a chance to rid himself of the smell of prison, she told me. Buying some new clothes too."

They discussed it for a while and decided to take the stolen items and go down to wait for him the next day. Ada didn't altogether trust his mother so, while Willie stayed in the shop, they went to sit with Mrs Spencer at three o'clock.

They heard him coming and Ada's heart was racing as she prepared for her first sight of him. She held the bundle of jewellery in her hands, still unsure how she would approach the revelation of their discovery. Her strongest thoughts were the loving greeting which she would have to share with his mother and Cecily.

She stepped outside, her arms ready to enfold him, but instead of running to her as she had imagined in her dreams, he ignored her and went first to the workroom and looked up at the light fitting. Disappointment and hurt, then anger, enraged Ada. Why hadn't she been his first thought after all these months? She ran across to the workroom and threw the jewellery and the notes in front of him. "Phil, is this what you're looking for?"

His mother followed her out and gave a scream.

"They're mine," he said in a low voice. "I paid for them."

"Paid? Not stolen? Mrs Watkins and Mrs Richards gave them to you, did they?"

"Paid for with the time I served in that place. They're mine."

Mrs Spencer gave another scream, grabbed the jewellery, ran back and threw the items onto the fire. Phil stepped inside and stared at it with no apparent concern. "I paid, the insurance paid, so how can you say it isn't mine?" He reached with some tongs and the poker and pulled them out, tipping coals onto the hearth while his mother stared at him.

Ada left the cottage and walked with Cecily to where they had parked the car. Nothing was said during the short journey and when they got back to the shop, Willie reported a few queries and orders for the next day, and went back to the stable to continue with his work.

"It's as though none of it happened," Ada said later, when they were preparing their meal. "My marriage to Phil, living with his mother, the happy times, then the arrest and imprisonment, it's all a horrible dream."

"I shouldn't have gone with you, Ada, love. You'll see him tomorrow and everything will return to how it was, you and Phil happy together."

"I sometimes think we should sell this shop," Ada surprised her by saying. "I'm not really superstitious but Dorothy has ill-wished us ever since Dadda left it to us. We've had nothing but bad luck."

"Bad luck, you call it? I call it Dorothy's vicious interfering. *She's* our bad luck, not our small inheritance."

"I mean it. If we didn't have the shop we'd be free to have some fun."

"Running this place *is* fun. Besides, where would we live? You'd go back to Phil and his mother but what about me and our Van?"

Later that evening, Van was out with Edwin and his parents, and Cecily and Ada went out to put some empty boxes into the stable. They looked around the smoke-stained walls and the charred beams where the upper floor had been burnt away. The loft had only been used for storage but it would be handy if they were going to increase their stock.

"We ought to think about getting this properly restored," Ada said. "Willie and Danny would do it. Willie has already worked out costs."

"I don't want Danny working here," Cecily said, then she stopped and listened. She smiled as they heard voices singing hymns, recognizing the strong voice of Horse and the tinny sound of his wife accompanying him. They opened the small door in the large stable door and looked out. The couple were sitting on the ground in the lane, eating what looked like cold soup from tins.

"Evening, miss," Wife said, waving her tin of tomato soup. Her mouth was like a cartoon with the lips and beyond bright red from the food.

"Wait there," Ada said and ran back to the house to give them half a loaf and some cheese.

The homeless couple had been responsible for burning the stable but aware that the cause of the blaze was mostly down to Van, the sisters had not accused them of starting the fire, insisting they had left a lamp burning. They were thankful that the couple had been unharmed. "Van did it because she enjoyed having a secret from us," Cecily said. "I worry sometimes that her resentment towards me will spill over and cause some serious trouble for us."

"She's young. What harm can she do? She'll soon be too busy having fun to worry about upsetting us."

"I'm not so sure."

"So we'll talk to Willie about replacing the loft floor?"

"Yes, and I suppose I'll have to accept that Danny will be helping. They work together, don't they?"

Willie had removed most of the debris from the fire and he and Danny made a start on cutting away the damaged beams and measuring for replacements. Danny delivered post each morning and worked in the afternoon. Willie joined him in the evenings and at the weekends when he could, but the Pleasure Beach was keeping him busy with deliveries during the weeks of high summer. So it was mostly Danny who was there whenever Cecily looked out of the back kitchen window, and Danny whom she heard singing as he worked.

"At least he's more tuneful than Horse," she commented dryly.

August Bank Holiday was warm and sunny. Cecily rose early and took a cup of tea in for Ada and for Van, who was already dressed when she went into her room.

"Edwin and I are playing tennis before the day gets too hot," Van explained.

Van was growing into a long-legged bronzed beauty. Her blonde hair shone with health and she was proud of it. She brushed it regularly and washed it frequently so it fell in gentle curls about her heart-shaped face. Her eyes were sky blue but with a touch of scorn in them which Cecily found disconcerting but the boys loved. The small mouth was perfectly formed but also wore a suggestion of discontent. Although this didn't detract from her attractiveness either, Cecily realized, only adding to the appeal she had for all the young men in her circle of friends.

She wondered idly if Van and Edwin would stay together, or whether the separation when Edwin went to university would end their long friendship. They looked so right together, her small features and slimness beside Edwin's powerful build, her fairness beside his dark good looks.

Cecily and Ada hadn't planned to go anywhere. Waldo was ill and the books he usually attended to needed some work. Then, being a Bank Holiday, there were the beach orders to prepare. Willie was already loading the van with the first deliveries before the breakfast dishes were washed.

They worked until midday, then Ada threw down her pen and suggested they went to the beach. "Van is spending the day with Edwin and we'd only be sitting here dealing with books that can easily be done tomorrow. It's daft not getting some fresh air while we can," she added, thinking of how Phil had been locked in his cell for most of the day, week in, week out.

She had gone to the house to see him often but he seemed to be unaware of her presence, hardly acknowledging her when she arrived, just a brief nod when she left. Pausing at the door she would hear him muttering quietly to his mother, then she was hurried out, Mrs Spencer insisting it was "too soon".

She tried to put aside the disappointments and prepare for a day out.

When the last of the orders had been piled onto the van and Willie was on his way, they caught a bus. The weather would have brought out hundreds of motorists and, with the visitors already staying and more trippers bringing extra buses to the popular town, parking would be difficult.

The buses were full too but they managed to find seats in separate parts of the overloaded vehicle, clambering in between children carrying buckets and spades and beach balls, and the harassed parents staggering with extra clothes, packages of food wrapped in white tea towels and bottles of "pop", shouting with little hope of success to their children to "be quiet". They began to enjoy the bustle and excitement. "It's like we're on holiday too," Cecily shouted above the noise.

"We are!" Ada shouted back, laughing.

The beach and the promenade were unbelievably full. The roar of voices and the screams from the funfair rides met them as soon as they alighted from the bus. People covered the golden sand and it looked as though there wasn't room for a coin to fall between them, but families still went down and somehow managed to find a space.

Ada pointed to the cliffs rising from the sand. "Shall we go up there?" she suggested when they finally reached the sea wall and looked down on the mass of people on the sand.

Cecily shaded her eyes to look. "It's just as crowded up there."

"Not as hopeless as this."

They threaded their way through the lively families, holding hands to prevent being separated, and by two o'clock were sitting on the grass high above the beach, laughing with the exertion and wondering how they'd find something to eat. The queue for the nearby cafe was long and even the ice-cream sellers below them looked likely to run out as hot, eager children jumped up and down with impatience, waiting for their turn to be served.

"Let's not try," Ada said. "I don't think I could face the battle." She found a packet of boiled sweets which were stuck to the paper bag but edible. They sucked them and watched the scene below; the sea with its border pattern of bathers, the pleasure boats leaving with full loads to sweep the bay then return to spill out its cargo of brightly clad customers and refill with more. The sky was a rich blue, the air still and very warm, even on the cliff top, and the noise from below a regular murmur that relaxed them.

They had been sitting there for more than an hour when, gradually at first, a change came over the sky. In the distance, darker clouds began to build and as they watched, indifferent to the threat they contained, a storm gathered momentum, rushed towards them, then, with a suddenness that made them gasp, burst right above them.

By the time they realized the angry clouds were not going to blow past them, it was too late. Heavy drops of rain touched their shoulders as they began to hurry to the path that would take them down to the promenade. Everyone was trying to leave at once, filling the narrow path, shouting, crying, pushing and struggling to stay in groups, mothers frantically trying to check that all their charges were with them.

Most were only half dressed, dragging cardigans on in a vain attempt to stay dry or at least warm as the rain came in a deluge. There were screaming youngsters wrapped in towels, badly packed baskets spilling their contents, people growling in frustration as they tried to put on clothes that stuck to their skin. The hurrying crowd was made up of the merry, the complaining, the anxious and the stoic.

"I wonder if Peter's here?" Cecily shouted over the roar of the cloud-burst.

"We'll never find him in this. If he's got any sense he's already on his way home." Ada's hands were slippery with the rain as she gripped the sleeve of Cecily's dress for fear of the crowd separating them. "Stay close. Remember, I didn't bring any money and you've got the return bus tickets!"

"Let's give Peter a try," Cecily said. "There's no chance of us getting a bus for ages — the queues will be around the funfair and back again."

Pushed and jostled, they made their way down the path and along the prom where the offer of shelter had attracted hundreds, who stood blocking the way, looking with smugness at those still struggling up from the sand.

"It's like a battlefield," Ada gasped, pointing at the beach. There were mounds everywhere, abandoned clothes, deckchairs toppled over as people ran past. The rain was making patterns in the sand and, at the water's edge, barely visible through the heavy storm, a boat was emptying its final passengers, who were searching wildly for the rest of their families, ignoring the rain, hoping to see a waved hand to guide them. The boat was hastily dragged up onto the sand and was lost to sight as the downpour increased in intensity.

76

Lightning flashed and thunder growled across the sky and screams echoed through the building. Pushing determinedly through the almost solid mass of people, Cecily dragged Ada behind her and pushed her way through to the green stall near the cricket ground.

Peter was there, in oilskins, trying desperately to fix the wooden shutters onto the front of his stall. He stared in disbelief as he recognized the two women, then put down the last of the shutters and ushered them inside, handing them some towels. "Dry yourselves and I'll make some tea."

He busied himself while they made a vain attempt to dry themselves. They were wearing thin dresses and their skin was wrinkled with the soaking they had suffered but neither was upset. "Summer rain won't hurt us," Ada said with a laugh, when Peter showed concern.

"A cup of tea and we'll be fine," Cecily added, but both were shivering as he handed them their cups and they drank gratefully.

"Where did you leave the car?" he asked.

"We didn't drive — we thought it better to rely on the buses."

"I don't think this crowd will get clear before late evening," Peter warned. "I think you'd better come home with me to dry out."

It took more than an hour to get away from the beach. Traffic was snarled up, with everyone determined to move at once, and with cars stalling and refusing to budge and rain still pelting down, the roads were chaos.

There was a blanket in the back of Peter's car and the sisters *cwtched* up together under its welcome warmth.

He eventually stopped in the middle of a terrace where, on a more normal day, there would be a view over the docks, he told them. On that day they couldn't see further than the neighbouring houses.

He told them to wait, then after opening his door, returned with an umbrella and hurried them into the house. Putting a match to the fire, he ran upstairs for more towels. "Sorry I haven't any spare clothes, unless you'd like trousers and a jumper in my size."

"Don't worry," Ada said. "Our dresses are thin and will soon dry."

"We'll look as though we were knitted," Cecily said, "so wrinkled we'll be, us as well as our clothes."

"Are you hungry?" Peter asked as he knelt to coax the fire to blaze. Cecily thought he might be a bit ill-at-ease with them there and decided he would prefer to keep busy.

"We're starving," she groaned dramatically. "We didn't have any lunch — only a boiled sweet."

"A sweet for lunch? I can do better than that."

They sat listening to Peter moving about in his kitchen and he soon reappeared with two beautifully presented omelettes each on a tray covered with an embroidered cloth.

"Who does the handiwork?" Ada asked. "That's something we've often wanted to learn but we haven't had the time."

"Or the skill," Cecily admitted. "This is a pleasant room. You look after yourself well, Peter. I can just imagine how hopeless Dadda would have been without us." In spite of the smile, she was feeling a deep sorrow for this kindly man, who spent so much of his time alone.

"My wife. She's been dead twelve years now. You cope because . . . life goes on."

Once they had eaten and were warmed by the now-cheerful fire, they sat and talked in their normal relaxed way. The brief unease Peter had shown was gone.

"Your husband is home, isn't he, Ada? Tell him I wish him well." Cecily glanced anxiously towards her sister. Ada still hadn't returned to the Spencers' home and refused to discuss Phil's plight and Cecily was afraid Peter's comment would spoil the visit, but Ada answered without hesitation.

"Yes. The time had passed, at last."

"Has he decided what he'll do?"

"I don't know. He never allowed me to visit, he won't talk to me even now and his mother doesn't tell me much. All the enthusiasm and optimism have gone. He could always make me laugh but it won't be like that any more. I hope he'll try to revive his printing business, though; it's all he knows. He'll cope, if people give him a chance."

"I'll do what I can to put business his way."

It was nine o'clock when they stood up to leave. Peter supplied them with woollen jumpers which hung on them like sacks, and insisted on driving them home.

"We'll look like a scarecrows' convention! What will your neighbours think?"

"I don't think they'll see us." He pointed to the window, where the rain was again falling.

The roads were still partially blocked with many broken down vehicles including a bus full of passengers, so it was almost ten before they got back to the shop.

"Will you come in?" Cecily invited.

Peter shook his head. "I'll call for my jumpers another day."

"Any time," Cecily said impulsively. "Call any time you have time to spare for us." She paused as she was about to run for the porch. "Peter? How long have we known you?"

"Eight years last January," he said at once.

"I remember. It was after Dadda died and we bullied you into opening your cafe early."

He smiled. "A businesswoman through and through. Don't let anyone underestimate you, Cecily. You have a fine mind for business and a real talent for getting the best out of people. Don't let anyone persuade you to think otherwise."

She wondered about his words that night. Was he telling her to keep away from Danny, who loved her but wanted to change her? That he was not the one with whom she'd find happiness? She knew that already. She's known it years ago but it didn't stop her wanting him. Seeing him and hearing him as he worked on the stable repairs was a daily reminder of that.

Weeks passed and still Ada hadn't returned to the Spencer home. Each time she called, Mrs Spencer

80

would open the door and shake her head and insist it was too soon for her to see him.

Peter came to lunch one day, bringing an order for some posters for Phil to print — Ada told him about Phil's refusal to see her and when they had discussed possible reasons, he suggested in his quiet way that maybe the statement purporting to come from Phil might be Mrs Spencer's own wishes and not Phil's at all. On the following day, Cecily persuaded her to go to the cottage, ignore the entreaties of her mother-in-law, and walk in.

Cecily waited in the car out of sight, hoping that the decision was the right one. When Ada hadn't reappeared in half an hour, she left the car and walked back to the shop.

Seeing her husband properly for the first time since the trial, Ada was shocked at how small he looked. The clothes he wore were too large, hanging on him as though they had been given to him by mistake. She watched as his mother put out the meal she had prepared for him. He sat in the chair, which had been empty for all the lonely months, staring as though dazzled by the generously filled plate, the white cloth and the shining cutlery. He didn't eat until his mother put the cutlery into his hands.

He was subdued, slightly bewildered and his skin was ashen. Ada chatted cheerfully for the pair of them, feeling like an outsider and wondering if she would ever see again the perky, lively man she had married.

Phil said very little, seeming to want only to wander around the house and the workshop and relearn everything that had once been so familiar. Ada followed him. He noticed even the smallest changes, like the clock which had gone from the kitchen and was tucked in a drawer, having refused to stop chiming once it had been wound. And the table, which had been recovered with fresh American cloth with a pattern of roses.

The workshop was changed too. The machines were heavily greased and covered with cloth. The window blinds long ago broken had been replaced by curtains.

"They'll have to go," he said in his quiet voice. "Too dangerous with machinery about."

"Of course," Ada said. "There's stupid we were not to think of that."

Phil lifted the covers and touched the machines, felt the blade of the guillotine, stroked the letter press and the litho printer. He examined them closely, for signs of rust or damage, she presumed. His pale and unusually clean fingers stroked them like pets.

"They'll need a bit of work but they aren't too bad. They could run again, I suppose."

"Willie's been in a few times to check them and grease them," she told him.

"If they do run —" He turned to Ada, his eyes haunted "— who'll give me work now?"

"Plenty of people," she said firmly. "I've already got orders waiting for you. Waldo wants you to print his Christmas offers and posters for the new season's jams. Peter Marshall has work for you and there'll be others once they know you're back in business."

"That won't keep us all."

"There's the shop and the business is growing. We're thinking of opening a second shop. I haven't told you that, Phil, I kept it as a surprise. We've been doing well, so you don't have to worry about money for a while yet."

Mrs Spencer had been following them, just staring at her son, not speaking. Her eyes were red with tears but now she said, forcing a smile, "They've been good to me, Phil. Every week without fail I've had a visit and some money as well as a box of groceries. Brought by Willie Morgan every Saturday night." She looked at Phil, who was staring at her, and she had to turn away to hide her tears. "Marvellous they've been."

"Go and make us a cup of tea, Mam," Ada said, seeing how upset she was. "Sinking for a cuppa I am, all this talking I've been doing. Not giving Phil a chance, am I, Phil, love?"

Phil seemed not to hear her. He was staring at the machines, wondering where he would find the strength to rouse them into life. He felt so weak and old.

Ada returned to live at the cottage and she drove herself to work every day but it was three weeks before he opened his arms to her and three more weeks before he shared her bed.

Her routine had returned to the way it had been before Phil's imprisonment and Cecily suffered agonies of misery at the emptiness of the shop premises with only herself and Van there.

"You wouldn't believe the difference one person makes," she said to Waldo when he called with Melanie one evening in late September. "I suppose it's because we're such good friends as well as sisters." She smiled across at Ada who sat with Phil near the roaring fire. Phil was constantly chilled, his face was pinched and pale, his shoulders drooped listlessly and his eyes were dull and lacking any spark of enthusiasm. She wondered how Ada could stand it.

"Sorry, but there's no chance of my coming back here," Ada said, patting Phil's skeletal hand. "Not now I've got my Phil back home. But," she asked hesitantly, "I've been wondering, couldn't we find work for Phil with us? We're opening another shop when we find a suitable premises — we'll need extra staff then and he doesn't feel up to restarting the printing business just yet."

Waldo flashed a warning shake of his head to Cecily, who took a deep breath and said, "Ada, love, don't you think you and I should discuss this on our own first? I mean, we always have, haven't we? And we can't talk about Phil as though he isn't here, listening to all the nice things we're saying about him, now can we?"

"You don't think it's a good idea!" Ada's voice startled them by its sharpness. "I knew that would be your answer!"

"I haven't given an answer. I don't make decisions. I want us to discuss it together, go over the ins and outs of it, decide where we could use Phil and if there's a place to offer him. We always decide together."

"Do we?" Ada's lip curled unattractively. "Like the way we discussed employing a girl to clean? First I knew about her was when she appeared in the kitchen. And the decision to change our wholesaler? And give a discount on accounts that are cleared each month? When you want to change my mind for me, *that's* when we discuss things! Cecily, I'm sick of being your skivvy."

"My what?" Cecily stood up in alarm, hurt and bewildered at the sudden outburst. "My skivvy? How can you think such a stupid thing? We've worked together since we were twelve and still at school. Together. Always together."

"I'm tired of people telling me I'm the dim one, playing follow-my-leader. This is important to me. I want my husband to work with us. It's a threesome we are now, not a twosome any more."

Waldo and Melanie were holding hands, heads down, unable to leave but wishing they were a long way away.

Ada fell silent, her fingers pulling at her handkerchief, looking briefly at Phil who was staring impassively into the fire. Cecily looked at Phil too and saw the hint of a satisfied smile.

"Phil?" she questioned. "Has all this come from you?"

He stood up and smiled at his wife. "Sort it between you! Come on, Ada, Mam will be waiting for us. Time we went home." He stood while Ada helped him with his coat and, without another word, walked through the shop and stood by the door.

"See you tomorrow, love," Cecily called as Ada fastened her coat and put an arm through Phil's. There was no reply and the bell tinkled with unnecessary merriment as the door closed behind them.

"That," Cecily said in a trembling voice, "was the first quarrel we've ever had."

"And orchestrated by Phil if I'm any judge," muttered Waldo.

"She knew she was wrong to ask and knew she was embarrassing you," Melanie said. "She's torn between loyalty to you and to Phil. He put her up to it for sure. He needed to know she was strong for him against you. We shouldn't begrudge him that, I suppose. He's been through a terrible ordeal."

"Caused by himself," Waldo muttered.

"But all those terrible things she said —" Cecily looked at Waldo, who smiled reassuringly and offered comfort.

"Oh, if you sat and thought for a moment or two I'm sure you could come up with a few complaints about Ada."

"Perhaps, but not enough to cause a scene like that."

"Before we go," Waldo said, picking up Melanie's coat, "about the second shop. Melanie and I have discussed it and think it's a good idea to hold off for a while, and this outburst makes me think even more that it's the right decision."

"It's the threat of war," Melanie said. "It seems likely that this Hitler will have to be stopped."

"Let's wait and see what news Chamberlain brings back from his meeting with Herr Hitler," Cecily said. "A second shop would be a good thing, if there's food rationing, for example. Our income would be cut drastically if we are limited on the food we sell." The friends parted, each to consider the possibilities.

★　★　★

As 1938 slipped towards its end, and the promise of "peace for our time" predicted by Chamberlain was no longer believable, people began to prepare for inevitable war. In December the government told of the plan to spend £200,000 on air raid shelters. The population still hoped for peace but their thoughts were on stocking food against the possibility of war.

For the sisters the second shop remained an idea, waiting for a decision on what kind of business it would be and where. The peace that was uneasy on a national front between government leaders was echoed in the shop between the sisters.

No more was said about Phil working for them and in Ada rankled the belief that the decision not to open the second shop was based on Cecily's unwillingness to accommodate Phil in his need to work, and nothing to do with Hitler at all. Phil was so subtle in the way he suggested it, Ada believed the opinion was her own.

Christmas 1938 was the quietest Cecily remembered. Only Peter came to share the Christmas dinner, Van having been invited to share the Richards' celebrations. She had been invited too but had used the excuse of Peter's longstanding invitation to refuse. The usual family gathering in the large sitting room above the shop wasn't even suggested; the remarks she overheard or were reported by so-called friends told Cecily that the "shameful Owen sisters" were not suitable company at that time.

It was Peter, too, who watched with her from the cliffs above the sandy beach as the New Year of 1939 began.

He called for her at nine o'clock and they went first for a meal in a quiet hotel out of town. Then, instead of going back to the shop, they drove to the beach. It was cold as they stepped from the car and he had wrapped her in the blanket he kept on the back seat.

"This is a funny place to watch the New Year begin," she said.

"Different." He smiled in the darkness. "Sometimes it's a good thing to stand alone and wait for something to begin. I remember on my birthdays as a child, standing here and looking out over the sea and imagining my life like a huge, empty blackboard, waiting for me to write something on it."

"I've always been filled with hope at New Year."

"I think this coming year will be full of unpleasant things. The writing on that blackboard won't show much fun."

"You really believe we'll be at war?"

"I hope not. Look, let's see what we can see written on your blackboard, shall we?" He pointed to where the faint line of surf showed in the blackness like a child's scribble and pretended to read. "Phil's full recovery. An even better year for Owen's shop."

"And you, Peter? What would you like to see written?"

He squeezed her shoulder, bent his head down a little so his chin rested on her hair. "Oh, just more of the same will do for me." For the first time he touched her cheek with his lips, then guided them back to the car.

"New Year is never a new beginning, is it?" he mused. "Threads drag over from one year to the next. Problems never cease on the stroke of midnight."

As he spoke the midnight chimes began to echo over Ada and Phil's resentment and unhappiness, over Cecily's inability to face the truth over her obsession with Danny, over Dorothy's spiteful nature and Peter's secret love for Cecily. Yet all these were insignificant as optimism faded while they waited for Chamberlain's government to dash their hopes and war to begin its ugly, destructive path.

As they approached the docks they stopped as hooters and ships' sirens filled the once-silent night. High-pitched whistles and deep blasts from the big ships all blending on the night air to perform the usual symphony. They stood for a long time, each with their dreams, then Peter drove her home, adding his car's horn to the rest, smiling at her in the darkness.

CHAPTER
FOUR

Willie had finished the stable repairs, the charred wood had been replaced and a new floor added with steps leading up to what once had been the hay loft. The place had been emptied of the stalls where the horses were kept and the hay feeders were gone from the wall.

"It makes me sad to think there are no more horses," Willie said as he stood with the sisters to explain what had been done. "Perhaps we should have waited. If this war is as bad as some predict, we might have to give up the van and go back to the horse and cart."

"It was lovely to ride on the trap, wasn't it?" Cecily said. "It made us feel special."

"Even our Van was pleased when Willie met her from school and she could ride home in style," Ada added.

Willie looked down the stone steps leading to the cellar. "You might like to think of making this into an air raid shelter," he suggested. "The government will be delivering shelters soon and you might be just as safe down there."

Ada shuddered. "I can't imagine having to leave our beds and go down there," she said. "Can't we forget the war for a little while?"

The year had begun like every other with talk of the weather, comparing it to previous winters, knitting scarves and hats to keep warm, reminiscing about the previous summer and looking forward to the next, but whatever the subject of the conversation, there was always a reference to the approaching war.

The rumblings of war filled everyone's mind. There were more insistent calls for volunteers for air raid precautions and fire watching and many other organizations intent on preparing for the troubles to come. The experience of the Spanish war encouraged councils to recommend building deep shelters, the Maginot Line quoted as proof of the strength of cement as protection.

Entrepreneurial businessmen advertised their services in strengthening underground rooms, making cellars and basements comfortable and safe. Other firms offered custom-built shelters complete with lights and sanitation. The sisters left the decisions and the work to Willie.

Their neighbours surprised them by saying they were selling their bakery shop. The premises was emptied and they moved somewhere away from the coast and its docks, hoping to avoid the worst of the bombing they were warned to expect. Several of their friends had done the same, two leaving by ship to go to America until Europe was clear of the German threat.

Cecily was still thinking about the shop next door. She and Ada had often considered buying a second shop but with the strained atmosphere between them she couldn't imagine their discussions being fruitful.

Without mentioning her intention, she went that day to talk to the solicitor who had dealt with their few problems and arranged to buy the shop.

She had no idea what she would sell but felt that, with Ada and Phil being so difficult, she had to have something of her own. Being on her own was more and more likely. Ada had once mentioned selling the shop and with a place of her own that wouldn't be such a disaster. She and Van would be able to manage. The sale went through quickly and her bank balance looked sick but she was pleased to know she had a place, a second way of earning a living for herself and her daughter.

Ada's only reaction to the news was a disapproving nod and a look of anger shared with Phil.

After the event, she told Waldo and Bertie. The only other person who knew was Willie. They depended on Willie for so many things. They paid him seven pounds a week now, double what most men earned, and considered it money well spent. Although he was only twenty-four, he was capable and mature and they trusted him completely.

Beside what he did in the business, he dealt with the care of the property, deciding when and how repairs should be carried out. He employed men, occasionally Danny Preston, to do the work, which he meticulously oversaw to make certain the work was correctly done. It was Willie who Cecily asked to do some tidying-up work on the shop next door. She and Ada dreaded the thought of a war, not least because of the threat that Willie would have to leave them.

Phil was never enthusiastic about any job they coaxed him to do. Although Cecily had not gone back on her refusal to employ him, there were occasional tasks which, if he had shown the slightest interest in doing, would have at least kept him occupied. But he preferred to set out a game of patience on the table in the room behind the shop and wait for Ada to finish work and take him home.

He had retained his prison pallor and Ada was determined that in this coming summer she would persuade him to get out on the beaches, to swim, relax and build up his strength and health in exercise, fresh air and warm sunshine.

The cellars were inspected by Willie and a man from the council who visited such places to assist in decisions about air raid shelters. They decided it would need strengthening but, when finished, would be large enough to hold six people comfortably. The couple who ran a nearby cafe, were invited by Ada to consider it theirs too. Willie suggested that if war became a reality they would need a key but the thought of a key being in someone else's hands made Cecily doubt the decision to offer them a place. Living alone in the rambling old building was bad enough without the fear of someone else being able to come into the yard without her knowing.

Jack Simmons helped with the work of strengthening the cellar. He no longer sold cheap fruit and vegetables in the rundown shop nearby. The business had failed and now with his wife, Sally, the three children and another on the way, he coped by managing an assortment of jobs, including selling ice cream from a pedal cycle cart in the summer and in winter by taking any job that offered. Twenty-four shillings dole was not enough to pay rent and feed and clothe them all. Cecily and Ada helped when they could, finding him occasional work and recommending him to others looking for a reliable workman.

The cellar was finished and duly examined by the sisters and Phil — who pronounced firmly that he would never use it. "Been locked up for too long," he said, peering into its dark and cold interior. "You won't get me down there, not if Hitler himself landed on the beach!"

Willie went home one day in March to find the living room empty. He thought Annette must have gone shopping and worried in a slightly irritated way: she was near her time and shouldn't go far from home. He stood on the doorstep and looked out, anxious for a sight of her. Then a voice called and he saw Gladys Davies running towards him, skipping in her excitement as she ran across the grassy lane.

"It's the baby!" she shouted. "Come quick it did. Your mother-in-law is with her. Lucky she was here, mind. The doctor's been and everything is fine."

She knew after the first few words that Willie wasn't listening. He ran up the stairs, leaving her at the door, still talking.

"Annette, love? Are you all right? Why didn't you send for me?"

94

Annette lifted the tightly wrapped bundle proudly and smiled at him. "Willie, everything is perfect, we have a little girl and her name, as you wanted, is Claire." She kissed the small, wrinkled face. "Claire, meet your dadda."

On 1 April 1939, Van celebrated her fifteenth birthday in two ways, by going skating in the evening with Edwin, which cost them a shilling including the hire of skates, and by leaving her position as third sales in the department store's fashion floor. She had been there six months.

Dorothy was disappointed: Van had been a successful sales lady, being forthright in her criticism of the choices of many wealthy customers and persuading them to be guided by her. This had led to a group of clients who would only be served by her.

Dorothy gloried in her niece's success, referring to her as "my protégée". She had explained at length the problems the poor dear girl had to face at home with criminals and a mother who was "very keen on men and not providing a suitable environment for an innocent and clever girl like Myfanwy", whispered behind an elegant hand. She convinced everyone that she had influenced the child for the better and was afraid of her falling back into the bad example of the sisters.

"What will you do, lovey?" Cecily asked when she was told. "Will you go to commercial college for shorthand and typing? That would be a useful skill to have."

"I'm coming to work here, in the shop."

Taken aback, Cecily blustered, "Well, I'd rather you began building a career for yourself, not bury yourself here in the little shop with Auntie Ada and me." She looked at Ada to see if there were signs of protest at the suggestion of a job for Van when no place had been found for Phil.

"Auntie Dorothy tried to persuade me to stay on in the fashion business," Van told her. "She said I was brilliant and, besides, she didn't want me to come home and work with you. She seems to think this shop will belong to her Owen one day and I should find myself a place where I can keep myself in the manner to which I'm accustomed. Whatever that means!"

"Dorothy is *twpsin*," Ada snorted. "It's our shop, mine and your mother's, and we've no intention of leaving it to anyone but you. In fact I'd rather leave it to Horse!" She glanced at Phil, who was concentrating on putting a black three on a red four and seemed oblivious to them all. "I doubt if Phil and I will have a child, but if we do, then half the business will still be yours and there's a good enough living for two, isn't there, Cecily?"

"Not if Owen runs it! He doesn't even know the cuts of bacon yet — he has to ask every time. And after all this time working with Waldo."

To Cecily's relief, Ada agreed that Van should start working with them but it was an uneasy few weeks as Van learnt the ways of the sisters. They had worked together efficiently for so long, there was no space for another to intervene. Van would go to do something

96

and find it already done, and would complain when one of them corrected her and told her to do something their way. She was far more difficult with Cecily, who found it more and more exhausting to work beside her and try to ignore the constant carping.

For her part, Van was enjoying herself. The opportunity to criticize her mother — and in front of others — was a joy. She used her half day to go into Cardiff and report her progress to Gran, a secret which gave her an added pleasure. She worked beside the sisters day after day and they had no idea she was in regular touch with their mother. The visits were even better now. Kitty's stepson, Paul Gregory, was home.

On the first day at the shop she had slouched aimlessly around, unwilling to be more help than she needed to be. Her growing resentment, fuelled by Dorothy, was clear, and the sisters wearied themselves coping with it and trying to ignore the disappointment and stifle their anger at her behaviour.

Van had once learned to dress the shop window and they decided that might be a good place for her to start, but she took all day on the simple task, ignoring their request to display more prominently the items with which they were overstocked and needed shifting. The final result was a mess. Cecily agreed that it was deliberately done, but slowly Van began to change. People commented on her dismal displays and this brought out a pride in her work and her interest grew.

She filled shallow boxes with straw and arranged apples and pears and oranges in polished rows which she decorated with a few leaves. She enjoyed the work and added some tins of fruit, which they wanted to sell quickly to make room for other things, some ribbons and even a few fluffy chicks on the baskets of farm eggs. She was soon entering into the work with greater enthusiasm, getting to know the customers and giving the sisters a little more free time.

In May the beaches were throwing off the mantle of winter and preparing for the influx of visitors in the next few months, but amid the gaiety and cheerfulness of newly painted signs urging people to eat, drink and spend their hard-earned holiday money in a hundred different ways, the undercurrent of trouble looming on the Continent was ever-present.

It was during that month, amid preparations for the first of the summer entertainments, that the first delivery of gas masks arrived and with them the realization that war was frighteningly real. The town was one of those being given a supply of household shelters, and auxiliary fire pumps were presented to assist in the town's defences.

It was also in May that, after encouragement, women busied themselves building supplies of clean white cloth to use as bandages as well as preparing for the evacuation of children from the danger spots when war was declared. No longer "if", but "when".

At the end of the month, a sea and air battle took place to enable the forces to demonstrate how and what the town could do to protect itself. There was a practice blackout and shops advertised aprons and blankets made of asbestos, which could be used to put out fires in the event of a fire-bomb attack.

It was frightening yet the organization of summer on the beaches went ahead as if the rumours were nothing more than the government's pretence to the German threat that they were ready and strongly able to combat any foolish attempt to begin battle.

Van played tennis with Edwin during the long evenings and skated and danced and picnicked on her days off. She was showing a quickness and an intelligent ability to deal with the running of the shop with its complex seasonal changes. Ada and Cecily were proud of the way she fitted into their ways. She had, after initial problems, become very reliable.

Ada and Phil continued to live with Phil's mother who, although looking frail, was still keeping the whitewashed cottage as neat and orderly as always, and producing a meal for them every evening. Ada tried in vain to be allowed to help, but apart from bringing home the shopping and paying all the bills, Mrs Spencer managed contentedly alone. She had never learned to read and took great delight in deceiving others and convincing them she could. She would listen while the news items were read to her, marking mentally the section of the pages where these were to be found.

With the absence of Ada while Phil was in prison, it had been Gladys Davies who read the main news items to her and she continued to do so. Gladys was impressed by the woman's memory as she pretended to read the paper, reciting without error all that she had been told.

"Fancy delivering post to foreign parts by aeroplane," she greeted Phil and Ada with one evening. She was referring to the newly augmented transatlantic Air Mail service. "A bit different from when that Amy Johnson flew to Australia in twenty days or so. Or when that man Corrigan went to fly to America, turned the wrong way and ended up in Ireland! There's a thing! Fancy if you posted a letter to Ireland and it ended up in America!"

She would prattle on as she brought dishes to the table, seemingly unaware of how little Phil contributed, although he occasionally laughed at her reminders of things long ago. She would take her son into his workshop while Ada did the dishes and talk to him of the customers he'd once served, hoping one day to see him rise out of his lethargy and start up the machines. But he would stare vacantly around him as if he were in a strange place with nothing even vaguely connected with his past or his future. Then he would walk back to the living room, crouch near the fire and play patience, while Ada talked about the happenings of the day.

He gave up playing patience in June and began counting things. Tassels on the chenille table cover, flowers on the wallpaper, bars on the grate, roses on the cloth covering the kitchen table. He would become agitated when his tired eyes refused to separate them and make him lose count. He would begin again and again, anxiously holding threads in his hands, or covering the roses with dishes as he counted, or touching the bars of the fire with the long brass poker.

The doctor called regularly and wanted to take Phil into hospital but Ada wouldn't hear of it.

"Can you imagine what it would do to his mother if he went away again?" she argued. "Besides, I want to look after him. Cecily helps and Gladys is wonderfully kind, I can manage."

When she told Cecily, her sister said, "With Van here to help me, you can spend as much time with Phil as you need until he's well again." She was startled by the vehemence with which Ada replied.

"No need! I'll continue *helping you*," she said. "Van gives us extra freedom but you and I, Cecily, are partners. I am not your assistant!"

"Oh, not this again," Cecily said with a groan. "When have you and I not been partners?"

"You've always treated me like a useless dogsbody!"

"Am I such a bossy woman that my own sister has to remind me of my place?" she asked Peter one Wednesday near the end of August. "I don't mean to treat her like an assistant, it just comes out that way sometimes, and I don't really think of our partnership that way. We each contribute what we do best."

"You're right. You and Ada are equal partners but your roles within the partnership are different. Ada is the hesitant one, the brake to hold you back and make you consider before you jump into a new venture. You, my dear Cecily, are the brilliant entrepreneur without whom she wouldn't have such a comfortable life."

"I do put her in the shade, then?"

"No, but the shade is where she is. If she were left alone to manage the business, it would continue well enough for a while, but you create the momentum and without you it would inevitably go downhill. No business stands still, as you well know. It's always changing, absorbing new ideas and projects, either growing or falling back. You push it ever forward but Ada, capable as she is, would be unable to stop that slide."

"You always make me feel better, Peter."

He smiled at her and said softly, "The feeling is mutual. I look forward to seeing you and never feel complete while we're apart."

Cecily was warmed by his words but didn't think about them too deeply. "I might not be able to come on Wednesdays for a while," she told him. "Ada needs to get away from the gloom of spending all her time with Phil and his mother. I've suggested we both learn to drive an ambulance. It seems certain we'll soon be at war. People say — as they did last year — that Hitler's only waiting for the harvest to be brought in before making his move. Last year it was a rumour but this year it seems inevitable. I think we should all do what we can and it will be a fresh interest for Ada and that's an extra incentive."

Willie and Danny had completed most of the work on a pretty farm cottage with a stream running through its garden and it was already sold at a healthy profit. They used the money to buy two other houses which only needed tidying and cleaning. They hired Jack Simmons to decorate, and dig the gardens between his ice-cream selling, and were pleased with his work. There were only two properties on which they had a mortgage. They now owned seven, giving the job of collecting the rents on Friday mornings to Annette.

"Isn't it time you and I packed up our other jobs?" Danny said as they went over their books in the comfort of Willie's living room. "Look, man, you've got a good living and Annette wants for nothing, but she never sees you. What's the point of working for Cecily when you could spend your time making more money on our own business? You don't need to work for the Watkins any more." He looked at Willie's face and guessed he was not convincing him. "You give up the shop and I'll give up the post, is it? We can both concentrate on what we do best — repairs and furniture."

Willie shook his head. "I can't leave them to cope on their own. They've always been good to me, and generous. If Phil Spencer had turned out to be a useful man, then I might have considered it, but he's about as much use as a paper shovel. No, while they need me I have to be there."

"Why didn't I marry Cecily? Fool, I was. What a team we'd have made, you and Annette, Cecily and me. Man, we'd have made a fortune in no time."

"Cecily's the brains there and you wouldn't be able to take it, seeing her dealing with workmen and architects and the like, every man being a threat. Fool you are, Danny, and it's unlikely you'll change."

"I have changed. I'd accept her now, flirting an' all. But it's too late, we've had too many false starts."

"What about Jessie? Have you tried to patch things up there?"

"I tried, yes, on that holiday someone treated her to. But she saw through me, knew it was really Cecily I wanted. Who can blame her for not accepting second best?"

"Perhaps someone should arrange a holiday for you and Cecily," Willie said dryly.

"Was it you?"

"No, but I have an idea who it was and before you ask, no, I won't tell you!"

"It's strange working at the shop. We've worked on the cellar for a while now, me and young Jack Simmons. Close to her I've been, seeing her every day, but not allowed to touch." He was silent for a while then said, "Hey, there's odd that Phil is, don't you think? He stares at Cecily in a way that makes me nervous. Changes coins from hand to hand, counting in a low mutter and watching her. You'd think from the expression on his face that he hates her. Scary it is, man."

"I know and it worries me. I've mentioned it to Cecily and Ada but they think he's all right, just a bit depressed."

"Wants locking up again if you ask me."

Danny and Jack Simmons had finished shoring up the floor of the stables with extra joists to make the cellar as strong as possible. The pillars were sea-soaked wood

104

bought from a ship-breaker's yard. The place had been cleaned and benches built around the walls for seats, or, if necessary, to use as beds.

"Come and see if it's what you wanted," Danny said to Cecily when the work was done. "Willie and I designed it, safe as anywhere in the town it is. Can I come and share it with you?"

"Room for six comfortably," Cecily said lightly, "or more if comfort isn't the priority."

"It's a bed I want to share with you, Cecily Owen, not a cellar with half a dozen others looking on."

Cecily stepped away from him, a tacit warning not to say any more, but he followed her into the cellar and took her in his arms. The strangeness of their surroundings took on the feeling of a sanctuary, a refuge from the rush and bustle of the world outside. Armoured against possible air raids, it was still benign, silent, a place without any of the implications of war.

A low-wattage bulb glowed orange from the ceiling, encased in a wire frame. In its light, Cecily saw a small spider audaciously building a web and claiming the place as his own. She looked around at the built-in benches and the cupboard made to hold blankets, food, candles and a first aid box. She looked everywhere except at Danny's face yet she knew he was looking at hers.

He lowered his head and his lips found hers waiting. "Cecily, why are we wasting all the best years? It's been so long. Let me move in — we'll make it legal as soon as the divorce is finally sorted. We can't go on watching the years pass without us being together. Together." He

105

whispered the word like a low groan. "You've defied convention before. Why not now? I can make you happy, I know I can."

Gradually his words slowed as desire threw them aside, speech wasn't important. He carried her to the leather-covered bench and they began to undress each other.

When they emerged from the stable, Phil was standing in the doorway of the back kitchen watching them silently. He turned around and disappeared into the house without acknowledging Danny's wave.

Ada saw the flushed cheeks and the dark-eyed look on her sister's face and guessed where she had been and with whom.

"What are you going to do about Danny?" she demanded. "Marry him or what?"

"Nothing."

After all the loving and the talk that had followed, he had said nothing to make her believe he had changed, that as soon as they were together he wouldn't resume his mistrust of her and anyone she happened to meet. "Nothing," she repeated. "Danny is Danny and nothing will change him. I'd be a fool if I can't accept it after all these years."

"We aren't a family for happy marriages," Ada said quietly, looking to make sure Phil wasn't listening. "There was Mam and Dadda, you bringing up a child without a husband, your dreams of Danny, and me . . ."

"But I thought you . . . you and Phil are content, aren't you?"

She smiled then and looked at Cecily. "It was Gareth I wanted, but he wouldn't consider me, not with you around to dazzle him." There was no bitterness in Ada's voice, only sadness.

"I thought he was long forgotten."

"We seemed so right for each other, Gareth and me; dancing, thinking the same about — well, just about everything, or so I believed. I'd have been happy with him, if he'd asked me to marry him instead of asking you."

"He's buying the other half of The Wedge I hear," Cecily said to fill the silence that followed.

Gareth had one of a pair of small, odd-shaped shops on the main road, called The Wedge. The doors angled in, with doors set into the triangular porch. He planned to buy the other half when it became vacant and to open it as a women's hairdressers, run by a manager. Gareth Price-Jones, with the over-possessive mother, who had been their dancing partner until Dadda had died and it had been more difficult to go out as regularly as before.

Cecily was surprised that Ada had felt a love for him. From the expression on her sister's face as she spoke of him, she guessed that Ada was casting her mind back to her hopes and dreams from long ago.

She shivered then, remembering the intent way Phil had been watching as she and Danny walked out of the stables. Perhaps he'd crept down and been watching them as they lay together. She shivered again.

That night, when Ada and Phil had gone home, Cecily went to play whist, an occupation she now enjoyed. Van was out with Edwin and when she got home, the shop was dark and the empty feeling she dreaded was there, a strong sense of emptiness, yet with shadows hovering like past memories, giving a feeling of utter and inexplicable sadness. If she and Danny were together, at least she wouldn't have to face walking into the empty house alone.

She went into the room behind the shop and filled the place with light. The kettle was making small purring sounds and she reached for the teapot before taking off her coat. On the table, as she turned to place the filled pot down, she saw a note from Van. She would be staying at the Richards' overnight. Cecily gave a sigh of disappointment. Tonight, for whatever reason, she didn't want to be alone. The house was even more cold and empty.

Van's bed was smooth as she glanced in as she always did, forgetting momentarily that the girl was not there. The bed looked unused, as though the occupant was gone forever. She shook aside the frightening thought and went back to the landing. From below she heard the big clock like the heart of the house — burlip, burlip — burlip, burlip — and she stood looking down into the blackness of the stairwell, willing it to continue, afraid it too would unaccountably cease. Afraid, but not knowing why, she left the landing light burning and went to her room.

She undressed with a continuing feeling of unease, hurriedly slipping on her nightdress and adding a dressing gown for its welcome warmth. It was one

108

o'clock when she drifted to sleep with the light still shining on the ceiling, an open book held in her hand.

She woke with the sickening sensation that she wasn't alone. Her eyes opened in alarm but all was quiet, everything in the room was as it should be. Perhaps Van had returned after all? She had left the bolts unfastened on the shop door in case she changed her mind. Her eyelids drooped again, drowsy and calling herself a fool for being afraid.

Moments later, as she dozed, the book slipped from the bed and a hand came out and caught it before it touched the floor.

Again something disturbed her restless dreaming, and she roused, afraid to move, with a return of the feeling that she wasn't alone. She opened her eyes, slowly this time, and saw Phil staring at her from the doorway.

"Phil!" She clutched the covers for their flimsy protection and sat up. "What d'you want? Why are you here?" The expression on his face terrified her. His eyes glittered in the pale face and his mouth was curled in a rictus of hate. His hair was spiky as if he'd recently risen from sleep.

"I've paid the price for my guilt, but you haven't," he muttered. "Filth is what you are, Cecily Owen, and you should be made to pay like I had to. Why should you get away without paying for your sins?"

The voice went on but she no longer listened. The only words she heard were "You should pay, you should pay" as though they were weapons with which he was beating her. He was mad. She had to get out of the room but how could she with him in the doorway?

"All right, Phil, you go home now and we'll talk about this later, all right?" She regretted the words as soon as they were spoken. How could she encourage him to go home to Ada? Who knows how his confused mind would make him behave with her?

She moved slightly as though to get up but he didn't change his position and he didn't stop staring at her in that frightening intensity.

Hoping that reasoning with him was the wisest way of dealing with him, she asked, "Pay, Phil? Why do I have to pay? What have I done?"

"Taken another woman's husband. Had a child by someone else's man."

She was startled. "What I've done has never harmed anyone."

"Illegitimate daughter, going with another woman's man. You should be punished, like I was. I did wrong but I've faced my punishment."

Slowly she rose from the bed, carefully covering herself as she eased back the covers. Her heart was painful in its drumming, she felt the beat of it in her face and throat. He stood watching her, his mouth slack, and she felt like a mouse at the mercy of a crouched, ferocious cat.

Then he seemed to snap out of the strange and dangerous mood, and in a normal voice, said, "All right, then, we'll talk about it later."

He left the doorway and she darted onto the landing and saw his shadow slipping down the stairs. She

110

followed without asking herself why she was suddenly so brave, only wanting to know how he had got in, to make sure he wouldn't do so again. He opened the back door and ran out, through the stables, and she heard the sound of the small door set in the big sliding doors open then slam behind him.

She ran back through the house and checked all the doors, slamming all the bolts firmly into their place. Willie would have checked the back door before he went; Phil must have unlocked both that one and the stable door ready for when he came back. She was trembling, wondering what to do, worried about her sister. If only there were someone near. The neighbours? No, this had to be kept in the family until it was sorted out.

Willie? No, it wasn't fair to worry him. Danny? Yes, he'd know how to handle this. She had to go to make sure Ada was all right.

Putting on all the house lights, she ran back upstairs and hurriedly dressed. Nervously she went back to the yard, which was illuminated only by lights shining through the windows. Starting at every shadow, frightened by a cat running in front of her, expecting to see Phil jump out from a corner, she reached the car and fumbled with the keys. She turned the starting handle and it fired at once. Pulling back the sliding doors, she backed out into the lane and it took all her nerve to get out and pull the heavy doors shut. She sprang into the driving seat and headed for the village, where Danny had a room. She had no idea of the time but the blackness around her suggested it must be two or three o'clock.

She stopped near his lodgings and glanced at Phil Spencer's cottage. There were no lights. She hesitated, wondering if she should go first to see Ada, make sure she was safe, but decided that with Phil so unpredictable, a man would be necessary.

She didn't know which was Danny's bedroom in the cottage were he lodged but presumed that he would have been given the one at the back. She guessed correctly — after throwing a number of small stones against the window she was rewarded by seeing it open and Danny's head appear. He came down and she clung to him and explained what had happened.

"In your room? How did he get in? Ada's keys, I suppose."

"No, when he ran off he went through the stable so he must have left doors open for some reason in his distorted mind. Hurry, I want to make sure Ada is all right. I'm so afraid for her. There's no telling what he'll do."

Danny knocked loudly on the door. It was Ada who answered, throwing open a window and demanding sleepily what he wanted at three in the morning.

"It's me," Cecily called. "Open the door, will you?"

They waited for Ada to come down the stairs and open the door. She was clutching a dressing gown around her and had a scarf over a head of curlers.

"Is Phil here?" Cecily asked.

112

"No. He often can't sleep and goes for a walk at night. He'll be back soon. Why? What's happened?"

"Can we come in, love?"

Ada stepped back in the narrow hallway and closed the door behind them. They went into the living room where the fire glowed a faint pinky grey. Automatically, Ada livened the fire and turned the kettle on its swivel. Whatever was happening, tea was an essential ingredient.

"Mind if I look around while Cecily tells you why she's here?" Danny asked.

Cecily told her briefly what had happened. She didn't mention that he had been in her bedroom watching her as she slept, but instead said he was in the house and the sounds woke her. "Confused, he was, and I thought I'd better get Danny and come to make sure you were both all right."

Both women looked up as Danny returned.

"Ada, love," he said, kneeling down beside her. "There's no easy way to say this. Your mother-in-law is dead. She's lying on the floor of her bedroom, laid out neat as neat."

Cecily saw the colour fade from her sister's face and reached out to hug her. Ada pulled away and went to the stairs, the others following. Mrs Spencer was in the middle of the room, dressed in a nightdress and dressing gown. Her hair looked freshly combed and she was holding a Bible in her hand.

"What happened?" Ada whispered. "She couldn't have died like that."

Danny ran to the corner to phone for the police and a doctor and then waited with the two stunned women, listening for their arrival, or that of Phil. The police were first and Ada seemed not to hear what was being said, although she answered the few questions they asked her; she was waiting for Phil.

It was Willie and Annette who opened the shop that morning. The rest of the night had been taken up with police, doctors, all asking searching questions. Cecily was at first as vague as she could be about the reason for arriving at her sister's home at such a time, and with Danny. But most of the truth came out before Phil had returned and explained in a most convincing and lucid way how he'd gone to fetch his sister-in-law to come and help him to tell his wife, who loved his mother very much. He added with a controlled sneer how his presence at night had been misunderstood by a woman whose sexual appetites were well known.

There were a lot of questions for Phil to answer, mainly about why he hadn't called the doctor and the police earlier. In this instance his answers were less clear and he spent a long time giving his explanations.

When they were free, Cecily took Ada back to the shop. "Best you come away, love, Phil will be talking to the police for a while yet. There'll be a lot to sort out. We'll come back later. Try and rest, then tomorrow you can start arranging the funeral, you and Phil."

They told Willie what had happened and at once he began to organize the day. He called on Jack Simmons, who would take the orders out. Willie would stay with

Van in the shop. Annette came to prepare food. She carried baby Claire Welsh fashion in a blanket around her shoulders and under the baby, keeping her warm and safe and allowing Annette to have her hands free. Victor came too and was excited at being allowed to explore the large house, the stables and the newly furnished cellar. He ran up and down stairs, and in and out of the house, banged noisily but tunelessly on the piano and thoroughly enjoyed himself. Once his morning tasks were done, Danny was his willing accomplice.

Cecily sat talking about what arrangements were needed. They ate very little. The police called several times with more questions but it was long after the shop had closed before Phil arrived. He was weepy at the loss of his mother. A constable accompanied him but seemed irritated rather than sympathetic. The weeping hadn't begun until they reached the shop and Ada could comfort him.

"Heart attack, the doctor thinks," the constable said.

"You'd think I killed her, the way they've gone on and on about me laying her out. Grieved I was, and wanting to do something for her. Can't anyone understand that?"

Cecily glanced at Ada. The possibility that Phil had murdered his mother had filled her mind all that awful day. "You'll stay here tonight, Ada, won't you?" she almost pleaded.

"No, we won't," Phil said. "They'll be bringing Mam home and we can't have her coming back to an empty house. We'll go back now."

115

"But she won't be home tonight, Phil," Ada said. "I think we should stay and go back in the morning."

"We're going home."

"D'you want me to go with you?" Cecily asked.

"Yes, that would be —" Ada began.

Phil just shook his head and, reaching for Ada's coat, helped her on with it and they left, Phil hurrying his wife away in a manner that frightened Cecily. She looked at the policeman, an unspoken question in her eyes.

"He won't harm her, if that's what you're thinking, miss. Sure I am that it was grief that made him act a bit peculiar, like."

But Cecily was uneasy. "He's been . . . unwell for a long time, you know." She was hesitant about blurting out the full story of the burglaries and the violence but the policeman clearly knew.

"An experience like he's had is bound to change a man," he said. "After all, it's meant to be punishment and a deterrent. We can't treat them so soft they don't think they've had to pay for their crimes, can we?"

He left them, with reassurances for Cecily and Van that they would be all right. Nothing had changed, the house was still the same comfortable home it was before this tragedy happened. Danny was still there, sitting in a corner while the constable talked to Cecily. When she had shown the constable out she turned to Danny. "Danny, you will stay tonight?" Cecily sensed rather than saw the slight reaction from her daughter. "We'll be a bit nervous after the events of last night, won't we, Van?"

116

"Yes, I'll stay. And we'll make sure the bolts are across, won't we, Van? We don't want any more night visitors."

Van just stared at him and gave an almost imperceptible smile.

Danny slept in the room that had been their father's. Cecily had changed the white counterpane for a blanket of blue and cream check to add some cheer to the cold and unwelcoming room.

"Thanks. I'd feel like a corpse myself sleeping in that white bed," he said with a grim smile.

He didn't use the wardrobe but left a few clothes scattered about the room, on the backs of chairs, across the bed and folded in piles on the marble wash stand, printing his identity on the place but suggesting his stay was not permanent.

The newspapers made a lot of the story the following day and it was Cecily who came out worst. Her story about Phil appearing in her bedroom and how, worried about his sister, she had driven to the village to make sure all was well, had been turned on its head by Phil. He had gathered his wits and strength for the purpose of making her look a fool. He insisted that he had knocked on the shop door and Cecily had told him to go away, refusing to listen to his story about the death of his mother. Cecily pretended to ignore the unpleasant lie to people who didn't matter but pleaded for Ada and Van to believe she had spoken the truth.

Only Peter believed her. She had gone to where he sat in the tea stall, selling ice creams and sweets and all the other needs of the visitors to the beach. She told him in detail everything that had happened and after that she avoided him, afraid that her company would bring him unpleasant publicity — and he didn't deserve that.

Van believed the unkind version and went to talk to her gran about it. Kitty tried to persuade her not to believe what had been the ramblings of a confused mind but Van was unrepentant. "My mam is always in trouble. Why should I think this time is any different?"

"Try to think about it honestly, Van lovey. Your mother wouldn't do what the papers are saying. You know her well enough to believe her."

Van smiled. "She'll get what's coming to her one day, you wait and see."

Kitty was worried about the bitterness in her granddaughter's expression and wished Cecily and Ada were willing for her to go and talk to them. They needed her and because of their refusal to forgive her for leaving them as she had, she was unable to help. "You don't think, with all this going on, they might agree to see me, do you?" she asked.

"I try, Gran, I really do but they say they'll never forgive you. Thank goodness I found you. I love you, Gran."

The business wasn't affected detrimentally. In fact, new or rarely seen customers filled the place, hoping for more facts or fantasies to add to the story that was buzzing around the town. There were some who came just to stare at the woman who invented stories about men wandering into her bedroom, and had shown no

118

concern when her brother-in-law had knocked on the door and told her his mother was dead, but had sent him away. It was sickeningly hurtful and she wished Ada had been there with her to at least refute the worse exaggerations that were bandied about and growing in strength and imagination day by day. But Ada didn't leave Phil's side during the weeks following the funeral and when they did see each other it was clear that Ada believed Phil's story about her refusal to help.

Danny wasn't around much. He delivered the post in the morning then spent the rest of the day in the workshop he shared with Willie until late in the evenings. Willie asked him one day if he'd seen Cecily.

"No, I don't want to get my name mixed with hers with all the rumours that are going on," he admitted.

"Got a reputation, hasn't she?" Willie said, and there was something in his voice that made Danny look at him. "And whose fault is that? What makes you suddenly feel innocent of it all? The woman is to blame, the man is just being a man, right?"

"I thought it best to keep away until it all dies down."

"Phil lied, and you damn well know it. But you're leaving her to face it alone. That's typical of you, Danny Preston."

Danny felt a tinge of guilt but not enough. He preferred to believe the story the papers had carried. Had she lied to the police and pretended that Phil had been in her room just to cover up her unkindness at refusing to help him? But no, that unwillingness to help wasn't in her nature. It didn't make sense.

Cecily was glad it had happened during the busiest time of the year, leaving her little time to dwell on the humiliation and accusations that filled the air around her.

Peter called one Sunday morning and invited Cecily and Van to lunch at a restaurant overlooking a beach a few miles out of town. She gladly accepted and the three of them set out in his car. Van seemed pleased to see him and chatted easily as he drove. As they ate, it was Van who brought up the subject of the night when Mrs Spencer died.

"Phil is a confused man," Peter said when Van was asking why the papers had been so unkind to her mother. "He'd been caught with stolen goods in his hands and prison was a punishment he found difficult to bear. He wanted someone else to be punished too, and even though your mother wasn't guilty of anything except in his mind, he chose to embarrass her like he did. I don't think anyone can understand why." Van smiled but she wasn't convinced.

Cecily was so glad to spend time with Peter. He was the only one apart from Danny who had heard the full story of that strange and frightening night visit. Phil's story had been more convincing than her own.

"You should have told the truth at once and not tried to protect Ada," Peter said as he and Cecily sat for a few precious moments of peace outside the beach cafe. "She must know how disturbed Phil is. You haven't saved her from anything — just delaying the imminent and inevitable crash. Changing your story led the police to doubt you."

"Too late now."

"Too late to stop Phil's stories but they're dying down anyway. Are you sure Ada doesn't believe you're telling the truth? She's an intelligent woman and she knows you better than anyone else does."

"She believed Phil then and still believes him. She insists he knocked on the shop door asking for help and I turned him away; that the story about coming into my bedroom was a nonsense. In fact, I'm being blamed for his depression. If I'd agreed to give him a job he'd be fully recovered now. That's what she believes. My own sister. Oh, Peter, I wish Mam was here."

"That's maybe what Ada says but I doubt she believes it. When trouble comes and there's no way out of it it's natural to look for a scapegoat."

"So I can add scapegoat to all the other epithets I've collected over the past weeks?" She laughed without humour. "Why not? It makes a change from whore!"

"Cecily, my dear, don't! You know who you are, and the circumstances which make people so unkind will fade into misty memory. Phil isn't going to miraculously recover, is he? And one day the truth will become apparent and Ada will have to face reality."

"I hope so, Peter. With Ada against me as well as all the rest, I'm finding it hard to take."

CHAPTER
FIVE

Two weeks after the funeral of Mrs Spencer, the events which were to change all their lives began. Poland was invaded by Hitler's German army in the early hours of 1st September and on the 3rd, war was declared.

It was a Sunday morning and the first night of the war was dark, with a moon hidden in an overcast sky. The blackout came into force immediately and people felt they had been transported to an alien land as they tried to make their way through the streets without the assistance of friendly lights.

They fell, bumped into each other as well as into lampposts and trees, and tripped over the cats which wandered, curious about the unusual blackness of the night. Dogs stood and barked their confusion and young people giggled helplessly as they made a pantomime out of finding their way home.

Special window net and tape were sold, both of which had to be dipped in water then fastened to the glass to hold it in case it was shattered, the tape in a criss-cross pattern and the net cut to size. Four and a half thousand Anderson shelters were ordered for the town and digging began on the deep holes needed to accommodate them. Vegetable plots, some cut in carefully nurtured lawns, were marked out and digging began.

People stood around in groups, watching the sky as if expecting a horde of enemy planes to swoop down on them, spreading death and chaos from the leading edges of their wings. Torches as well as car and bicycle lamps were allowed, but these had to be more than half covered with black paper to reduce the beams to a thread. A few lights showed from houses where the blackout restrictions weren't taken seriously but as the air raid wardens began their beat, these were swiftly snuffed out.

The air raid sirens did a practice alarm and followed it with the sound of "all clear", but hundreds of people had not been told about the rehearsal and they ran, clutching their valued possessions, down the nearest shelter and spend the night there, coming out the following morning to be teased and laughed at by friends.

Everyone was busy making sure they didn't fall foul of the new regulations. Many made wooden frames which they covered with blackout paper. These were pushed into place to cover the windows every evening and they stood, bulky and inconvenient, against a wall during the day. "Put that light out!" became a regular call during the hours of darkness.

Cecily and Ada sewed thick curtaining for the window between the living room and the shop and were convinced that it was a lot of work for what must surely be a brief war.

Their greatest worry was the possibility of Willie having to leave them. They depended on him for so many things. Already thousands of soldiers, sailors and air men had been called away from the town and Willie and Danny were in the age group to join them. One hundred and fifty-eight-thousand troops were transported across the Channel to begin the task of halting the German army in its march of occupation. A million — mostly children — were evacuated from areas considered to be potentially dangerous and all theatres and cinemas were closed, fearing the large number of casualties if a bomb landed on one of them.

Ambulance training was increased and as Ada and Cecily were by this time quite expert on the cumbersome vehicles, they began training others. Dorothy found a niche for herself at one of the new Citizen Advice Centres, one of 200 set up to assist if homes were destroyed and families scattered. As the risk of conscription loomed ever closer, hundreds of couples made hurried plans to marry.

Among these were Gareth and Rhonwen, who met at the register office with only Rhonwen's daughter, Marged, plus two friends to act as witnesses, were married and went back to live at Rhonwen's terraced house near Dorothy, on Snipe Street.

Gareth told his mother while holding Rhonwen's hand and with Marged giggling behind him. He knew his mother would be shocked but decided that one shock, giving her no chance to try and dissuade him, was the kindest.

"But you're leaving me all alone, and with Hitler about to invade," she wailed, wiping her long nose with a cologne-soaked handkerchief. Gareth didn't point out that he would probably be joining the army and leaving her anyway.

"No, Mam, you don't have to be alone, there'll be plenty of soldiers looking for accommodation. Take in a couple of boarders. By looking after them, you'll be doing your bit towards winning the war. We'll help with cash, you won't go short." He knew he'd taken the coward's way of beginning his marriage, but with the threat of call-up he didn't want to go away without having someone of his own to come back to. Telling his mother before the event would have been a sure way of getting it postponed.

Gareth, Rhonwen and Marged walked towards the neat house on Snipe Street and stopped at the top of the hill leading down to Owen's shop where they bought fish and chips to take home for their wedding breakfast.

"Tomorrow," he told his wife and stepdaughter, "we're off on a week's holiday and we'll have grand food every day." But on the following morning, Danny brought them a letter stating that the hotel he had booked had closed, taken over by the army for the duration of the war.

Ada was worried about Phil. He seemed untouched by the talk of war; it all went over his head as unimportant as an announcement that tomorrow it might rain. He still wandered about at night and for a while she wondered if he'd gone back to his old ways and begun robbing houses. But no talk of burglaries reached her and their finances were only what she provided.

He rarely slept in her bed; the sheets on his side were still untouched in the mornings although there was sometimes a dip on the counterpane where he had lain for a while with a coat wrapped around his shoulders, staring up at the ceiling. He still came to the shop with her each morning and returned every evening, not speaking to either Cecily or Van. Ada spoke of him to the doctor, who visited him occasionally and who offered little hope of an improvement, but said nothing about his behaviour to Cecily.

Cecily guessed from the drawn expression on Ada's face that all was not well but since the accusations levelled at her by Phil, she didn't risk opening up the subject of his mental state, although she was seriously worried.

Danny had started visiting again, arriving as Ada and Phil left each evening, sharing their meal and listening to the wireless for a couple of hours: programmes like *Band Wagon* with Arthur Askey and Stinker Murdoch provided a good laugh. Comedy shows were very popular; an easing of tension was necessary during the early weeks of the war, when every time the sun went down there was fear that this might be the night when the bombers would come.

The shelter below the stable was stocked with emergency food and a bottle was filled with water every evening and placed against the back door, to be carried if they should hear the dreaded siren and have to run to the shelter.

Cecily and Danny both noticed that Van's door was never fully closed. Perhaps she was standing guard against Danny's nocturnal wanderings towards her mother's room. But Danny was careful and although he spent many hours with Cecily, they were convinced she never knew. A fifteen-year-old sleeps soundly.

Familiar faces began to disappear as men joined the forces; some driven by the thought of regular if small wages to help their families. Others were goaded on by brothers, cousins and friends who had already joined and among the first to go were Gareth, the sisters' cousin Johnny Fowler, and Jack Simmons.

Waldo was losing all his shop assistants and was regularly advertising for replacements. The situation was repeated in every business in the town and people with the right experience were hard to find, especially as the factories offered more money.

Gareth left his barber shop with its newly acquired "other half" in the hands of his one-time apprentice. His plan to open the second half of The Wedge as a ladies' hair salon was abandoned until after the war ended. The second half was simply an enlargement to the original business, giving more space for people to wait, and for display shelves on which he offered combs and brushes and shampoo for sale. The contraceptives remained hidden in a drawer and referred to as "a packet of them, you knows" by his customers.

Owen failed his medical, much to Dorothy's surprise and Owen's relief. Young David, the sisters' red-headed

127

one-time assistant, joined up. Winifred Rees, the girl who helped with the housework, left too, hoping to find better paid work in the factories which were advertising for people to fight the enemy by making bullets and shells for our fighting men.

News of the fighting was sparse. The local papers made big headlines over items like whether or not to supply milk to all school children instead of those proved to be in need. Gareth's mother gained notoriety for a while having been fined ten shillings for a blackout offence. There was no mention of any air raids that might have taken place in other parts of the country, and no mention of the landmines and barbed wire fences being placed around many of the beaches.

The first local deaths of the war were bizarre. A soldier was shot by a guard on the docks who thought he was a spy. Several people were knocked down in the blackout and a car ran into the river, the driver unable to see the road in an intense storm. All victims who had never heard more of battle than the practice air raid.

It was during a mock air raid, another to test the organizational skills of the defence services, that the first death to affect the sisters occurred. During the noise and the sounds of the terrifyingly realistic mock air attack, Waldo died.

He woke from a deep sleep to the sound of heavy guns protecting the docks, forgetting in his fright that a practice had been planned. He woke Melanie and tried to carry her to the shelter and suffered a heart attack before he left the bedroom. He died almost immediately, still holding Melanie in his arms.

128

Cecily refused to believe it when the news was brought by Owen early the next morning. She stared at the fat, red-faced boy as though it were his fault, her eyes wide in gradually dawning grief.

"Waldo? He can't be! He's always there when I need him. He can't be dead, he'd never leave us." She rang Peter to tell him, crying as she said the dreadful words, and he promised to come at once. "No, not yet. I have to go to see Melanie."

"I'll wait at the shop. It's sad to lose a friend. Be brave for Melanie, love."

She repeated the denials over and over in the time it took for Ada and Phil to arrive, and as she went up to tell Van, and as she walked through the house to where Willie was stocking the first orders.

She was still telling herself it wasn't true as she ran up the hill to the main road where the large store stood, already — to her imagination — looking forlorn and engulfed in sadness in the dark early morning. No light showed. Within, everything was still and silent. What would normally have been a thriving activity with the staff behind the locked doors preparing their counters and displays for the time when customers were admitted was utter stillness. It was as if it too had died in the night.

The side door stood ajar and she went inside, wondering what she should say. What if the rumour was false? What if she blurted out something so terrible and Owen had got it wrong? Waldo wasn't dead. He'd just suffered one of his attacks. Anger filled her against Owen. The stupid boy, he'd got it wrong.

She stepped inside the dark shop and knew at once it was true. The staff stood about in small groups and anxious faces. A ship without its captain, Cecily thought as they greeted her with lips stiff and refusing to smile, eyes that did not meet hers.

"Is it true?" she whispered to Tomos Small, the manager, whose father had been on the docks when her father had died. She held her breath for that last moment of faint hope, until he nodded.

"And Mrs Watkins? Is she at home?"

"Yes, Miss Owen. She sent word to me and through me to others and now she's home. She particularly asked that you were told, miss. I sent Owen as he's related, like. I'm sure Mrs Watkins would be glad to see you, miss."

It wasn't far to walk back down to collect the car, but irritated by the delay, she wanted to walk, run, depend on her own self to get there and see her friend. She nodded to the staff, muttered a few words of sympathy and went outside. Willie was standing at the kerb, his flat cap in his hand, the other on the door of the car.

"Thought you might need a lift," he said. "Terrible sorry I am about this. Dreadful shame. I know what a good friend he's been to you and Miss Ada."

"Thank you, Willie." She cried then, at his thoughtfulness at turning up at the right moment. "Waldo has been a good friend, yes. And so have you," she sobbed. She got in and he drove in silence to Melanie's house.

It was a large house, set on a corner and painted white. It was unusual in that there was no garden wall or hedge, but flowerbeds and green lawns running from the house to the pavement. The green grass was a splendid setting and the slope rising from the road gave the house an elevation which added to its impressive appearance. Today, although dawn had broken and the sky was bright with the promise of a sunny day, the blinds were still drawn.

As she stepped from the car and walked up the drive, Cecily saw there were lots of people inside the house. Through the open front door she could see them standing in small groups and from the kitchen a woman appeared carrying a tray of teas. Melanie saw her and came to meet her, looking smaller and somehow frail, shrunken both in size and personality by the tragedy.

Cecily clung to her friend and their tears flowed, each silently grieving for Waldo, who had added so much to both their lives.

"I knew he was ill," Melanie said when they had recovered a little. "But somehow you refuse to accept what the doctors tell you. Death and illness are what happens to other people, not to this kind and loving man who made my life one long pleasure." She gave a deep sigh then added quietly, "He told me you are mentioned in his will and to arrange a reading when we are all together."

"I'll do whatever you want of me. Would you like me to sleep here for a few nights?"

"Thank you, my dear, but there's no need. The servants will still be here. Such a pity we never managed to have a child; it would have been such a comfort now."

"You have a hundred friends. I doubt if Waldo ever made an enemy." Cecily smiled. "Come on, I don't know about you, love, but I'm sinking for a cuppa."

"Stupid, really," Melanie mused, "how we drink tea as if it somehow solves the problem by dilution."

"If only it were that simple to drown sorrow," Cecily said, guiding Melanie to where a cup of tea was offered.

The funeral was a very large one and the main road was closed by it. Everyone who could find a place beside the kerb on that cold, wet day stood and lined the route. Others stood at open windows and in doorways and shared in the farewell to a favourite citizen. The cars made a procession that stretched out of sight in both directions and seemed to go on forever.

Afterwards the house was full to overflowing with mourners and it was late in the day, with the family and close friends still there, when the solicitor called Melanie, Ada, Cecily and Van to join the widow to hear the contents of Waldo's will. Cecily was anxious, watching Melanie for signs of stress as she ushered her sister and daughter in front of her into the silent lounge.

There were seven people present and Cecily found a seat near the door and waited for Mr Grainger to begin. He looked thinner and older, but his eyes were as sharp as when he had read the will of her father, Owen-Owen, almost ten years before.

The will began with the bulk of his estate being left to his wife, Melanie. For her there were the properties, the shares and most of his fortune. The second largest amount, to the surprise of everyone present, with the exception of Melanie, was left to Van. The shop was hers with enough money for it to be run for her until she gained control, at the age of twenty-one.

"Myfanwy will need a capable manager and someone to guide her and help her to fully understand the way a large grocery store is run. In this the will continued, 'I know my dear wife, Melanie, will willingly and lovingly assist Myfanwy Owen in every way'."

Then came the announcement Cecily had dreaded. She felt Ada's hand reach for hers and grip it tightly as Mr Grainger spoke into the silence that was almost a hum.

"The will goes on 'Myfanwy is my daughter. Mine and Cecily Owen's and I am proud to be able to tell of this at last, even though I won't be present to receive the congratulations of you all. I wish her every joy and happiness as my successor at Waldo Watkins' store'."

Mr Grainger coughed and looked down at the papers in front of him, troubled and tense. Melanie smiled across at Cecily and blew a kiss, a comforting and reassuring gesture that made Cecily want to cry.

It was Van who spoke first. She turned to stare at her mother, a glance then at Melanie who was sitting, pale-faced, near the fireplace, watching her, then back to an equally pale Cecily. "Why didn't you tell me?" she spat out at her mother. "My father living in the same town and you didn't tell me!"

"The decision was mine and mine alone." Cecily was surprised at how calm she sounded. She was not looking at Van, but at Melanie, who had not moved a muscle, apart from the smile for Cecily, as the announcement had been made. "It was *my* decision, Van, *mine*, not yours. It was my wish that you were not told, but Waldo obviously decided differently. I don't want you or anyone to think that this news alters in any way the character of Waldo. He was a fine, honourable man who offered his friends nothing but love and kindness."

"A fine pair you were!" Van glared at the sisters. "Bringing me up pretending my mother was a stranger, that you'd taken pity on me, an orphaned child. And all the time my father was there, in my life, but unknown to me." She turned to look at Melanie. "Did you know?"

"Not until two weeks ago. Waldo told me when he knew he wouldn't live long enough to hand over the shop when you reached twenty-one, as he had hoped. Only when he was sure I knew and understood did he write that in his will."

In some ways this was as great a shock to Cecily than the announcement. There hadn't been the slightest sign in Melanie that she knew. Nothing had changed in the relationship; she had been as affectionate and loving as always.

She turned to look at Van, distress on her lovely face, her breathing heavy and uneven. If she had known Waldo had planned to reveal this, she would have spoken to her daughter, prepared her. But then, what was a good way of learning something like this?

Numbly they listened to the remainder of the bequests and when Mr Grainger closed his file, Cecily stood beside Melanie, still afraid the gentle woman would show the disgust and contempt that she deserved. But Melanie hugged her and said only, "We must talk, my dear."

Van, standing at the back of the room, who Cecily began hesitantly to approach, stormed to the door and shouted, "I hate you! All of you!" Cecily tried to run after her but Melanie held her back.

"Let her go, my dear. She needs to be alone to digest all this. Come on, let's go back and face the others. It has to be done." She put an arm around Cecily and Ada, and walked back to where the remaining guests were waiting to hear the remainder of Waldo's last will and testament with curiosity and anticipation of some gossip to share.

Cecily pulled herself free and ran outside after Van. She found her standing outside the door, calm and coldly composed.

"Don't worry, Mother. I'm going to see Edwin and I'll be home at ten. Don't worry, I'm not suicidal or anything, I just want to talk to Edwin."

"But Van, lovey, I need you with me at this moment. We need each other."

"I don't need you! I want you out of my life! You can spend the next few years wondering how I'll pay you back, because I will. You'll regret the way you've treated me. Now I'm going to find Edwin. Don't make a scene, I'm not a hysterical child! I want him to know before someone else tells him. You can understand that, can't you, after a lifetime of secrets?"

"Shall I come with you?"

"No. I don't need my hand held. I'm not a child and I want to tell him myself."

"And you'll be all right?"

"I'm all right. Tell Auntie Melanie that I'm sorry I shouted." She turned and walked away.

Dorothy had obviously learned that Van had inherited the shop. As Cecily re-entered the house, her sister-in-law's loud voice was heard to say, "My Owen will have the Owen's shop now, of course. Eldest son of the eldest son. Owen-Owen he's called, named for his grandfather. It's his by right and Waldo obviously understood this."

No one answered her, except Owen, who shushed her and whispered, "Mam, I don't want the shop! I want to keep my job at Watkins' and if you upset them I'll be kicked out!"

Everyone finally went home, leaving Cecily and Melanie sitting next to each other, the departures a sea of blurred faces, the parting comments unheard, though automatically answered. When they were alone, Melanie said to Cecily, "Tell me about it, dear."

"It wasn't an affair. He was — I know this sounds stupid, but he wasn't really unfaithful to you. It was a momentary thing. A weakness at a time when I was vulnerable and he was caring and kind."

"It was after you'd cancelled your wedding to Danny, wasn't it?"

"I came to talk to you, as I'd always done when I was upset or worried or needed guidance. Danny had just made it clear that once we were married he'd expect

136

me to give up dancing and we'd move from the shop to live in a couple of rented rooms which he could afford to pay for, and I'd have to settle down to what he called normal married life. I laughed. I honestly thought he was joking. He wasn't. We argued and, as you know, I called off the wedding even though the banns had been called. I was distraught.

"I came here but you were out and he comforted me. Then things got out of hand. It was so sudden we were both taken unawares and the comforting and the being comforted went out of control. It was my fault, I expected too much of him and, well, that brief encounter resulted in my becoming a mother. It was my fault, Melanie. He never stopped loving you for a moment."

"That was how he told it to me, but he took all the blame on himself," Melanie said softly.

"From the moment it happened, all his concern was for you. A few months later, when I knew I was carrying his child, we talked and I agreed to go away and invent a story about a friend. There was never a suggestion that I had an abortion, nor did he ever suggest I might have her adopted."

"So, now everyone knows. At least, your Dorothy knows, and that's much the same thing!"

Cecily frowned. "Why did he do it, d'you think? It seems cruel on both of us, as well as a hurtful shock for Van."

"He must have thought we could cope with a sixteen-year-old scandal. As for Van, she has a life ahead of her and now it's without secrets, clean and pure and with no possibility of unpleasant surprises."

"He was probably right. Unpleasant, but best dealt with and put aside."

"He'd thought it out and his decision was for the best. I believe that. He always made the right decisions."

"I'll send Van to talk to you as soon as she's calmed down, Melanie."

"No, dear. Don't send her. Tell her I'd love her to come. There are many things to discuss." She smiled then. "Just think, I'm a sort of mother at last."

"More than that. Friend, mother and loving aunt, all rolled into one. Van is very lucky."

The major effect of the news breaking that Van was Waldo's child was Van leaving the shop and going to work at Watkins' store to begin learning about the running of her inheritance. The other main change was that Danny, distressed by the notoriety and the widespread gossip, also left the shop and returned to live in the room next door to Gladys Davies.

That good lady told him he was a fool. "There's a lot of character and strength in a woman who decides to bring up her child without a husband," she said. "She knew she'd have to face disapproval and a lot of unkindness if the truth came out, yet she took the chance. Now it has come out sixteen years on and she's facing the world with a defiance that forbids many from openly criticizing her. She's a brave and remarkable woman who deserves the support of her friends. If you can't see that, Danny Preston, you're a fool and she's better off without you!"

Danny was speechless under the onslaught of her angry words. His anger rose too, but as he began to look pompous and tell her he wasn't the man to be associated with such an affair, she called him a hypocrite and worse.

"Where have you been staying these past weeks? In your own bed, were you? Hardly whiter than white. You're thinking about yourself, as usual, not her. Afraid of people calling you names instead of standing up for her. People calling you names never does no harm, not to a strong person it doesn't!"

Danny told her to "Shut up, woman" but he was ashamed of leaving Cecily to face her critics alone. He was a hypocrite and worse, he admitted to Willie as they worked on a hall table for Bertie Richards.

"Too late now, it is, to go back. I always do the wrong thing, Willie. Every time. Why is that, d'you think?"

"Gladys is right. You put yourself first *every* time and that's why you get it wrong *every* time."

"You have to think about how circumstances will affect you," Danny protested. "Everyone does that."

"But you never work through to the point where you can consider anyone else. Too quick to condemn you are. If you thought for someone else you wouldn't keep digging holes for yourself to fall into, one after another."

Danny grinned at the picture Willie created, of scrambling out of one hole only to fall into another.

"Damn me, you make me sound like a demented rabbit!"

"Worse, Danny. Rabbits rarely end up alone and that's what'll happen to you." He rubbed fiercely at the wood he was sanding. "Caring is what it's about. Whatever Annette does, I'm her man and I'll never let her down, and she knows it."

He pointed across the road to the Spencers' white cottage. "See Ada and Phil? He hasn't brought her much happiness, has he? But would she think of leaving him? Damn it all, man, you want your arse kicked till your teeth rattle!" He walked off in unaccustomed anger, which showed in his swift, long-legged gait and in the head, lowered to his chest, and the arms rigidly held at waist height with balled fists.

"Annette," he called. "I need a kiss, a cuddle and a cup of tea — in that order."

Peter Marshall came frequently to see Cecily and Ada. They were tempted not to go out, even to the whist drives that had been a recent pleasure, or to the training sessions which went on with increasing urgency, preparing for the raids which must surely come. They both pretended it was not because of the half-whispered remarks, or the refusal of some husbands to allow their wives to attend a class held by them. Peter made them face the truth. "You're allowing yourselves to back down and that will never do," he said. "Come on, we'll all four of us go to the whist tonight."

140

Ada was surprised when Phil showed enthusiasm for the idea and for a while they went regularly. But Phil lacked concentration and frequently messed up a game with careless play and Ada backed out of going. Cecily, now she had faced her friends, continued to go regularly with Peter as her partner. There were several Wednesday afternoon dances where tea was served and patrons had the choice of dancing to records or playing whist. Gradually Cecily learned to ignore the remarks about her past from the few ill-mannered people who refused to allow the talk to die down, and enjoy the afternoons with Peter and their friends.

Ada's life became a routine of shop to house, and house to shop, with little besides. Phil followed her around and spent most of his time staring into space with only an occasional game of patience to alleviate his irritating stillness. When he did move, he would frequently look behind him as if trying to catch someone creeping up on him. He would turn a corner or go through a door then bob back again, suddenly, as if trying to surprise an imaginary follower. Ada gave up asking what he was doing; his replies were vague and often referred to something she had said hours before.

When Cecily spoke of his odd behaviour and tried to express her concern, Ada reminded her of her unwillingness to help when he was still well enough to be helped. However unreasonable, Ada blamed her sister, at least in part, for Phil's continuing illness.

In more lucid moments, Phil encouraged her anger towards her sister, insisting insidiously that Cecily thought of her as an assistant and not a partner who could make decisions. Defiantly, Ada employed a boy to help, without discussing it with Cecily, in readiness for when Willie had to leave them.

The business at the beach was long finished for the summer and with so many of the beaches barricaded off from public use with rolls of barbed wire and mined areas, there was general concern that the summer visitors on whom so many businesses depended would not come the following year. The brave words that it would all be over by Christmas were no longer believed, even by the most optimistic.

Thanks to Willie, other sections of their trade grew. He had sought out owners and captains of seagoing ships and once they increased their stocks to accommodate the new lines, they had attracted some very useful extra business from the docks. The crews of ships, and the dock workers that serviced them, needed food and other stores, and the cooks dealt with Owen's shop in increasing numbers due to Willie's hard advertising and the shop's convenient position not far from the dock gates.

The premises next door, which Cecily had bought but never opened, was packed from floor to ceiling with stores. Orders went out in the van driven by Willie, or one of the sisters, although Willie didn't like them going to the docks now there were sentries and armed guards to satisfy; their dedication and thoroughness was a reminder of the danger of being found in the wrong place.

Relations were still strained between Van and her mother, but one day she came to talk to Cecily and invited Willie and Ada to listen to what she had to say.

"As it's all in the family now, don't you think it would be a good idea for us to deal with these large shipping orders and contracts at Watkins'?" she said when they were all sitting in the room behind the shop one Wednesday afternoon. Before they could discuss this surprising idea, the shop bell gave its tinkling warning and Peter walked in.

Cecily told him what had been suggested.

"It makes sense, doesn't it, Peter?" Van said enthusiastically. "Mam and Auntie Ada would have less to do and it would still be in the family."

"But you'd have to employ extra staff, wouldn't you? That would be a mistake, with everything covered satisfactorily as it is at present. You're likely to lose your manager soon with the call-up underway, and if you manage to find the staff you'll be increasing your costs and your mother and Ada would have time on their hands here. Another thing is that with the shop next door, the stock is easily available. No, Van, the work being divided between the two stores works perfectly. A change would be too costly."

"Peter's right," Cecily said. "It sounds fine but there'd be an excess of people here and a shortage up there. Besides, it's Willie who found the extra business for us. I don't think he'd like us giving it away."

"Willie could come and work at Watkins'."

"Oh no!" Willie was adamant. "I don't want a change and besides, they need a man here, specially now with the risk of bombing and God knows what else. No, the sisters are my responsibility. I'm staying here."

"Well, forget the girl you employ to replace me. That's one less."

"There isn't one. Annette comes in if it's very busy, but other than that we manage."

"You wouldn't like Owen, I suppose?"

There was a chorus of dissent.

The talk went backwards and forwards, mainly between Cecily and Van but with the others adding their comments, and although the young girl was competent in putting her case forward, and Cecily was proud of her skill in debate, they all agreed that things were best left as they were.

When the sisters were alone, apart from the silent Phil, who sifted through the hot ashes and appeared to be counting those of a certain size, Ada had a change of heart.

"D'you know, Cecily, the more I think of it, the more I'm convinced it would be for the best for Phil and me."

"But how?"

"I'd be able to stay home a bit more if there were fewer rushes to get out the big orders. We are short handed at times even though we didn't admit it. And Phil is so much better at home." She glanced at her husband, kneeling on the rag rug in front of the fire. "He talks more and even goes into the workshop and looks at the machines and thumbs through the old order books. I really think that if we were home more of the time he might break out of this strange mood and start taking an interest in something again."

"All right, I'll talk it over with —" She almost said Waldo, who was no longer there to advise. "I'll talk to Peter and Willie again."

"Oh, you will, will you?" Ada said quietly. "What's happened to us? Why can't we ever make a decision, just you and me?"

"Oh, don't go on, Ada love. I know you think I'm overbearing and forceful. Don't start again. You and I have always talked things through with others, like Waldo and Bertie and Peter, haven't we? And you must discuss things with Phil too. It's how we come to a good decision, throwing ideas to and fro."

"Go on then. Get Peter on the phone. Ring him and tell him you want to discuss our business affairs with him. Not us, but *you*!"

"Ada!"

"All right, I do see you need to talk to someone else besides me but it shouldn't be so obvious that you want him to tell you what you want to hear."

"He made his comments on the facts Van gave us. I'm not asking him to agree with me and tell you you're wrong!"

"Aren't you?"

Ada stood up, reached for their coats and offered a hand to help Phil up off the floor. His face was bright red from the heat, his eyes bland but remarkably blue against the bright skin. "I wish I had just some responsibilities here," Ada said. "You make all the decisions and I'm just good old Ada. 'There's lucky

Cecily is to have good old Ada to help her.' That's what people say!"

And those words are Phil's and not yours, Cecily thought sadly, but she didn't say it aloud.

She went to the shop door and waved them off, filled with melancholy, then reached for the phone.

"I know it's the wrong thing to do, and I agree with all your reasons for refusing," she told Peter, "but I'm sick of confrontations with Ada. I want to do as she asks, just this once."

"I have a strong feeling that this is a serious mistake, Cecily," he warned.

"I'm sure too, but I'm so tired of fighting."

"No, you're not. You've always tried to please too many people. Van, Ada, your father, and Danny, of course. Why not please yourself over this and say no? I believe it could land you in a lot of trouble."

"I am pleasing myself," she lied. "I'll hand over all the big contracts we've worked so hard to get. Let Van deal with them and enjoy the extra freedom."

CHAPTER
SIX

The air raid sirens went frequently during the winter months of 1940 but no bombs fell. People began to hover at the entrances of shelters, much to the consternation of the wardens, looking up at the sky instead of huddling in the cold comfort of Anderson shelters or the larger, concrete street shelters with their entrances protected by walls of sand bags. Rationing began, but to many the war was still unreal. When the first air raid happened, people were devastated with shock.

It was after the shop had closed and Ada and Phil were just leaving, having stayed for a meal. Willie too had stayed late but as the siren began its wailing warning, he left.

"Annette has the children to look after, best I get straight there," he explained, pulling on his coat. "It's probably another false alarm but you never know." He went out and tried to start the car, which spluttered futilely and coughed its refusal to budge. He thought about going back and asking Ada for a lift but decided against it. She'd probably stay with Cecily until the all clear. He slammed the car door and set off to walk. Using the back lanes it wouldn't take long.

In the shop Cecily recommended that Ada and Phil should stay but Phil was restless.

"I can be home in five minutes," Ada assured her. "The streets will be empty." Then she remembered that Van was with Beryl and Bertie and unless the neighbours climbed the wall and used the cellar, Cecily would be on her own. "No, you're right." She handed Phil a flask to fill with tea. "Best we stay."

They carried a tray of tea and biscuits, which Cecily took from the shop and took precious moments to note in the relevant book in her meticulous way, and went down the cellar.

Willie was aware of the sound of planes first, as he ran along the dark lanes between the houses. Then he saw searchlights sweep the sky attempting to pinpoint the enemy. Guns boomed and the war was suddenly real. The bombs, when they came whistling down, seemed to be aimed at the docks, but he knew that didn't ensure Annette's and the children's safety. He ran as fast as he could, ignoring the shouts of wardens telling him to take cover, looking up at intervals to try and follow the battle going on above him. Searchlights and the small explosions and traces of smoke and flares lit the scene and at times was as bright as day. So much for the blackout, he thought as he cut across a field, taking the shortest possible route home.

The battle in the sky followed him. A plane flew across his path followed by another, smaller fighter. The crump of a bomb filled the air with a roar like nothing he had imagined, as it landed only streets away from the open ground over which he was running. The blast lifted him off his feet and he was stopped abruptly and painfully against a tree. He was winded and terrified at the strength of it. It was as if an impatient hand had swept him out of its way and thrown him hard against the tree. He regained his feet and recovered his breath and ran on.

Unbelievably, houses were falling like children's bricks as he reached the streets again. The night was filled with loud cracks as window glass shattered and rumbling as walls collapsed. Fires had already broken out and were illustrating the horrifying scene, growing with alarming speed. The horror of it filled his mind with wild imaginings and intensified with every passing moment.

Buildings blazed and the crackling increased in volume. His ears were filled with the roar as greedy flames engulfed everything in their path. Bricks clattered, slates winged through the dust-filled air. People and animals bolted past him, crying, screaming; he was crying too, and calling for Annette. He was trapped in a nightmare of terror and confusion but he didn't stop to help. All he could think of was Annette, Victor and Claire.

A small spaniel darted across his path and he fell headlong. The demented creature was trapped by him and it crouched against a wall, panting, its eyes wide, its whole body trembling. Willie picked it up, pushed it under his coat and ran on.

Stumbling over debris, his mind stupidly identifying broken pieces of wood as window frames, door panels, troughing and fence posts as he swerved around them in a zigzag path to get to his family.

He talked to the dog, telling it not to be afraid, that he was safe now, that the bombs were falling somewhere else, far away. He saw a plane making odd, jerking sounds coming across his path, the engine labouring. The plane dropped lower and lower and he saw with amazing clarity a parachute released and come floating down, beautiful in the glow of the fires. Then he cried as it touched a burning house and was enveloped in flames.

He was still crying as he opened the door of the Anderson shelter he and Danny had built, half underground, in his back garden. He fell into Annette's arms and she soothed him as he had soothed the dog.

"I found him," he sobbed. "I couldn't leave him, he was all alone."

The morning following the raid was a scene as strange as any Cecily could have imagined. She had already checked that Van and the others were unhurt, but when Peter came, they walked up to see the damage to Waldo's store and make sure Van was coping.

In the streets people were walking about, silently looking at the devastation. Children followed their parents searching among fallen masonry for shrapnel and whooping with delight when they found a piece large enough to stand in a bedroom as a trophy.

Numerous dead cats and dogs were found and men were already sweeping away the rubble, clearing paths and disposing of the sad sight. In the square, almost a

150

hundred pigeons had died, apparently of fright, and were also swiftly taken away.

Waldo Watkins's store had been damaged. Workmen were boarding up the huge space where glass had shattered. Women were out on the pavements, brushing away the evidence of the night, chatting cheerfully to disguise their fear and shock. Cecily and Peter went into the store and found Van there, organizing the staff who were cleaning up the dust that had blown through the broken windows and preparing to get ready for business.

Although she was only seventeen, she expected to be obeyed and was having a little trouble making the team do what she wanted, her voice raised and her hands on her hips. "A proper little scold," Peter said with a chuckle.

"We'd better leave her to it," Cecily said. "She doesn't need our help to sort them out, does she?"

Owen was there, sitting on the stairs, idly holding a bucket and mop, apparently content to sit while others did the first and worst stage of the clearing up.

"He intends to wait then give the floors the final impressive wipe to universal applause," Peter whispered.

Owen dropped the bucket and stood when he saw them watching. "Mam's all right," he reported. "And she said to tell you Annette's all right too."

"You were hurrying to tell us and stop us worrying, were you, Owen? There's kind."

"Yes. As soon as I'm not needed here," he said, slowly reaching for the abandoned bucket.

"Willie came first thing to tell us just that," she said angrily. "So now you won't have to bother yourself, will you? Go back to your sitting down, you lazy, useless creature!"

"What?" he said in amazement.

"You heard!"

Picking their way through broken glass, pools of water and soggy cardboard, they stepped warily past ruined and drunken displays. The floor was littered with smashed bottles and jars, the contents of which were unrecognizable. They gave off a weird mixture of smells: sweet, sour, pleasant and foul. As they left the shop Van was still shouting at her staff and Cecily was gratified to hear her start on Owen.

The day was slow to start. Few came shopping during the morning as most were clearing up either their own mess or helping others. Ada and Phil were still there, having decided to wait until the roads were clear before driving back home.

"We're so relieved you and your family are unharmed, Willie," Cecily said when he returned to the shop. "Running through all that, it's a miracle you are safe. Luckily, none of us is harmed and the only damage here is a broken slate on the back kitchen roof."

"Umm." Willie hesitated, looking at her with a frown. "That isn't the only damage we have to worry about." He beckoned her to where Ada and Phil couldn't hear. "It's their house," he whispered. "When I went back after coming to tell you we're safe, I saw the Spencers' cottage and the workshop were both gone."

Her hands flew to her face. "Oh no! How will he cope with this?"

"Will you tell them or shall I?"

"We'll do it together." She began to shiver, thinking how close she had come to losing her sister and how difficult it was going to be for Phil to accept another loss.

Ada was preparing lunch for them all.

"Ada, love," Cecily said, trying to control her shaking limbs. "I — we — have something to tell you."

But it was Willie who said, "It's your house and workshop. It's all gone. If you hadn't stayed here last night you'd be gone too, so try to think of that."

Cecily reached out to hug her sister, the shock of the near tragedy filling her throat with bile, but Ada turned for comfort to Phil. Willie saw the look of distress on Cecily's face and his strong arms went around her and he held her while she cried.

"There's clumsy I am, to say it straight out like that," he said. "Never did have no finesse." Ada and Phil stood together, neither of them showing any emotion. Willie and Cecily continued preparing lunch but no one ate. Her sister took Phil up to the bedroom and they came down looking calm and unaffected by the loss of their home.

The rest of the day was busy with callers. Melanie came to tell them she was moving away, further into the country away from the docks, which were a natural target. Dorothy came as they were about to close the shop and the sisters were shocked to see how dirty and dishevelled she was. Her eyes were red-rimmed to exhaustion.

"We've just finished digging people out of Grant Street," she sobbed. "The whole street went down like a pack of dominoes. One dead. And fourteen injured." She tried to hold on to the cup of tea into which Ada had poured brandy, but her arms trembled so much that Ada held it while she sipped. "I've been helping with the digging, then driving over rubble and I don't think my body will ever stop shaking," she said between sips of the reviving drink. "Lucky you two were that it wasn't the night you were on duty."

"Shamed I am that I didn't stop to help when I heard shouts from the houses that were hit," Willie said, "but I was demented with worry. All I could think of was getting home to Annette."

"No one would blame you for that. Certainly not me," Dorothy said.

Dorothy seemed to have forgotten her anger towards them over Owen's inheritance and called often between her many activities for a brief rest and a snack. They knew she hadn't really changed, she still occasionally showed her tendency to spitefulness, but today she looked too weary to argue or even raise her voice.

"Our house is gone," Ada told her. "We haven't been to see how bad it is yet but Willie thinks it's beyond repair. It will have to be completely rebuilt."

"And you haven't been to see it?" Dorothy was surprised.

"Phil says he isn't ready to face it. We'll go when he's ready and not before."

"Come on, we'll go now." Phil jumped up as if offended by her words.

"Not now, love, it'll be dark soon. Let's go tomorrow, is it?" Ada coaxed but he reached for their coats and would accept no further delay. Ada shrugged and they set off to examine the ruin of their home.

They walked through the house and yard into the stable, which once held horses but was now a garage for the van and the cars, and Ada helped Phil to pull back the heavy sliding doors. She drove the car out and went back to close them but she stopped and smiled as hymn singing reached them from nearby. Horse and his wife had survived the raid.

"They sound near." Phil frowned and looked around. With the car chugging ready to go, they walked to the corner and to where the lane met the street. Ada pointed to the empty shop once rented by Jack Simmons and now owned by Cecily. It had new tenants — undoubtedly illegal ones.

"Their home must have been damaged too," Ada whispered.

The window of the shop was gone, allowing the enthusiastic singing to swell out into the evening. The hymn tune was recognizable but not the words.

"This isn't much of a place, Horse, this isn't much of a place," sang Horse's wife.

"I damn well never can please you, why don't you shut up your face," was Horse's reply, keeping to the melody of a favourite hymn.

"Give over, you two," an angry voice yelled from the darkness at the end of the lane.

"That's old Zachariah Daniels in his shed," Phil whispered. "At least his place survived."

"This shed'll collapse on me one day with you two kicking up that flamin' racket," Zachariah continued.

"Jesus wants me for a flower in His garden," Horse's wife sang brightly.

"The sooner the better!" Zachariah snapped with un-Christian-like fervour.

Ada was glad of the smile to break the tension. She glanced at Phil, who was chuckling as she drove up the lane and on to the main road.

"Zachariah hasn't got much," he said thoughtfully, "but what he does have keeps him content. A donkey, an old cart, a shed to live in and a few sacks to keep him warm."

"Wouldn't do for me." Ada shuddered.

"No, but some want too much. Cecily aims too high."

Ada didn't reply. When he began talking about Cecily he often became upset and she didn't want that now, with him having to face the ruin of his home.

The white-painted house had not been bombed, but the boom of a heavy gun had weakened the walls. A window had blown out and the resulting draught had swung the curtain across to where a fire had started. Gladys had been in the habit of lighting a fire occasionally to keep the house aired and it was this that had started the blaze. It was fire that had destroyed the building, splitting the walls, breaking glass and setting fire to the furniture then the ancient timbers. It had

156

happened after the raid was over when most people had gone back to their beds, so the first few flickers of flame had not been seen and the building had smouldered gently, unseen and unheard.

Ada held Phil's hand firmly as he went to look at the damage. Defying the warning on the roped-off garden to "Keep Off", he went into the shell of the once-neat house where the smell of burning made Ada feel sick, and looked at what was left. He hardly paused in the living area but pushed his way dangerously through charred furniture and fallen beams, and splintered window glass and out to his workshop. She watched with tears in her eyes as he touched the twisted metal, naming the recognizable machines in a low mutter. Burnt paper was all that was left of the order books, broken glass the only evidence of the dyes and inks he had once used.

"Thankful I am that Mam didn't live to see this," was all he said, before walking away from the destroyed building.

Van was always anxious after the town had suffered a serious air raid. The drone of the enemy aircraft became a regular sound but she didn't fear for her own life — like most young people she thought she was immune, that terrible things only happened to "others". But she was always afraid her grandmother would be killed and that fear had her hurrying to Cardiff at the first opportunity to reassure herself that Kitty Owen was safe.

She always slowed at the point where she would have her first sight of the grey stone terrace in the quiet street. She avoided looking for as long as she could, afraid the house would be gone and a pile of stones the only remnants of a secret she had kept from her mother and Auntie Ada. She loved Gran, but she also loved the secret.

On one of her visits she almost bumped into Willie, who was on a similar errand, making sure his mother and sisters were unharmed. He was standing at the gateway of his mother's house talking to someone hidden in the porch. She darted back into a shored-up empty house which was roped off and covered with warning notices about its unsafe condition. Stepping beyond the ropes she slipped around the fractures and crumbling walls to peer back in time to see Willie leaving his mother's house, turning once or twice to wave. She waited a while, then hurried on to where Gran lived in a similar house a few streets further on.

Gran was pleased to see her and after reassurances on both sides that no one was injured, Van updated her grandmother on the trivial (yet to Gran precious) news of the family.

Kitty Owen was small and still attractive, and she dressed with a skill that disguised the unpicked and resewn garments and cut-down and remodelled outfits she wore. She looked forward to Van's visits and the slight connection with the family she had rejected, although seeing Van revived her guilt at the way she had run out on her "duty".

158

That Van had been scarred by the way she had been treated was clear. Kitty also knew that by leaving her family, by not being there when the truth of her birth was revealed, she had further added to the girl's distress. Van's resentment of her mother's denial of her for those early years worried Kitty and she tried gently to ease it away but Van closed up, a door slamming in her mind whenever she tried to explain the reason for the lies. When she did mention the subject it was to insist that she would one day pay her mother back for her dishonesty and the shock of the eventual revelation.

Van always wanted the latest news about Paul Gregory, Kitty's man-friend's son. He seemed to hold a fascination for the girl, and she saw him as exciting and worldly compared to other men she met. Today there was nothing to be gleaned as Gran had heard nothing from him since Van's previous visit.

"He's safe, though, isn't he, Gran? You'd have heard if he'd been hurt or been killed?"

"I'm sure as I can be that he's safe. Just unable to write. You'll see him again soon for sure," Kitty promised, hoping as she did so that Paul was nothing more serious than a youthful "crush" on her granddaughter's part. Paul Gregory was not the kind of man for Myfanwy Owen to marry.

As Van was leaving, Kitty asked the question she always asked.

"Van, lovey, is there any chance yet that your mother and Auntie Ada would be willing to meet me? I know what I did was terrible, but after all these years surely they've forgiven me at least a little? With this war on we

159

shouldn't let it go on any longer. I think I'll write to them — a letter wouldn't hurt and they might reply. It would be such a joy to see my girls again."

"Leave it to me, Gran, I promise I'm trying to persuade them but now isn't the time. Trust me, I'll find the right moment soon and do all I can to persuade them to talk to you. But not yet." She hid the smile of relief as Kitty agreed to leave it to her a while longer.

As she walked to the station for the train home, Van's thoughts were on Paul and it was because of that that she allowed herself to bump into Willie again. He spoke before she had time to find a corner in which to hide. It was at the station and they were obviously catching the same train.

"Van? What are you doing in Cardiff? Not shopping, from the lack of shopping bags."

"Oh, I did come to shop but I couldn't get what I wanted," she explained airily and without conviction.

Willie didn't question her further but showed her the coconut matting for which he had queued for an hour to get for Annette. Then, as she obviously didn't want to talk about her day, he talked about his mother and stepfather and his sisters and how they were coping with the air raids and shortages with good humour and even a sense of fun.

"This blackout's a bit of a lark," he told her. "This friend of their queued at the chip shop in the dark but as she got near she realized the chip shop was next door and she was queuing at a men's lavatory. There's soft she must have felt. And I wonder what the men thought she was doing there?" He looked at her to see whether she was amused at the story. "Even I lost my way here once. Took a wrong turning and almost walked into the canal!" He chattered on, all the time wondering what she had really been doing in Cardiff.

Over the next few weeks a number of serious raids hit the town. People who had been slow to erect their shelters hurriedly finished them and made sure they were stocked with food and blankets. Beside the docks, the targets were warehouses where food and ammunition were stored. The stocks were regularly replenished as it was from these and similar places that the forces were supplied with numerous food items. Owen's shop was again offered contracts mainly because of the convenience of its position. Cecily was delighted but again Van insisted that the larger Watkins' store was better placed to deal with them.

"We've got a cold room for a start, Mam," Van argued. "And we've got the space to stock these large quantities."

"Space isn't a problem," Cecily reasoned. "There's the shop next door besides the stable loft. We can use the stable too, if we leave the van and car in the street."

"But you don't want the worry. A big order is quite a responsibility."

"I'm quite capable . . ." Anger began to flare.

"Mam, you have to face it, Willie is likely to be called up any day and how will you manage with only Uncle Phil to help? No, it's best, really it is, for me to take it off your hands."

161

Ada pleaded with her to agree and Peter added his voice to Cecily's protest.

"I'll find you someone when Willie goes," he promised. "Don't let your business be whittled away after all you and Ada have done to build it up."

"The business isn't sliding, it's growing all the time." Cecily argued. But she didn't look fully convinced as she added, "Van only wants to ease our burden until things get back to normal."

"Then there's the problem of Phil. Ada will expect him to be the one to help when Willie goes. I don't like to think of you being dependent on Phil. He's obviously ill. In fact, I feel very uneasy about him, Cecily."

"Perhaps he would be better with more to do. I refused to help him, give him a job here and . . . Peter, there's something else. Van wants me to leave the running of the shop to Ada and Phil and go up to help her at Watkins'."

"What? Leave the running of your business to Ada and Phil?" He made no attempt to disguise his dismay. "Cecily, my dear, you can't seriously consider that?"

"Phil is a bit better now. They'll manage well enough, just until we can all get back to how we were, when this war is over."

"It's your business that will be over if Phil and Ada take charge, and all the best of it is going to Watkins'," he said solemnly. "And as for getting back to how we were, I doubt we ever will."

One day Van phoned and asked Cecily to come at once. Leaving Ada and Phil to deal with a small rush of customers, Cecily ran up the hill, worried abut the urgency in her daughter's tone. She found Van in her office with a nervous-looking Owen. Tomos Small, her manager, was sitting opposite her and books were opened across her desk.

Tomos Small had very short hair, cut well away from his ears, giving him a naked look, no place to hide. He was flushed, his ears shining and his skin moist. His eyes, behind the thick lenses which were the reason for him not being in uniform, were wide and staring with shock.

Van stood and offered her mother a seat where she could examine the ledgers spread out before her. Van pointed a finger to a number of entries in the stocktaking sheets.

"All of these have been altered, to cover losses of several hundred pounds," Van explained. "This man has been robbing me blind and has used this method of disguising the fact."

"What have you to say, Tomos?" Cecily asked quietly.

Tomos began to bluster, hoping to bluff his way out of the situation, briefly confident that he was able to out-talk two women, one of them a seventeen-year-old girl. His words were cut short by Van's voice telling him not to waste their time by lying.

Cecily was impressed by her daughter, at her sharpness in spotting the neat alterations to the listed items and the totals at the end of each column. She remembered the way Van had played as a child, not with dolls but with pretend shops, and how she seemed to understand the language of arithmetic with such ease, seeing figures in her head and solving problems with exceptional ease. It had served her well.

When blustering failed to get him out of trouble, Tomos pleaded innocent error. Then, when his whining was met with only a stony glare, he returned to trying to use his greater experience to unnerve the young girl.

"You can't tell me how to run a piddling little store like this! I've managed big-huge London company stores, I have!" he said contemptuously. "You? A kid like you? Damn me, it's always important to cover yourself against losses, didn't you even know that?"

"So," Van asked calmly, "which is it to be? A mistake? A genuine business practice? Or downright robbery?"

"It's you, interfering and trying to tell me how to do my job!"

Van stopped him with an edge of steel in her voice. "I'm not telling you anything, Mr Small." She turned to her mother. "I should tell the police but I won't." She turned back to the man now standing deflated and utterly humiliated. "I've spoken to Mrs Watkins and she agrees that you go. But if we hear any insults or foolish talk from you, the police will be informed and I have the books, in your handwriting, and two witnesses to this interview, evidence that will imprison you. One more thing. I won't be giving you a reference."

The man went without another word and after a moment Van dismissed Owen, who had sat silently and nervously throughout the interview. He wondered if he dare slip out for a bun while Van talked with Auntie Cecily but decided not.

Cecily was surprised to see that Van was trembling. It had been an ordeal for a young woman. She held her daughter's hand. "Van, lovey, I'm so proud of you. You handled that better than most men I know. How d'you do it?"

"Determination to let them know that being a girl doesn't exclude me from having a brain!" She slumped back in her chair in which she had sat upright and authoritative when Tomos was faced with his crime. "I'll be short handed now, Mam. Will you come to help me? All the staff are being taken away and it takes so long to train someone new. This food rationing is added work too, having to total up the fiddling counterfoils and fill in dozens of forms."

"You don't mean every day, do you?"

"Please, Mam."

"I'll talk it over with Ada and Phil tonight, and see if Peter can think of a better solution."

Phil had improved since the loss of his workshop. It was as if it had released him from the guilt of his failure to restart his printing business. Seeing the mangled remains made it clear to everyone that he could no longer contemplate working there. He had begun to take an interest in the shop and had even borrowed a horse and cart to buy what fruit and vegetables he could find, out of town, for the sisters to sell.

Supplies of fruit were dwindling owing to the shortage of pickers and the problems of transport. None came from abroad as shipping was needed for men and the means to make weapons. The items Phil bought from small growers and farmers were a boon to the local people and an additional profit for Owen's shop. Rabbits were a good off-ration meat source and Phil sometimes returned with half a cart load, which he gutted and displayed hanging in rows above the shop windows and were quickly sold.

"Could you two manage without me for two or three days a week?" Cecily asked as they sat down to eat. She was hesitant to commit to going to Watkins' full time. It was too much to expect Ada to manage the business completely. She had told them, with some pride, about how her daughter had sacked her manager. "Owen is worse than useless, he's a liability! Bertie helps when he can and Melanie calls every week, but Van needs someone there all the time, really."

"Go full time then, if that's what you want to do," Ada said cheerfully. "I've been in the shop as long as you. I can manage. Phil will be here some of the time. Pity about Willie having to go but we'll manage, won't we, Phil, love?"

"It's definite then? Willie has to go?" Cecily sighed deeply. "I was hoping he'd manage at least a deferment."

"He's going, but Annette says she'll come when she can."

"Annette won't be able to do much — she has baby Claire and Victor to deal with, bless them all, and she'll be without Willie too, remember."

"We've discussed it and Gladys Davies will look after Claire until she starts nursery school."

"That's settled then." Cecily hid the irritation she felt at everything being arranged before they had discussed

166

it fully. Wasn't that what Ada always accused her of doing?

So Cecily's routine altered again and disrupted her peace of mind more than other changes had done. She couldn't accept leaving the shop every morning in the hands of Ada and Phil, afraid it wouldn't be run the way she had always insisted. She still wanted to have the reins in her hands, feel the pulse of it throbbing through her veins as she had ever since their father had died in 1930.

But once in the large store and ensconced in the office overlooking the shop floor, she found so much to do, experiencing a similar challenge in the vastly different trade, her dismay was quickly put aside. It was only in the evenings, when Ada and Phil discussed the happenings of their day, when they told her things they had done that she would have handled so differently, that she felt cut off and no longer a part of her home.

"Dig for victory" was a growing cry during the first years of the war. Besides the allotments, which flourished under the care of older men, boys and a great number of women, plots could be seen in unlikely places. Women were planting potatoes in the gardens of bombed-out houses. Along the banks of streams and road verges, the soil was turned and planted when it became obvious that ships were no longer getting through regularly and the need for home-grown food was increasing.

"Every time a ship is filled with food, it means fewer guns and less support for your boys" the newspapers warned. But apart from growing thyme and parsley in tubs in the yard, there was little Cecily could do to help that particular call.

At the end of 1941, food was rationed further by the introduction of a points system. Each ration book included a page of small tokens which had to be exchanged as well as money for various tinned and dried foodstuff. This added to the burden of the shops and they had to be counted and used when they gave their orders to the wholesalers. It was a boring task which Cecily found waiting for her both at Watkins' store and at home.

There was so much to do that at times she felt she was riding a merry-go-round that was out of control. Working all day with Van, rushing home to prepare a meal before dashing out to attend lectures on putting out incendiary bombs, starting savings groups, or helping Dorothy organize a flag day in aid of comforts for the troops. There was the fire-watching rota, meaning loss of sleep, and it seemed sometimes that she dragged herself from one place to the next in a semi-doze.

Peter came regularly and helped in many ways, delivering orders and collecting goods from the whole-salers, which had changed its address after being hit by an incendiary bomb. He was there when Danny came to say goodbye.

"I'm joining the navy, me having a bit of experience, like," he said excitedly. "Damn me, it's bound to end soon now, with Willie sorting out the army and me soon in charge of the navy. We'll be back victorious before you've had time to miss us."

Cecily sat close to Peter and listened to the three men discussing the latest news of the war, and arguing about the rights and wrongs of it all. She was feeling older than her years. This war was robbing her of her youth. She showed no more emotion than the rest when Danny shook their hands and kissed her and Ada with the same amount of affection before departing for the station. She stood in the shop porch, the door closed tightly behind her to stop any light showing, and there wasn't a waver in her voice as she called her final goodbyes. Only Peter guessed how she was feeling.

"Come on, Cecily, my dear, I feel like going to the pictures. Margaret Lockwood's on in *The Stars Look Down*."

So they queued in the dark street and went in to the picture house to be transported away from the present and into another world where their problems and fears were far away. Cecily was glad of Peter's utterly reliable friendship and of the hand which held hers with such understanding.

On the home front, 1942 was a year of scrap collecting. There were arrangements for gathering waste paper and to aid this valuable recycling, children were admitted to the pictures free if they brought two pounds of paper. In that way, three tons were collected. Bones were valuable too to make glue, foodstuff for animals and fat for lubricating heavy guns — the rumblings of which filled the air night after night as raids continued.

The salvage drive also included rags and tin and iron and other metals. Saucepans and frying pans were shown on posters flying through the air in an effort to persuade people to part with any surplus utensils. Railings disappeared from gardens, all taken to build planes, the householders were told. Rubber was another need and heels from shoes and boots and hot water bottles were all gathered in.

At Christmas time, people were asked to save string and wrapping paper from their parcels. Ada began a string collection in the shop adding every piece that was brought in until she had three balls, one measuring more than three feet in diameter and which would hardly go through the door when the collectors came. There were appeals for books and nearly 40,000 were pulped as well as a thousand being added to depleting libraries and 13,000 sent to the forces. Again picture houses helped, allowing children in free when they carried four books.

There was an unusual appeal, this time asking householders to invite members of the forces into their homes and allow them a few hours of luxury away from camp. This the sisters felt unable to support — their lives were far too full — yet they hoped that somewhere, someone would be kind enough to give some comfort to Gareth and Willie and Johnny Fowler and Danny.

Cecily fell into bed exhausted most evenings, having begun her work at six and worked on her many activities until late in the evening. She took no part in running the shop and was too weary to do more than ask a few questions about its progress.

One morning, as she stood waiting for the rain to ease before running up the hill to start her day with Van, she became aware of how empty the shelves were. Rationing had cut down dramatically on the foodstuff but there were other lines available. Tinned food no longer filled the shelves behind the grocery counter; the vinegar barrel was missing from its stand. There was no chicken meal or dog biscuits. Small shelves Willie had made to hold the spices their cosmopolitan customers demanded were no longer there, only marks on the paint showing where they had once stood. The top shelves where soap, scouring powder, mop heads and brushes were normally displayed were empty, or filled with old cards advertising things they no longer stocked.

"Ada, love, why are the shelves so empty?" she asked, looking round for some sign of rearrangement.

"We don't see the point of ordering stuff we rarely sell," Ada said. "When Phil and I do the ordering, we check to see how long since we last ordered the item and if it's slow we don't re-order once it's gone."

"But Ada, that's the way to let a business die! It's because we stock so many items that people come to us. We save them walking up to the main road. Remember how we painstakingly built up the stock after Dadda died? How happy we were to do it our way? If once a customer comes and can't find what he wants we've lost them to the shop where they do find it.

Don't you see? Ours is a handy shop, selling everything."

Ada's face showed incipient anger. "It's my responsibility now, mine and Phil's. Van agrees with us and she knows about business. She advised us to avoid overstocking on things that sell only occasionally. We know what we're doing, holding only fast-selling items and forgetting the rubbishy stuff that's only money lying idle."

Cecily was horrified, finding it difficult to believe that Van would give such illogical advice, but she backed away from the confrontation which, from the look in Ada's eyes, was highly likely if she continued.

"Go on, you, up to make a fortune for Van," Ada said after a moment, to allow the anger to subside. "Phil and I will see to everything here."

That night, when Ada and Phil were in bed, Cecily went down to the shop and examined the books. It was a disaster. The points system had discouraged people from buying from Owen's shop. With so little choice they had taken their points and their ration books elsewhere. Not even to Watkins' she noticed. They'd be too embarrassed, her being there to note their disloyalty. No, it was probably Lipton's or the Home and Colonial who had their business now. "Oh, Ada, what have you done?" she said aloud.

She couldn't sleep so she settled down to write some letters. Since they had been called up, she wrote a weekly letter to Gareth and her cousin Johnny Fowler; him with the disobedient hair, who at thirty-two, still seemed too young to be amid the horrors of war. Willie also received a regular letter since he had reluctantly left them to serve in the army, a short time before Danny.

Willie didn't receive the letter she wrote that night to dull her mind from the realization that Ada had lost the business they had so painstakingly built. He was injured only hours after she wrote it, and although it followed him to various hospitals, he was home before it caught up with him.

Annette didn't know how badly Willie had been injured. In his letter telling her he would be coming home while a wound healed, he didn't explain the nature of the problem.

"With you expecting again, he wouldn't want to frighten you, leave you imagining something worse than it is," Cecily said after reading the letter.

"But his writing, Auntie Cecily. All skewiff it is. It isn't his eyes, is it?"

"Try not to let your imagination run away with you, love. He doesn't say he's being invalided out, does he? Just home for a wound to heal. That doesn't sound too bad, having him home for a while, does it?"

Later that evening, Cecily had a phone call. It was from Willie, asking her to be with Annette when he came home. He refused to explain his injury and, guessing it troubled him to talk about it, she didn't press for details, just promised to be there.

"I'm coming down tomorrow afternoon," she told Annette. "I feel like mitching I do. I haven't had an afternoon to myself for ages. All right if I come for a cup of tea, love? And see you and the children?"

She sat in the neat living room, where Annette knitted a tiny woollen vest for the baby expected in time for Christmas, and they talked about everything except Willie.

He walked through the door without either of them seeing him come down the green lane and across the road. Annette gave a cry and ran to him. Then she pulled back, staring at him, searching for a sign of discomfort, and asked anxiously, "I didn't hurt you, did I?" She looked him up and down, then she saw that the lower part of his sleeve looked odd. Willie, her capable, clever, talented Willie, had lost a hand. She pressed a hand to her mouth and her agonized eyes stared at Cecily.

Cecily picked up the three-year-old Claire and said firmly, "Well, you won't want us around for a while." She kissed Willie, adding, "Willie, I'm so glad to see you safe home with us. Whatever's happened, you're home where you belong. And that's the very best news for us all. Now, Claire and I will go to the park for an hour, right? Then we'll meet Victor from school. We'll all have tea when we get back." She forced gaiety into her voice as she dressed Claire and went through the door and up the green lane, then, to Claire's amazement, she sobbed uncontrollably for almost ten minutes, grieving for Willie and for all the others whose lives had been irrevocably changed.

When she calmed down, she pushed Claire on the swings, rode with her on the roundabout and helped

174

her up the long slide which should have gone for scrap but which some kind person had seen fit to overlook. Then she bought a shilling bar of chocolate with the sweet coupons she had intended to save for Christmas. After an hour she met Victor and they walked back down the green lane to share the treat after tea.

Willie didn't mention his lost hand. Cecily stayed to have tea with them and heard more news to upset her. Willie told them that Jack Simmons was dead, the bright, quick-tempered boy who had lost his job at Watkins' after fighting with Willie so many years ago. Cecily wondered how his family would manage and wished she knew them well enough to call. She didn't even know where they lived.

All the way back to the shop she cried. She was so tired and depressed and told herself that was why it was impossible to hold back the tears. But what chance was there of having a break? Perhaps a few hours over at the beach sometime would help. It was the end of summer and, despite the war, a busy time. When she and Ada had run the shop it had been their busiest time too but now the beach trade which she had enjoyed so much was, like so much of their business, in other hands.

Injured soldiers appeared on the street in growing numbers, bandages, plaster and crutches giving endless variety to the signs of battles against Hitler's armies. On the streets children played amid the ruins of houses, playing at war, thinking it an exciting game. One day on the way to visit a customer with a complaint, Cecily was horrified to see a small pair of boots sticking out of a pile of rubble. A child had obviously been caught in a fall of loose and dangerous walls. She went in and began scratching away at stones and bricks to find a cheeky dirty face grinning up at her. "Ever be 'ad, missus?" he called as he ran off. She chased after him and slapped his dirt-stained legs and he yelled with all his might.

"I'll tell our dad about you," he wailed, running into a nearby house, to return a moment later with a large, unkempt man who began complaining about her treatment of his son.

But although at least a foot taller and five stone heavier, it was he who backed away from Cecily's anger. She asked several people where she could find Jack Simmons' family and no one knew. That made her angry too.

CHAPTER
SEVEN

Amid all the tragedies, arrangements were made to encourage people to stay at home instead of travelling further afield for their holidays. People needed to have fun and each town was determined to provide plenty. Dances and fun days, children's choirs and the town's silver band gave concerts and entertained locals and tourists alike. The Pleasure Beach, with its beautiful golden sand, remained open and free from the dangers of mines and barbed wire, and the shops and stalls flourished.

There were Punch and Judy shows, swing boats and roundabouts on the sand, free entertainment from small groups of actors and clowns. Fancy dress competitions were always popular and talent shows brought out the most enthusiastic singers that ever faced an audience, plus a few brave comedians.

Although most of the regular summer staff had moved on to war work, the tea rooms continued to open for business with older women and young girls taking their place. The town was a haven amid the tragedies and deprivations of war.

It was a forced defiant gaiety during those wartime summers and Cecily worked with Dorothy and dozens of others, when her full schedule allowed, to help make them a success. Schools stayed closed for two more weeks, and the children were bronzed and healthy despite restrictions on food.

Danny came home on leave but didn't call to see Cecily. She learned from Willie that he spent his precious time with either Jessie or Danielle, who was now eight, or with Willie and Annette, where they discussed plans to take on a trainee when the conflict finally ended.

The war effort continued to keep Cecily and hundreds of others busy for hours of each day. There was a special Wings For Victory savings scheme to raise £250,000 to build four Lancaster bombers and ten Hurricanes. The following year a penny a week collection saved to send parcels to a growing number of prisoners of war. Every moment of every day was filled and there were still requests for more help as new schemes began.

"At least," Cecily told Peter, "it doesn't give me much time to worry over what's happening at the shop!"

Gareth came home on leave and he and Rhonwen called to see Cecily and Ada. Cecily thought he looked well as he smilingly thanked her for her letters.

"And thanks for looking in at The Wedge to see that everything is running smoothly. I don't know how you find time for all you do."

"By not thinking about it!" she said with a laugh.

Johnny Fowler was another who called when he could manage it. They were surprised to see that his hair was now very short and standing stiffly up all over his head.

"Poor dab," Ada said. "He looks like a paintbrush."

Johnny's difficult hair clearly didn't worry him, as he called one day in 1943 to tell Cecily and Ada that he was getting married.

"I met her in Somerset when I was on a forty-eight," he told them, smiling widely. "She's with Mam now. Already making arrangements, they are, for the wedding. On my next leave it'll be. You'll all come, won't you?"

"What's her name, what does she look like, what does she do?" Cecily demanded, encouraging him to talk as he obviously wanted to.

"Her name's Sharon and she's thirty-seven," he said proudly. "Got three daughters she has: Victoria, Debora and Leonora. Little beauties they are."

They all wished him luck and promised to attend the wedding and filled his haversack with cakes and a few sweets and waved him off affectionately.

The sisters had a second visitor that day. Late in the evening there was a knock at the door and it was Ada who answered it, shading a torch as she opened the shop door to avoid trouble from the ever-vigilant wardens. A man she didn't know stood there, and he seemed hesitant to explain who he was.

"This is a bit difficult, like," he said. "I've got some news. It's about — oh, hell, can I come in? It's as dark as looking up a chimney out here."

"Phil?" Ada called, and the man stepped back as if expecting trouble.

"I want to talk to Miss Cecily Owen and Mrs Ada Spencer," he told her.

"You'd better come through." Phil pulled Ada aside and allowed the man in, leading the way to the back room, where Cecily opened the door once the passage door was closed.

The man was very large. His army greatcoat looked as if it were padded, Cecily thought. He had black hair cut short, and his bull-like neck was red with the chill of the night. His dark eyes looked around the room as if selecting the best position and he chose a chair and sat with his feet close to the fire, without being invited to do so.

"It's about your mother, see," he told them. "There's been an accident. Well, not an accident, more an act of God, you might say." He might have gone on waffling around the subject for an age if Cecily hadn't intervened.

"Our mother?" She and Ada drew close and reached for each other's hand. "What about our mother? Who are you? Where is she? What's happened?" They asked questions in turn, confused and frightened by what they were about to be told.

"It's your mother, see, Kitty."

"What about her!" Cecily demanded.

"Well, she —"

"For heaven's sake, man, say it!"

The sisters moved closer, thinking the worst, guessing it was her death he was trying to tell them but refusing to say it for him. She was dead, the mother they hadn't seen for many years and who had never contacted them.

"It was a bomb, see. Direct hit on the house. Dad's dead and Kitty, your mother, well, she's on her own."

Relief hissed out of them like air from a punctured balloon. They both felt relief peppered with anger for the devious way they had been told. He had put them through agony for nothing.

Ada was the first to find her voice. "And who are you?"

"I'm Paul Gregory. It was my dad who Kitty — your mam — you know, lived with, like."

As he went on, their anger changed to sympathy.

"My dad's gone and I haven't got another soul in the world, except Kitty. My own mam threw me out when Dad went to live with your mam. I don't like to think of Kitty being on her own, see, with me in the army and never there to look after her. I thought I'd tell you rather than write. She wants to see you, sure of that I am, but she isn't sure of a welcome, see. I thought that if you wrote a letter I'll see that she gets it. Fond of your mam I am. She's been good to me has Kitty Owen."

His voice distorted as he spoke and he swallowed a lot as if clearing his throat of sobs. Cecily and Ada felt sympathy growing, but then Cecily caught an expression in the young man's eyes and felt a chilly, stomach-churning shock. The eyes were cold and calculating and showed no real distress at the bereavement he was talking of. It was an act. He was pretending to feel the emotions of a broken-hearted son. She was frightened by him and wanted him gone. He was a stranger getting in the way of thoughts about her mother returning. She wanted solitude and the chance to think, to take in the news of her, but instead here was this man faking grief at the death of a man they didn't know, whom they hadn't even met. The man who had taken their mother from them.

She tried to ignore him and allow her thoughts to dwell on her mother, whether they would be strangers after all the time that had passed, or friends. But Paul's presence refused to allow it. He sat there waiting for her to speak. What did he want? Why couldn't he see they needed to be left alone?

Ada was still clinging to Cecily, until Phil peeled her away, taking her into his arms and leaving Cecily standing alone. She realized that Ada was sobbing, and Phil was whispering to her in a soothing way, and Cecily moved away from them, fussing over cups and saucers.

"Do you have time for a cup of tea? Or do you have a bus to catch?" she asked the soldier, hoping he would take the hint and go. "We mustn't take any more of your time." It didn't sound very polite but the silent way he was staring at her made social niceties irrelevant.

After a silence that went on too long, he said, "Tea? I'd rather something stronger, Cecily." He smiled disarmingly and she felt ashamed. He had come to tell them about their mother being on her own, using his precious leave to do so. She was just being fanciful thinking there was anything other than kindness in his expression.

"Take off your coat, boy," she said then. "Look in the cupboard over there and you might find a flagon of beer."

He stood to take off his greatcoat and in the uniform underneath he looked equally large. His battle blouse stretched across his huge chest and the sleeves bulged with muscles. Three stripes showed him to be a sergeant, the badges that he was a gunner. He found the flagon and a glass and settled to enjoy it. Phil watched but didn't complain about not being offered to share it. Phil had a strange ability to make himself unnoticed at times like this, almost invisible, when someone else was taking all the attention.

"And you are Paul? Paul Gregory?" Ada rubbed her reddened eyes. "I'm afraid we've seen nothing of Mam since she left with your father. She was always sickly, mind, and we brought ourselves up, so we didn't get really close to her even before she left."

"Sickly? Auntie Kitty, as I call her, has never even had a cold since I've known her! Full of fun she is, a damned good laugh. Hell, yes, she makes the house ring with it."

The sisters looked at each other. Could there have been a mistake?

"Our mam? Lively and full of fun? But — you're sure you've got the right place? I mean, silly things happen in wartime and it doesn't sound like our mam. An invalid, she was. Spent a lot of time in bed."

"She's your mother all right. I'd have recognized you two easily from the photographs she has on her bedside table. Damn me, she talks about you enough too. I'd have known you two anywhere."

"And our mother is lively? And a lot of fun?" Ada delved into a drawer and handed him a photograph of their mother.

"Yes, that's Auntie Kitty. She said your father made her into an invalid, trying to make her into something she wasn't."

"Rubbish!" Ada said at once.

"Was it?" Paul poured himself the last of the beer. "She said he wouldn't allow her to do anything except stay in the house and mind the girls, who didn't want minding. She escaped into the life of a bedridden old woman, to be pampered, to read books, listen to the wireless and dream of a life where she could be herself."

"I don't believe any of this." Cecily agreed with Ada.

"You don't? You're Cecily, aren't you? You'll never marry, according to Kitty Owen, until you find a man willing to allow you to be yourself. She says you're a free spirit and will never make the mistake she made. Is she right? I don't see a ring, so perhaps she is and you haven't found the right man yet."

"You are impertinent!"

He smiled and nodded agreement.

Cecily wanted to throw him out. She watched him drain the last of the beer and go to the sideboard to find more. He was big, confident and intrusive, an alien in their safe living room.

184

Paul waved a new flagon at Phil, who sat beside his wife, leaning forward in a protective way, poised to leap up to defend her.

"Want a glass?" Paul asked. Phil shook his head.

Cecily's brain was struggling with confused thoughts. The way he had walked in, found himself a place at their fireside, and told them things about their mother's life had disturbed her. His grating personality made her postpone her thoughts on her mother until he was gone. She wondered how she could help him on his way.

The second flagon of beer was half emptied and she watched as he refilled his glass. As the liquid went down, so the moment of his departure drew closer. She wished Phil would take some and make the moment come sooner.

Paul Gregory looked at her over the rim of the tilted glass and his dark eyes closed slightly as if he were smiling. Had he guessed her thoughts, seen her discomfort? Was he prolonging his stay to torment her? There was something frightening about him. She wasn't imagining it. She was unable to control a shiver of apprehension from travelling down her spine.

They heard the doorbell tinkle as it opened to admit Van. She and Edwin had been to the pictures and Cecily hoped he would come in, although he rarely did. Van walked through the shop and went into the passage to hang up her coat. She poked her head around the door.

"I've called to pick up the order book. Uncle Bertie said he wanted to have a look at it," she called out. "I'll stay tonight as I want to have a chat." Then she saw

Paul and, recovering from the shock of seeing him, demanded rudely, "Who are you? You aren't taking in lonely soldiers now, are you, Mam?" The words were directed at her mother but she stared into the appreciative eyes of the soldier, not showing with even a flicker of a smile that she and Paul had met often at her grandmother's house.

Almost sullenly, Cecily introduced her daughter to Paul, who stood up and held Van's hand for what seemed to Cecily an interminably long time. He too hid the fact that he and Van were friends.

"So, you are Myfanwy." He smiled, showing strong white teeth in a wide, aggressive jaw. "My sort of cousin by non marriage, you might say."

"You are not related," Cecily said at once.

"Now there's a lovely thought," Paul said. He was admiring Van, who stared back boldly, her young face slightly flushed and very beautiful. "Seventeen and never been kissed?" Paul teased. Cecily saw the charm being turned on as Van and Paul sized each other up. She was upset, wanting him to go, never to appear again, wishing Van wasn't looking at him in that way.

"Good for us to meet at last. Like my own family, you are."

Ada laughed and the sound cut into Cecily's agitation. She turned to see Ada and Phil watching the young couple with obvious delight. They clearly didn't share Cecily's unease.

Ada stood then and whispered in Cecily's ear, "Don't tell her why he came. We'll tell her about Mam later, when we're on our own." Cecily nodded agreement.

186

"Well, thank you for coming, Paul." Cecily implied it was time for him to go.

Van said, "Sandwich, anyone? I'm starving and sinking for a cuppa."

Cecily's heart dropped as Paul at once nodded. Ada nudged Phil and went with him into the back kitchen to prepare food, leaving Cecily and Van with the young sergeant. It came out then, his father's death and why he had called. He went on to explain why Kitty and his father had never married.

"My mam refused to divorce him, see, so even when your father died, they still weren't free. But that didn't stop them being happy, damn me, no. There wasn't a more content pair in the whole town, I bet a shilling. She had to work, of course, cleaned at some swanky houses near Roath Park. And she did a few hours at the corner shop."

"Mam hated the shop!" Ada protested.

"Never! Loved it she did, flirted something awful, mind, terrible she was. The male customers loved it and spent more than they intended just for a glimpse of her smile. A proper flirt she was and my ol' dad loved it. Knew she was only having fun and belonged to no one but him, see. Well met them two for sure."

When Paul eventually left, he and Van seemed to have become friends. It was she who walked through the dark shop with him to see him on his way. Cecily waited in an agony of suspense for Van to come back. It was so unlike her daughter to be so friendly on such brief acquaintance. Peals of laughter rang out, hers high and merry, Paul's deep and with a tone that another time and with another person Cecily would have found infectious.

The door bell jangled at last and Van came into the room. Cecily saw from the flushed cheeks and the shining eyes that her daughter had enjoyed the encounter. Excitement didn't show that clearly when she had just parted from Edwin Richards.

It was about Edwin that Van wanted to "chat". "He's joining up," she told them. "The deferment is over and he leaves tomorrow."

"Why didn't you tell us before?" Ada asked.

"He only told me tonight."

"Then why didn't he come in? Why aren't you staying there to see him off?"

"I wanted to talk to you, to explain."

Cecily frowned, wondering what was coming next.

"Edwin hoped we'd become engaged before he went away."

"Van! That's wonderful!" They all chorused their delight.

"I said no. I'm not ready for such commitment. I haven't even got control of the shop yet. There's a lot I want to do before having a husband and children. I — I don't even know if Edwin is the one."

"You've been close ever since you were born. Being only two years older than you, he's always been your protector."

"Perhaps the length of time we've been together explains why there's no excitement in the prospect of being his wife."

188

"I hope you don't think someone like Paul Gregory and the excitement he offers is a better long-term prospect!" Cecily asked.

"Perhaps. He's certainly different!" was the disconcerting reply.

Cecily lay awake for hours that night, thinking about the implication of what her mother had told Paul. It seemed her mother knew her better than she knew herself. The refusal to marry Danny and accept his terms although she both loved and desired him was clearer to her mother than it had been to herself and eerily closer to her mother's life than she would have believed. She found it amazing that where she had been unable to put it into actual words, her mother had explained it simply and had been able to make Paul, a complete stranger to her, understand.

It was then it began to be real. A hope that she and Ada and their mother might meet and talk, without the recriminations that might otherwise have come between them. She thought of Danny too, knowing her decision not to marry him had been a wise one, even if not until now fully understood. She felt a greater loneliness than ever, knowing that Danny would never again be a part of her life or her dreams. She knew her future lay in helping Van to achieve a full and happy life, while she, Cecily Owen, faced a future unfettered by a loving partnership. Her chances had all gone.

She sat up and switched on the bedside light, which Ada and Phil had given to her on her thirty-seventh birthday, and reached for a book. She had just found her place in *Pickwick Papers*, which she found to be a pleasant way of cutting off the worries of the day, when the low growl of a siren warned of an air raid.

She hurriedly slipped on the trousers she had recently taken to wearing and a thick jumper, and hurried downstairs, calling to Van, Ada and Phil. They settled at once in the cold cellar. All except Cecily had been roused from a deep sleep and had no difficulty in returning to its blanketed comfort.

Cecily, still in her sleepless state, sat and stared into the dark corners of the barely lit room listening to the drone of planes and the thudding of guns, apprehensive that the next moment would contain the blast to take them all, as it had taken Mam's coalman.

Morning came and apart from the lingering smell of gun smoke and the sight of children searching for shrapnel, there was nothing to show for their disturbed night.

Neither Ada nor Cecily had suggested that Paul Gregory should call again, so it was a surprise when Van announced that Paul was coming for Sunday lunch one day in September.

"Lovely," Cecily managed to say, swallowing her dismay. "I'll ask Beryl and Bertie, and Edwin if he's home, shall I? It's time for him to have some leave, isn't it?"

"No, Mam. No one else. Just Paul and me."

"It's not as if he's someone we like," Cecily confided to Ada and Phil later. "He just breezed in off the street and sat as if he'd the right to be here. He's supposedly the son of the man Mam lived with, for heaven's sake! That makes him a nobody in my estimation!"

There had been no reply to a brief letter Cecily had given to Paul, so they presumed their mother still had no wish to see them. The thought made Cecily resent Paul Gregory even more. Ada thought differently.

"But Cecily, he's got no one and him a soldier too. I think we ought to make him feel a bit welcome, at least till the war's over." Ada sighed and added, "We don't know what will happen to him. Just think of poor Jack Simmons and all the others who aren't coming back. He could be gone like them in a matter of weeks. And just think of fighting a battle and then not having anywhere to go when you get a bit of leave. Terrible that must be."

"You aren't suggesting he comes here, are you?"

"Big he might be but he's only a boy. Shame on us if we don't offer a little bit of hospitality. What d'you think, Phil, love?"

"I agree. Best for us to give a bit of kindness to a homeless soldier." He smiled at Cecily, a gloating smile, guessing how afraid she was that Van would be taken in by the big bold, handsome sergeant. "Van writes to him every week."

"I know it's unreasonable, making too much of Van's friendship with him," Cecily told Peter later. "There's nothing wrong with the boy and Van writing to him — well, that's a kindness and nothing more. Van isn't a fool and she's well able to judge herself. But will she? Or will she be taken in by the glamour of him? He is glamorous; big, handsome and worldly wise and so . . . so bold. He has eyes that see everything and he smiles as if what he wants is there for the taking."

"With so many women looking for a man to replace those who have been lost, what he sees usually is his for the taking! But the confidence could be just an act. He might be less sure of himself than he pretends."

"Please, come on Sunday and judge for yourself," Cecily pleaded. "Just come, as if it's a longstanding arrangement."

"Van won't be pleased."

"No, Peter, but I will."

So Peter came and ignored the surprised and disappointed look on Van's face. He handed her a small parcel. "This is an un-birthday present," he said with a smile.

"Thank you." The words were spoken sharply. She didn't unwrap the gift but put it on one side, guessing it was perfume, refusing to be pleased.

They ate roast chicken at that difficult meal, Phil having gone into the country and bought one in exchange for sugar and tea, filched from the shop. He still went occasionally with the borrowed horse and cart and brought back what he could buy or barter. He brought back duck eggs, rabbits and mushrooms, sometimes cucumbers and tomatoes and on rarer occasions onions. Fruit, too, in season, reached the shop via his deliveries and queues would form as patient customers stood, hoping that the rare treat wouldn't be sold before their turn came. Ada proudly told the others of his skill in finding the luxuries they would enjoy today.

It was Paul who carved the chicken on Van's insistence, glaring down her mother's protests, although Phil, whose job it usually was, would have made a better job of it.

192

Van seemed to treat the day like a celebration for herself and Paul, ignoring Cecily when she made a comment that didn't include him.

Peter was quiet. Only Ada and Phil seemed unaware of the tension in the artificially cheerful group. They listened to Paul's stories abut life in the wartime army and laughed at his jokes, even though some were more crude than they were used to. He used the head of the table, where Van had placed him, like a stage, from where he watched his audience and played them like an expert.

When the meal was finished and they had moved the chairs back to enjoy the port he had brought, he went into the passage and came back with two boxes. One was the size of a biscuit tin, the other was small and tied with ribbons. The largest was opened first. It contained an iced cake and bore the words MUVANWIE AND PAUL.

"Sorry about the spelling." Paul laughed. "That's the closest the cook could get to Myfanwy. He owed me a favour, see. Got something on him I have. So here we have a cake made with butter." He winked at Van. "Nothing but the best for my girl, eh? And iced by one of His Majesty's soldiers. Specially for you, Van." He leaned over and kissed Van slowly, and with sounds of satisfaction.

Cecily looked nervously at the smaller parcel then back to the cake, afraid to ask why Van's and Paul's names were together. Peter reached and held her hand.

Van laughed excitedly as Paul released her and pointed to the second parcel. "And now this one?" she asked.

"Yes, impatient girl, you can open it now." He sat smiling, his dark eyes darting to Cecily and back to Van, in suppressed excitement as Van's small, slender fingers pulled at the ribbons and removed the wrapping. Van was smiling too and Cecily had the horrifying sensation that this was a charade especially arranged for her, some tormenting scheme intended to make her squirm. It was becoming unreal, as though the two people in the centre of it were strangers. She gripped Peter's hand tightly.

As she had been dreading from the moment she saw it, the package revealed a jeweller's plush-covered box. Van opened it and gasped in delight. The electric light caught the glitter of diamonds as a ring was lifted from its bed of velvet and handed to Paul. He took Van's hand and after kissing the palm, slipped the ring onto her third finger. "Well?" he said to Cecily. "Aren't you going to congratulate us?"

Cecily looked at her daughter and asked quietly, "Why didn't you discuss this with us, Van?"

"No need. I'm nineteen and in eighteen months I'll be twenty-one. Paul and I don't intend to marry until then so I won't need your permission, will I?"

"Permission? No. But it would have been nice to believe we're important enough to be included in something as important as this."

"Surprises. That's what life should be, Cecily," Paul said cheerfully. "Don't think I won't look after her properly. Just because you see me in the uniform of a sergeant doesn't mean that's what I'll always be. No fear. Under this khaki there's a man going places."

194

"To a grocery shop?" Cecily asked, sarcastically.

"Damn me, no! That's Van's territory! No, I have plans of my own. Don't know exactly what I'll do but by the time this war's over, I'll be ready to get started. Don't doubt it."

Belatedly congratulations were offered and Cecily asked Paul how long he was staying.

"I have to go back tomorrow, Cecily."

Hearing him use her name grated on her. He was altogether too bold, she decided, then shuddered at the even worse prospect of him calling her Mam! "And will you get leave again soon?" Her voice sounded artificial and stilted, even to herself.

"I'm not supposed to say, really, but I'm training some boys now for the big push that's coming in a few months," he said conspiratorially, "so I'm not far away. I'll be back in a week or two. I can't stay away now I've found my Myfanwy." He smiled at Van, who was still admiring her engagement ring.

"Come and help me take the dishes out, Van," Cecily said, and when Van followed her carrying some plates, she said to her, "Fortune hunter! I thought you'd have more sense!" She rattled cups angrily.

"He'll share the shop when it's mine to share, Mam. And perhaps he is excited at the prospect of marrying a wealthy woman, but I don't intend to spend my best years alone, like you! I'm not stupid. I'm well aware of the dangers. Paul and I will be partners but I will hold the reins, of that you can be certain." Van's eyes were glittering with excitement.

195

Van went back through the passage to the living room and through the open door Cecily heard laughter ringing out. But she wasn't a part of it. She was isolated, ostracized by her lack of joy.

She heard the clatter of china and tensed herself for Van's return but it was Peter who came back with a laden tray. Silently he stacked the dishes and when she began to wash them, he took a towel and dried them.

"I shouldn't have said a word," she muttered miserably.

"It's often the best," he agreed, "but the suddenness of it would make any caring mother anxious, specially when she dislikes the man."

"What d'you think of him? You're well balanced and just distant enough to judge without prejudice."

"I don't think he'll be enough for Van. She'll tire of him before her twenty-first birthday."

"Today was stage-managed for my benefit. She's scoring points for some reason I don't understand. She might be stubborn enough to still marry him. Knowing I disapprove could be enough to make her go through with it. Maybe the fact that there's a connection with Mam has brought the opportunity to hurt me. Oh Peter, I've made such a mess of bringing her up — the lies, all the pretence, they've ruined the chance of us being close and loving as we once were."

"She'll come round, when she's got it out of her system."

"She'll do anything to harm me and make me unhappy. I think she hates me."

Peter put down the white cloth and put his arms around her. "Cecily, dear girl, you worry too much. However hard you try, you cannot protect Van from every danger, avoid for her every pitfall life brings. You have to accept that she'll make mistakes. All right, perhaps you said more than you ought, but whether you did or not is irrelevant. Van is nineteen and whatever she is, she will remain. Come, my love, cheer up. Let's go back in and you can smile your wonderful smile at them both."

She looked at him, seeing the kindly friend of so many years and hugged him almost shyly. "Peter, what would I do without you? You're such a good friend. How long has it been now?"

"Thirteen years last April." He kissed her lightly on the cheek and she turned impulsively and kissed his lips. With an arm casually around her waist, they went back into the living room with smiles that were genuine.

Van and Paul were standing and Paul was putting on his army greatcoat.

"Where are you going?" Cecily asked.

"For a walk and a cuddle in the dark," Paul replied.

"We'll have to start saving our clothing coupons now," Ada said happily. "Won't it be lovely to have a wedding in the family? All the relations here. You can have all my coupons, Van, love. What about yours, Cecily?"

The next morning Cecily went out and spent eight of her twenty-six coupons — which had to last for a year — on a pair of worsted slacks for two pounds fifteen shillings, and a full-sleeved blouse using six more and two pounds sixteen shillings. A pretty nightdress cost one pound and ten shillings and used six coupons. Defiantly she returned to the shop and spent the remaining six coupons on eight pairs of stockings at a shilling a pair.

CHAPTER
EIGHT

Throughout that summer and autumn there were a few air raids but most times the enemy planes flew over the town without causing any trouble. Nuisance raids they were called: a plane passed over and the warning would sound, forcing workers to leave their benches and causing a loss of production. Gradually people became less worried and would hesitate before going to the shelters; some ignored them completely. A few bombs were dropped in the area but there was no return to the fierce attacks of earlier months. One theory was that if a plane had a bomb left after a previous attack somewhere further north, the crew would drop it rather than take it back to Germany, and they were indifferent about the target.

Cecily spent her days at Van's side in the office overlooking Watkins' shop floor, trying not to worry. She tried not to think about Van writing to Paul every day and waiting for his next leave with undisguised excitement. She tried not to think of the way Ada and Phil were allowing the business to slide deeper and deeper towards unrecoverable failure. It was all so difficult and if she tried to discuss either problem she risked an argument, so she worried, but spoke of it only to Peter.

Ada and Phil seemed to keep themselves busy in spite of falling trade. They still had a few customers registered for weekly rations but these were much reduced. Butter and cheese were down to two ounces per person per week and most weeks there was only one egg. Fuel was restricted too; the coal allowance was not sufficient for a daily fire during the winter, and logs were a popular extra. Magazines were full of recipes for wartime cooking: eggless cakes, fatless sponges, and there was Spam and the famous dried eggs.

Watkins' store began to build up for the Christmas trade by having small allocations of tinned fruit. The store was decorated with a few streamers to add some cheer, but in Owen's shop the shelves remained empty. Phil still went out on the cart but rarely brought anything apart from rabbits. These sold quickly, a queue forming before Phil had taken them from the cart.

Annette called with their youngest child, whom they had called William, and explained that, try as she might, she couldn't persuade Willie to return to the shop. "He just sits and mopes, except when Danny comes home on leave and that isn't very often. In fact, it's months since we saw him," she told the sisters.

"Shall I come and see him and ask him to come back?" Cecily suggested. She was tempted to show Annette the books and point out how much they genuinely needed his advice and encouragement, but loyalty stopped her. It was too easy to offend Ada these days.

"I don't think he'll be persuaded, but please try, Auntie Cecily. I'm in despair, I really am. I'm tired of talking to him."

"And talking isn't all you've been doing, is it?" Cecily said with a chuckle.

"No, you've guessed. There's another baby due in June. I can manage four children," Annette said wearily, "but please get Willie from under my feet!"

"Let's hope the war is over before he's born."

"I'll go on Sunday," Cecily told Peter. "In between fire drill and first aid and teaching a lot of new girls to drive ambulances! It seems we just get them used to the heavy vehicle then they take their skills to the forces."

They went late on Sunday morning and were invited to stay for lunch.

"No, loves, I can't," Cecily said, seeing the small piece of lamb they were prepared to share. "Ada will be expecting us back. I only came to have a word with Willie." She looked to where the twenty-nine-year-old sat, with a length of wood under his damaged arm trying to shape it into a hobby horse for four-year-old Claire. Seeing him struggling, she decided to use every argument she could to get him back, and forget her loyalties to Ada and Phil.

"I'm so tired these days, I'm likely to fall flat on my face and snore in the gutter," she told him, waving her hand in an ineffectual attempt to push her hair from her eyes. "That long the days are, I wonder why I bother to go to bed for the few hours I sleep." She took a deep breath and went on. "It's Phil partly, Willie. You know he's a bit, well, a bit odd. He spends a lot of time driving around in the horse and cart, most days coming back with nothing, and Ada is left to cope on her own. I'm with Van all day and I have to come home and cook a meal, then, between all the voluntary work, I deal with the books. Not the ordering, I'm not allowed to do that. I order too much apparently and it isn't sensible. How they explain how having no stock to sell is sensible I can't explain."

"I did wonder about the empty shelves but Ada explained about Van dealing with the big orders to save you worrying about them."

"That's only partly true. The bulk of the day-to-day business is still in the shop but they're running it down and down. Quite honestly, there soon won't be any business to worry about. Between them they've lost three quarters of it already."

"What will you do?" Willie asked.

"Please, will you come at least for a little while?"

"I don't like leaving Annette to get three children into the shelter if there's a raid. I'm needed here."

"I know you have your own business to get back on its feet, but could you come and see if you can persuade them to start building it up again? You know the business as well as I do and Phil might not object if you make suggestions about increasing the stock and encouraging our old customers back. I don't know what I'll do if things go on like this for much longer."

Willie stood up and walked around the room. "What's the point of me being there? What can I do with one arm?"

"More than most can do with two!" Cecily snapped. "It was your arm and that's terrible but it wasn't your brain, was it?"

Peter beckoned to the children and took them out into the garden, with Annette following.

"It's easy for you to talk," Willie argued.

"I never dreamt you'd be the one to feel sorry for yourself, Willie Morgan! I'm working an eighteen-hour day, running here, running there, trying to do the work of three and watching the business — that you and I built — go down the drain like the water from scrubbing a filthy floor!"

She glared at him, her blue eyes wide in feigned anger, her fingers crossed behind her back. Her relief, when she heard him chuckle, was enormous.

"All right, you big bully," he said. "But if I feel I'm not pulling my weight, I'll pack it in, right?"

"No. That's not right! Starting with built-in defeat isn't for me and it isn't for you either."

Peter laughed all the way back to the shop. "You're a formidable woman, Miss Owen." He smiled. "A suit of armour and a pack of dogs wouldn't be enough to persuade me to take you on when you're really determined."

"Did I overdo it?"

"No, my dear. Like everything else you do, it was perfectly correct."

"Flatterer!"

So Willie agreed to go back to the shop, leaving Annette and Victor and Claire and William to get to the shelter, if necessary, without him.

"We managed while you were away, love, and we'll manage now," Annette assured him affectionately. "Go to the shop and promise me you won't try running home through an air raid again."

"And you promise to take the children and your precious cargo to the shelter the minute the siren starts."

She put her head on one side. "Willie, you never used to boss me around."

He smiled, told her she was the most beautiful wife in the world and set off for the shop.

At the end of his first day he reported to Cecily that all was definitely not well.

"There isn't much on offer at the wholesalers but Ada is refusing to buy anything," he complained. "Things are so desperately scarce that she could sell whatever she can get. But no, she seems to get more satisfaction from emptying yet another shelf and putting up a board to hide the gap. She washes the shelves and does the windows every Monday regular, and boasts that the shop was never so clean. They've stopped selling fresh fish altogether, as Phil can't bear the smell, so that order has gone completely, although I might manage to get it back."

"I'm so worried, Willie. Every time I try to explain to Ada about widening her stock, she jumps into a rage and looks to Phil for support against me. He says I've given her responsibility and should trust her to do what's best. The truth is, I *don't* trust her. I suppose I never have."

He patted her shoulder in a comforting way. "Get this damned war over then we'll start again, but it'll be harder than before — restrictions won't vanish overnight. And there isn't as much fresh ground to cover as when you took over from your father."

"It's all there for us. We're using Watkins' for the big contracts so they're safe. It'll all come back. All the beach trade too, and the shipping orders. I deal with them through Van's store so they'll come back once Van no longer needs me at Watkins'."

"It's hard to imagine it," Willie said, "the men and women coming home, food rationing just a memory, goods coming from abroad to fill the shops. It will all happen, but I'm afraid it won't be for a while. Perhaps this time next year we'll see encouraging signs."

"However long it takes, we'll get the shop going again." She lowered her voice. "I just wish Ada hadn't lost so many of our day-to-day customers. Small people, small orders are what we started with and they're still our mainstay, or would be if she hadn't lost them!"

"Van will return the big contracts, will she?"

"Of course." Cecily laughed. "If I want to handle them, that is. It's all in the family, isn't it, and it doesn't really matter whether they're dealt with in our shop or hers."

"Will you stay at Watkins' when Van is twenty-one? Have you thought of a manager for her?"

"Plenty of time for that — 1945 is when she'll be celebrating. Besides, being twenty-one doesn't change anything. She just takes over the business officially. And what's the point of looking for a manager now with all the young men in the forces? No, it's the end of the war that will start things moving. Then we'll sort everything out and I'll come back to where I belong."

"Best for you too," Willie said firmly.

Christmas 1943 drew near without any prospect of the conflict being brought to an end and for Cecily and Ada, the occasion offered only the promise of a few days' rest and quiet. Peter was the only extra person they had invited. They anticipated this restful oasis in their lives with pleasure, but in fact the house was constantly filled with callers and they had little time to relax.

Although they expected no one else, extra food had been stocked, just in case. Peter brought cakes, pasties, a loaf and some tinned meat, bottles of beer and some sherry, again, just in case. "Anything you don't need we can give to Horse and his wife so they too can enjoy Christmas," he said.

Gareth was home on leave and he called with Rhonwen and Marged — who was now twenty-five, and in the Wrens. Willie brought his family, plus the dog he had rescued during an air raid, and Danny, who looked very strange with short hair and without his earring.

"He arrived just as Annette and I were leaving," Willie explained. "I told him you'd be pleased to see

206

them. Jessie and Danielle are with him." He looked at her to see if there was a sign of dismay, but she covered her surprise well.

Cecily hugged Victor and Claire and picked up baby William as some sort of defence as she walked through the shop to greet Danny and his family. She almost hid behind the baby as she said, "Danny. There's lovely to see you." She turned to the small, red-headed woman at his side, who was hesitating to enter. "Jessie! Welcome. Come in, all of you." Still hugging the baby, she led them into the living room. She was trembling. How could Willie be so insensitive?

Once inside, leaving coats draped over the counters, it was obvious the room behind the shop was too small. Peter went through to the back kitchen to fill kettles for the inevitable cups of tea, allowing her time to greet them all.

"Come on, all of you," Cecily said brightly, "I think we'll go upstairs to the big sitting room or we'll fall over each other." She ran upstairs, leading the procession of visitors, and put a match to the fire, and fussed over it for a while, glad of the excuse to avoid looking at Danny. When she did, he came over and kissed her lightly on her cheek and at once did the same to Ada.

"A Happy Christmas," he said. "You're both looking lovely."

Peter forgot about tea as Ada and Phil opened the drinks cupboard and took up bottles of port, sherry and lemonade, Willie produced a couple of flagons of beer and Cecily searched for sufficient glasses for them all. Since the bombing, they had packed away their best glasses and china in the cellar and were using cheaper ones. She apologized for them as she handed round drinks and snacks. She was still on edge at Danny's unexpected appearance, his wife watching her, trying to understand, perhaps, what it was her husband saw in the agitated woman.

When everyone was supplied with a drink and some games found for the children, she sat and allowed the talk to flow around her. It was easier than she might have thought. Danny still got to her and she supposed he always would but the occasion, with so many people present, was quite pleasant. Her heart calmed to its normal beat and the initial tension faded away. Danny and Willie had plenty to discuss, being friends and business partners, and the children were an easy distraction when things went quiet.

Rhonwen and Gareth were obviously very happy and Cecily felt momentarily bleak at the reminder that she might have married Gareth if his mother and Dorothy hadn't interfered. But there was no jealousy, only regret that she was alone and everyone else part of a couple.

"Where's Phil?" Ada asked as she added more precious fuel to the fire.

"He won't be far — he's looking for more drink, I expect."

"I'd better go and find him. We'll need more coal and logs brought up." She went downstairs, leaving the chattering group and calling to her husband.

He was outside. She found him in the back lane standing looking up at the sky, his arms around

Zachariah's donkey, singing softly in duet with Horse, who was heard but not seen.

"Phil, love? Why aren't you staying with our visitors? All friends we are and wanting you with us."

He went on singing for a while, using the correct words to the carol, in company with the irreverent Horse, who was making up his own, then looking at her as if seeing her there for the first time. "'Ell of a quiet night. Makes you wonder what's waiting for us up there. It can't last, you know, not this quiet."

"Nothing lasts, Phil, love. But we can enjoy the peace while it's here, can't we? Come on now, come and sit beside me. Not complete without you beside me am I?" She eased his arms away from the donkey and ignoring the strong scent of the animal on his newly knitted jumper, walked him back into the stable, locking the door behind them. Horse's loud voice was a background murmur in the still night air and, for once, he sang the correct words to *God Bless Ye Merry Gentlemen* in his sometimes melodious voice.

They paused a while and listened. It was dark and stars shone like pinholes in velvet. He seemed in no hurry to go inside but she coaxed him through the door, pulled the blackout curtains across and shivered. "Come by the fire, you must be frozen, standing out there talking to a donkey."

"Not much coal left," he said inconsequentially. "Five hundredweight to last more than a month. Wasteful it is to light the fire upstairs."

"You're right, love, but it's Christmas. Perhaps you could go out on the cart and buy some more logs?

Good at finding wood you are. Remember last year, how you found enough to see us through the winter? Great help that was." Talking to him all the way, she led him upstairs to rejoin the others.

"Willie," she said briskly, "out of that chair. Let Phil have a warm." She settled Phil in the seat near the hearth and set about helping Cecily to refill glasses and find more food.

It was while Cecily was downstairs collecting a few more bottles of cider they'd just remembered that more visitors arrived. Johnny Fowler, looking thinner and more bony than ever, came with his bride-to-be and her three daughters. Cecily kissed them all and ushered them into the ever widening circle around the roaring fire.

Sharon was over-made up. Her hair was fluffy and badly bleached, her clothes were too tight, her figure was one that made all the men sit up. But she was delightful and soon a friend to them all. The first impression, of an overdressed, vain young woman lacking in taste, faded at once in the warmth of her personality.

Her three daughters, all fair and very alike, were soon playing happily with Victor, Claire and Danielle. Victoria was six, Debora five and Leonora only four. Johnny was so proud of them his face shone in a constant smile.

The room was large and the fire made smaller by placing fire bricks at each side of the grate so less coal was needed to fill it. The fire was not really large enough to heat the room but the crowd added their warmth and soon cheeks were rosy, people spread further away from the hearth and the room became pleasantly warm and filled with chatter and laughter.

Marged sat on the floor and involved herself contentedly with the children. Cecily smiled affectionately at her, thinking how little the years had changed her. She was still a giggling, childlike young woman, for whom every day was a joy. Peter played the piano and they sang some of their favourite carols, and even moved the rugs back and danced for a while to tunes they knew so well.

By the time they had relaxed into that stupor following too much heat and a surfeit of food and drink, Cecily no longer felt ill at ease with Jessie. Annette knew her well and included Cecily in their conversations. Danny seemed content to sit next to Willie, leaning over occasionally to help him with food, or an empty glass, and Cecily felt a growing joy, aware that at last she was over him. Silently she thanked Willie for inviting him, even though she had wanted to curse him when they had first arrived. She supposed that her mother's words, delivered by Paul Gregory, had helped too.

"Sharon and I will be married next April," Johnny announced after a whispered consultation with his fiancee. "We hope you'll all come. It'll be a small, wartime wedding, not as grand as we'd like but —"

"It will be at the register office," Sharon apologized, "and no proper reception, but we want you all to be there. You will come?"

"Try and stop us!" Cecily said and, after a brief consultation with Ada, added, "And we'd like to hold the reception here."

The news of the wedding and the discussion following delayed the departures and it was almost two o'clock before the party ended. A little drunk, decidedly merry, they all trooped through the shop, giggled their way into their coats and, carrying the children between them, went off up the hill, still talking, laughing and bursting into occasional song.

Peter kissed Cecily and Ada and thanked them for one of the happiest Christmases he could remember.

Phil was the only one not to enjoy the impromptu party. For most of the evening he had sat in a chair near the fire, staring at Cecily with ill-disguised dislike.

"So much for our quiet couple of days," Cecily said with a laugh, as all but Peter had disappeared from sight. "And tomorrow we've got Bertie, Beryl and Melanie, and, who knows, even Van might favour us with a visit!"

"Pity she chose to stay with Beryl and Bertie," Ada said. "I don't know how she can, not after telling us she's going to marry Paul Gregory."

"He didn't get leave anyway. Thank goodness for small mercies."

"Perhaps he did and is staying with our mam. After all, she's been his unofficial stepmother for years and there's bound to be a strong bond between them."

"Why doesn't she get in touch?" Cecily wondered. "Why can't she face us?"

"She must hate us for our remind of the past and the way she let us down."

When Peter left after helping to clear the dishes, Cecily no longer felt tired. She sat down and thought about the surprisingly enjoyable evening. With Danny and Jessie and the wedding plans of Johnny and Sharon, Gareth and Rhonwen so obviously happy, the experience of having the house filled with children's laughter and of how glad she was to have Peter always there to support her, it had been memorable indeed.

She made a cup of tea and settled down to write some letters. There was no point writing to Gareth and Johnny, who had shared the evening with them, but she did anyway. They would soon be back amid the horrors of death and destruction and a reminder of the happy evening would be welcome. She wrote her usual weekly letter to Edwin too, and sat, looking at the envelope, wondering how and where he was. She hadn't seen him since Paul had given Van his ring and had no idea how he felt about it. She described the seasonal events including their Christmas evening but didn't mention Van at all.

CHAPTER
NINE

In March 1944 another savings scheme was announced, this time to assist the soldier. The target was £250,000 and Cecily, with many other volunteers, went out collecting on an extra evening, trying to encourage new savers as well as chivvy the regulars into contributing more.

There was a weariness on the faces as people went about their tasks, and a shabbiness about the town. The bomb damage had been cleared but the gaps in the once-neat terraces were a constant reminder of past horror and grief, and the possibility of more. Queues formed outside every shop as more and more food items came under the heading of luxuries and as soon as news came of a delivery, women would stop what they were doing and run to join the line of patient shoppers. Beside food, items like shaving soap and razor blades were enough to encourage people to wait for hours, enjoying the chatter and sharing the complaints, strangers for a brief while becoming friends.

Van's twentieth birthday was in April and Cecily and Ada spent a lot of time considering how best to celebrate it. They planned a family party and invited all the family members who were able to come. Everyone would contribute at this time of shortages and even neighbours who weren't invited offered a few small additions to the food being gathered for the tea party.

Uncle Ben, who sang in the choir and who, when he spoke, boomed so loudly the china in the cabinet rattled, hadn't been in touch with them since the revelation of Waldo being Van's father, and the reading of the will. His second wife, Auntie Maggie, strongly disapproved of Cecily, whom she considered to be a shame on the family, and she took pleasure in talking about it to make sure no one thought she would forgive. In this she was supported by Dorothy, who had always considered the Owen shop should belong to her son, Owen-Owen, named-for-his-grandfather. Invitations were sent out to them and, although no reply came, Cecily and Ada hoped they would come and end the disagreement.

Lists were made of who was invited, and what food they could provide, and on the Sunday before the party Van went out early in the afternoon and ignored their request for her to go over the list to make sure no one had been left out. She told them to go ahead with the party but that she wouldn't be there.

They argued, demanded to know what she would be doing that prevented her attending her own birthday party but she was vague. "I have already made arrangements for a celebration," she said airily. "I might be seeing Paul if he manages to get leave."

"Van," Cecily asked quietly. "If you know Paul Gregory, you must know where your grandmother is."

"I do know, but she won't have anything to do with us. I've tried but it's no good. She will not agree, so forget it — there's no chance of her offering you a reconciliation."

"A reconciliation? For what? We didn't do anything. It's us who have to forgive her for running off and leaving us without an explanation."

"Maybe she sees it differently. Maybe Granddad knew more than he told you. Either way, she won't consider meeting me or any of us," she lied. "It's probably your fault, Mam, you causing all the embarrassment and shaming the family by having me, don't you think?"

Cecily reacted to the cruel remark by walking away sadly, wondering if her daughter would ever return to the loving, affectionate person she had once been. Surely the truth would be faced and dealt with soon?

"I suspect she is in touch with Mam," Ada said. "I also suspect that what she has just said is rubbish, invented to offend you. She's got some growing up to do, our Myfanwy! But what can we do about finding Mam? The only address we have for Paul is his army address. Knowing she's in Cardiff isn't enough to find her and I don't think Van will help us, do you?'

"Surely Van wouldn't lie to us about something like this?"

"Oh yes she would," Phil said. He began laughing uncontrollably. "This is something your Myfanwy would just love. Hates you she does, Cecily. And if she can find a way to hurt you she'll take it!"

216

"Stop it, Phil," Ada said. "You're talking rubbish. Forget it, Cecily," she added in a whisper. "Poor Phil, he gets very confused at times."

It was embarrassing but they rang, called and wrote to cancel the invitations, and instead put the tinned and dried food aside for a different celebration.

In April, a week after Van's twentieth birthday, Johnny Fowler came home to marry his Sharon. She wore a dress made from muslin onto which she had painstakingly sewn beads of blue. Ric-Rac braid decorated the hem and neckline and the effect, although hardly smart, enhanced her figure and smiling face and made her a beautiful bride. Her daughters followed her as she came out of the register office with Johnny, and stood near her with bunches of flowers in their hands, while Willie took photographs. His clumsiness with the camera was ignored; no one offered to help as he held the camera awkwardly between chest, chin and injured arm. This was something he was determined to do himself. The bridal group waited patiently, smiling, until he succeeded in gripping the camera securely with the shortened arm while his strong hand took several pictures for their album.

Annette gave the children tissue paper, which she had cut into rose-petal pieces for them to throw over the happy couple. There were two cars, hers and Peter's, to provide transport for the guests. The children's clothes were obviously home made and cut from other garments. It was garish and cheap and Cecily's heart went out to them. She was glad they had done what they could to make Johnny and Sharon's day special.

She kissed the bride, surprised at the thickness of the make-up Sharon used and wondered suspiciously if she was in fact older than the thirty-five years she admitted to.

The journey back to the shop was a poor imitation of the procession when Ada and Phil were married. Willie had helped to wash and polish the cart which Phil occasionally borrowed and with streamers added made from old lace curtains, the newlyweds and the three little attendants set off in style, waved off by a crowd of well-wishers.

Family and friends went back to a meal of Spam and Duchess potatoes with a variety of vegetables, mainly from tins. The cake was small and only a sponge, but it had two layers and was decorated with icing sugar scrounged by Dorothy in exchange for some tea and added to the meagre spread.

The guests included Peter, who spent a lot of time helping Cecily attend to the diners. He was by now fifty-six and balding but to Cecily he seemed not to have changed at all. Johnny talked to him for a while about what he planned to do when he was out of the khaki uniform he had worn for his wedding. Dorothy and Owen presented the couple with a pair of pillowcases stored since before the war. Gareth was fortunate enough to have leave and he and Rhonwen brought a box filled with rare items like soap, a torch complete with batteries, shaving cream, a few cups and saucers, a beautifully polished copper kettle and an embroidered tablecloth.

"These are a few things we spared from our cupboards. Now this is your real present." She gave the excited couple a table lamp with a shade representing a thatched cottage. "I painted it myself," Rhonwen told them. "Everything we buy is so plain, I hope you like it."

Willie and Annette gave them a pair of towels for which they had to part with some clothing coupons and for which she queued for an hour. There were gifts of money, which Sharon immediately gave to Johnny to put in their savings.

"I don't want to risk spending it unwisely," Sharon said. "You're in charge of our expenses now, Johnny."

The guests stayed long after the meal was finished and at ten o'clock no one showed any sign of leaving.

"What will we do for food?" Ada whispered. "They're all starving again and there's no more bread on the loaf!"

"I've got two loaves at home and there's a tin of Spam and some pickle," Dorothy offered. "I'll fetch them, shall I?"

"Let me go," Cecily said, but Ada insisted that she should do it. "Tired you are and it's a long walk but not worth getting the car out."

She whispered to Phil, explaining where she was going and at once he said, loudly, "Why you? Why can't Cecily go?"

"I offered. I don't mind, really I don't."

"Then I'll go with you."

She laughed. "Get up and you'll never get your chair back! No, stay and enjoy the fire, love." She threw him a kiss as she went downstairs, with Dorothy's key, to collect her coat.

It was cold outside, the kind of chilliness that seemed to get inside the forehead and make ice in the blood. She hesitated about going back and taking the car — an extravagance but tempting. She put a scarf tighter around her neck, pulling it as low as possible over her face, holding the ends across her mouth. She hurried to 7 Snipe Street, holding Dorothy's key in her hand.

As she turned the corner, away from the vicinity of the docks and the blast of cold air coming from the sea, she slowed down, thankful for the slight relief. She was passing some tall, abandoned houses that had been slightly damaged by air raids but which appeared to be sound. At least, no attempt had been made to demolish them. She stopped to rearrange the scarf and became aware of cracking sounds. Looking up curiously, she felt something falling around her and touching her shoulders. She used her torch. Glass. It looked like broken glass. What could be happening?

She heard the sound of approaching planes and forgot the glass, thinking about the possibility of a raid. What should she do if the siren sounded — run on to Dorothy's and shelter under her table or run back to the wedding party? There wouldn't be room for them all in the cellar and she chuckled at the vision of them finding places under the stairs and other likely places in the old house.

She stood against the abandoned house, still undecided. Phil would worry if she were out alone in a raid. He might come looking for her. Best she went back. Ignoring the call of a man across the road wishing her good night, listening to the increasingly loud drone of the approaching planes, trying to decide from which direction they were coming, she was unaware of a group of young girls who passed on the opposite side of the road.

The throbbing engines were above her and an added sound began that terrified her, glass cracking like gunshots, the rumbling of falling masonry, the screams from the girls walking past. Then a thundering noise that seemed to go on forever. There was a raid yet no siren had sounded; the neglect outraged her and made her forget momentarily her vulnerability out in the open with not even a sandbag wall to protect her. Still she dithered about whether to go to Dorothy's or back home, stumbling a few steps this way and a few steps that way. Before she had finally decided she had to go home, the rumbling increased and the wall against which she was crouched moved and dust fell across her. She wasn't hurt. She would get up and walk away as soon as she had calmed her breathing. The sounds eased and stopped, then in the lull she heard them begin again, breaking glass and the gentle tinkling as the pieces landed somewhere nearby at first. Then more sounds as walls within the building weakened; a sound like water dripping, increasing into a flood. The falling water sound grew louder and suddenly became a roar and everything went dark and silent. The silence was as terrifying as the darkness. She knew she was deaf, the sounds were so completely shut off from her. She tried to move then and found she could not. She was frozen with fear. She listened but had no idea for how long, and gradually her hearing returned. There was a clatter as the last of the loosened bricks tried but failed to resist the pull of gravity.

Another long time passed and she managed to stand, her legs shaking and trembling so she had to take hold of some of the masonry to steady herself. "I've got to get home," she murmured aloud. "My husband, he'll be that worried. Came out for bread I did."

"Hang on, love, better worried than widowed so don't make any sudden moves or this lot might land right on top of us." It was the man who had just come out of the public house nearby.

"I have to get home, my husband will be worried." Ada looked around at the pieces of brick and mortar that surrounded her, dust filling her mouth and nose and making her cough. Slowly her eyes became adjusted to the gloom, which was exacerbated by the increasing dust.

The man who had spoken to her held her arm and she grasped his hand. From the faint smell of fish emanating from his sleeve, he was a seaman, probably from the fishing boats that still worked from the quieter part of the docks.

"You're one of the Owen sisters!" the voice said in surprise. "What are you doing out at this time of night?"

222

"I was going to fetch something." She frowned in confusion. "I can't remember what. Shops will be closed before I get there now." She closed her eyes and rubbed her sleeve around her nose and mouth to clear the filthy dust. "Why didn't the siren sound?" she asked.

"Siren? There hasn't been an air raid, missus. This old building decided it's had enough and just collapsed."

"Just move slowly and we'll be safely away from it in no time," a second voice called and she crouched down and felt a strong desire to go to sleep and dream away the events of the past minutes. But sleep was a long way off; she was wide awake and wondering if Phil was somewhere near and whether he was hurt, and why they were there.

With the two men guiding her, she moved with cautious care and when she saw the light of a couple of torches approaching she was convinced it was Phil looking for her. She called and, as disappointment came, she began to weep, silently, with hardly a sound. Someone tried to wrap her in a blanket, "For the shock," they explained. She pushed them away, assured them she was all right and insisted she was going home. Again she went in the wrong direction. As she turned, confused and looking for Phil, and the men protested and tried to persuade her to wait for the ambulance, the rest of the walls fell and this time window glass was a chord of musical delicacy heralding the roar of more falling masonry. It was only a few seconds before she lost consciousness.

At the shop, the Owen family waited with increasing anxiety. Cecily stood beside Peter, glad of his strength. He began to plan their search ready for the moment when they decided they couldn't wait any longer. Phil walked up and down in the confined space of the room behind the shop, groaning to himself. He was carrying Willie's dog, comforting the animal as though it shared the worry of his missing wife.

"She'll be all right — she's met someone and staying for a chat." Cecily repeated the words more to convince herself than the others.

"Perhaps there's been an air raid and we didn't hear the siren?" Dorothy suggested. "She'll be sheltering at my house. There's the Anderson shelter."

"Or under the stairs," Owen added.

Cecily and Peter shared a brief look of amusement. That was the pantry, a magnet to Owen, raid or not. She felt a pang of remorse for thinking spiteful thoughts at such a time.

Rhonwen was kneeling on the floor with Marged, playing snakes and ladders with Victor and Johnny's new stepdaughters. Cecily saw Gareth watching them affectionately. "We're very happy, Cecily," he said. "I'm so lucky."

"That's easy to see." Peter smiled. He sensed Gareth's need to talk and he moved so Cecily stood closer to him.

"I'm so glad, Gareth, love." Cecily laughed softly. "I don't think you'd have been so content with me. Just as well your mother stopped you marrying me, wasn't it?"

"Mam didn't stop —" He grinned and Cecily thought how boyish he still looked, with his straight hair and rather large ears and the shy expression in his sparkling light brown eyes. "All right," he admitted. "I did listen to Mam." He looked nervously at Peter before telling her, "I still love you, you know. Not in the way I love Rhonwen, but there's still a strong affection. There's fun we used to have at the dances, eh? That's why I can ask you something."

"Anything," Cecily said at once.

"I'm going back tomorrow and I think we're in for some . . . big trouble . . . if you know what I mean. If . . . if I don't get back, will you see that Rhonwen and Marged are all right?" He hushed the automatic protests about to come from Cecily and Peter. "There's the shop, and if you keep an eye on it, just to see that the manager is doing his job properly, they'll be all right financially. Rhonwen's an innocent and someone could easily diddle her out of everything. Just keep an eye, if I'm not here to look after her, will you?"

Cecily kissed him affectionately and said, "I promise."

Gareth moved away from Cecily and winked at Peter. "You can budge up again now." Peter laughed and moved to Cecily's side. He placed an arm on her shoulder and she held his hand.

"Time we started looking for Ada," Phil said in a wavering voice. He pointed to the clock which showed them she had been out for more than an hour and a half. He went out into the street, running, calling her

225

name. Before anyone else had reached the shop door, he was out of sight.

"Best we wait here for him to bring her back. She's sure to be at Dorothy's. Then," Gareth added slowly, "if she isn't there, we'll do what Peter suggests and go in different directions until we find her."

"Of course she's at my house," Dorothy said confidently. She gave Cecily a hug. "Don't worry, Cecily, your Ada will be all right."

Cecily thought those were the first kind, sympathetic words from Dorothy for years and shivered at the thought they might be an augury of all the kind, sympathetic words to come.

They stood in the porch watching for Phil's return. All the wedding party were there, none wanting to go until they had news of Ada. Peter stood beside Cecily, his large hand holding hers. When Phil reappeared, his voice reached them before he came in sight. "She's not there! She's not there!"

Fears that she had been knocked over or attacked by someone hoping there was money in the bag she carried swelled and reassurances were no longer heard. Willie rang the hospital but they hadn't heard of an accident nor had they admitted anyone resembling Willie's description of Ada.

From then on, through the darkness, they went to search the streets. Willie left Annette and Sharon to look after the children. Peter and Cecily were instructed to wait at the shop for when Ada came back. "And that," Cecily tearfully told Peter, "is the hardest of all."

226

Sharon wanted to help with the search. "She's my family now," she argued. "The girls are sleeping and Annette is here." But Johnny looked at her ridiculously unsuitable shoes with their satin-covered, high heels and decided his wife would be a liability on the streets.

"Make some tea," he suggested. "That'll be really helpful."

Those looking for Ada came and went continuously, Phil running, his eyes wide with fear at each failure to find his wife. Several saw the fallen ruin of the building under which Ada had been buried, and saw the men clearing the rubble without a thought of Ada being involved. Barriers were in place keeping people away from the workmen and they accepted that without question. Still they wondered whether there had been an air raid without any of them hearing the siren.

"That or an unexploded bomb," Willie decided.

At three in the morning Johnny regretfully had to leave. "I have to be back in camp soon — it's the six o'clock train or I'm in trouble."

Cecily hugged him and Sharon. "Sorry your day has been spoilt with this worry. We wanted it to be perfect for you both."

The bridal couple thanked her for all she had done and Sharon promised to ring later to be told that Ada was safe. "As I'm sure she will be," Johnny added.

The little family walked up the hill to the main road and off to the rooms Johnny had found for them. Sharon, who still wore the high-heeled shoes, carried Leonora, Johnny carried Debora, and Victoria, who was only six, was holding her mother's skirt and walking behind. The children were still in their bridesmaid dresses but Sharon had changed into a red satin dress in her bedroom, which was now cluttered cheerfully with oddments of the wedding ceremony and its aftermath.

Gareth also had to return to his unit but Rhonwen offered to stay.

"No." Cecily smiled stiffly, her face unwilling to give up the frown of dread that had begun when Phil had returned from the first fruitless search. "Go on, you, and see Gareth off properly. Good luck, Gareth, love. And Rhonwen, come and see us often while he's away. And come if you've any problems we can help with. Me, Ada, Peter and Phil, and Willie as well, we're always here, remember."

Gareth gestured his thanks with a nod and, with his arms around his wife and stepdaughter, went home. Cecily shivered as they turned for one last wave. "It's almost as if he's saying goodbye," she whispered to Peter.

He put a reassuring arm around her. "He'll be back, and you won't feel so sad when Ada is found."

Ada became aware of a draught of air. Dust-carrying air that cooled her face, chilled it and eventually roused her to realization of where she was. The dust tickled her nose and she tried to move her head to ease it and found she could not. She shouted with shock as her hair was pulled against the restriction. Her voice wasn't loud but had enough force to send eddies of brick dust floating up over her face.

228

Light began to shine through the gap via which the cool air came, and she could see motes of brick dust sparkling in the early sunshine. She ached terribly, especially her legs, but when she tried to move them to ease her discomfort, they were held by something painful, like broken brick, she surmised, then she went back to sleep again. She woke after only a few minutes and thought of the people who had helped her the first time and wondered vaguely if they were all right or whether they too had been covered in rubble as she had. She wriggled a little and debris shifted noisily. She had to get back to Phil. He'd be so worried.

There were no sounds coming through the gap in broken timber and rubble. Just her thoughts, which seemed to her to have been spoken aloud, the silence was so intense. She thought she had better call, but dust filled her mouth when she tried and it was such an effort. Someone would come: Phil would be searching for her, and Cecily. They wouldn't be long. She was unaware of the men carefully moving aside the bricks, not realizing she was suffering from deafness — the reason for the eerie silence. She wondered if there was anything in telepathy. If she thought about him deeply, calling to him where she lay, would Phil hear her? She concentrated on him, visualizing his face, thinking his name over and over, but sleep caught her and she drifted into a dream of a warm place, a soft, silky bed and a soothing drink gliding down her throat, easing away the dust.

The next time she woke it was with a sense of movement; something was happening nearby. Then her ears cleared and she heard brick clinking on brick and murmuring voices and she thought it was Phil. Perhaps he had heard her, and was there, on top of her premature tomb, digging down to find her. She had to call to him, tell him she was all right — "Phil" — but the intake of breath made her cough instead. The regular sound of bricks being moved ceased. The low voices sounded more urgent and someone said, "Anyone there?"

She coughed to clear her throat and managed to say, one word at a time between coughing, "Yes — Ada — Spencer. Is — that — you — Phil?"

The words had been heard, instructions were shouted, eager hands began to move the rubble with greater urgency and the voice continued to talk to her, soothing, encouraging, reassuring. She cried when the gap widened, bringing light and air, and was closed again but it was quickly reopened, widened and a face finally peered down at her; a dirty face, with a warden's helmet above it.

"I'm Ada Spencer, of Owen's shop. Will you tell Phil and Cecily I'm all right?"

Ada was taken to the hospital and a warden called at the shop to tell them Ada was safe.

Phil ran up the hill as soon as the words were spoken, not stopping to wait for any further news, but finding time to call to Cecily, "This is your fault, you bitch! Sending her out at that time of night like she was your servant! If she's harmed I'll kill you, bitch!"

Cecily gasped at the shock of it and Peter held her, supporting and half carrying her to a chair beside the fire. "It's the relief. He isn't a stable man and he had to hit out at someone once he knew she was safe. He'd been preparing himself to be told she was dead, you see. Then all the tension had to come out. Forget what he said, as he certainly will once he sees Ada and finds her unharmed. The warden told us she had no more than cuts and a few bruises. A miracle, he said. And remember too that he was here and could have easily gone instead, or gone with her, couldn't he?"

Cecily listened to Peter's words, too stunned to cry. "I feel so alone," she said later when everyone had gone and the shop was open for business. "Van marrying that Paul Gregory, Ada wrapped up in Phil and not caring a jot for me, ignoring the way he insults me. I have no one, Peter."

"I care for you, Cecily, you must know that." He held her and said, "I know this is probably the worst possible moment, but will you marry me? I've loved you ever since you first came to the beach and persuaded me to buy from Owen's. I've hesitated all this time to ask you, thinking I'm too old, or that you love Danny, but now, with tragedy all around us, don't you think we should take what happiness we can, while we can? It's an uncertain world and tomorrow might be too late."

Cecily clung to him and after a moment, said, "If I marry you, it would be for all the wrong reasons. To have someone of my own, someone to put me first, a man who belongs to me and shares my joys and sorrows."

"I'll accept that." For the first time in the fourteen years since they had first met, he kissed her with unrestrained love, his lips taking hers in a slow, all-enveloping possession. She responded with warmth and a passion that surprised her and with tears falling, as she saw an end to the empty years.

They were married during the first week of May and for their honeymoon went to see Betty Grable and Robert Young in *Sweet Rosie O'Grady* at the pictures. Cecily wore a silvery lace dress with a swathed bodice and a full skirt. It was sleeveless and with it she wore a white, flimsy stole. Rhonwen had made her a beautiful hat of the same material as the dress and trimmed it with feathers filched from a hat of her own. The sleeveless style caused a few frowns of disapproval but Cecily laughed them away.

"It's all I have that's remotely suitable," she said, "and I needed to take out the sleeves for Rhonwen to make the hat!"

Peter wore a grey suit with double-breasted waistcoat, a watch and chain across it. Chamois gloves hid his grease-stained fingers and a grey hat added distinction to his tall and generous figure. All his clothes were hired.

Ada was there, fully recovered from her ordeal when the building collapsed. She stood beside her sister in a cream dress, also defiantly sleeveless, with a generously pleated skirt and a top with pleats falling from shoulder to waist. A straw hat borrowed from Rhonwen was swathed in cream chiffon and had a large, artificial rose at the front.

Phil refused to come and Van too pleaded an urgent meeting that prevented her being at the register office.

If Cecily was hurt by the absence of her daughter and brother-in-law, and her still-silent mother, she didn't show it by the slightest frown. For Peter's sake she was radiant and he was ridiculously proud. The glow from them promised happiness that nothing could tarnish: not a sulky daughter, or an indifferent mother or a brother-in-law filled with hate. Peter came to live at the shop, presenting his ration book to Cecily with a bow. "My love, my life and my ration book. What more can I offer?"

There was something else. Cecily and Ada were delighted when he suggested renting his house over beyond the beach to Johnny and his new family, Sharon and the girls could move in straightaway and have a home ready for Johnny to come home to. Cecily was filled with pleasurable excitement when they went down the next day to talk to Sharon about it.

The horse and cart came into use once again, this time with the owner driving it as Phil typically refused to help. Sharon and her girls, together with their possessions, left the rooms they had rented, and moved into Peter's house. "I doubt it will ever be tidy again," Cecily warned as they watched Sharon ineffectively trying to put clothes into already overfull drawers and cupboards.

"What does it matter? It's hers now, hers and Johnny's, and I hope they'll be happy here." He gave her a hug. A scream from the kitchen preceded by a crash made him add, with a chuckle, "And what are a few plates between friends?"

233

* ★ ★

There was an air of gaiety about the town, as if everyone was waiting for some stupendous event. Cecily felt it in the urgency of preparations already underway for the entertainments for the summer season. These began earlier than usual and Willie's children came into the shop one day with their dog, who had won first prize for the waggiest tail, in the novelty dog show in the park. Claire wore the rosette in her hair and her face glowed almost the same colour, with pride.

The local papers were filled with small but cheerful announcements. Boating was to be allowed on Sundays at last, to the disapproval of some but the delight of many. Susanna Foster and Nelson Eddy entertained audiences with their performances in *Phantom of the Opera*. Everything that wasn't bad news was celebrated. No one seemed worried by the fact that coal ration was reduced, or that food rationing was very tight, testing the ingenuity of mothers to feed their families. The women were convinced it would be the last year of the war; the end of Hitler and his armies were talked about and cheered in public houses and joked about in the music halls. Only in the secret silence of the night did people fear that the conflict would go on forever, that their menfolk would never return.

Rumours about a Second Front, to bring the war back to Europe and wipe out the German army in a great, triumphant effort was partly the reason for the surge of optimism. There was a vibration in the air telling the exhausted population that something stupendous was about to happen and tensions ran high and showed in exaggerated laughter and enthusiasm for anything that was pleasurable.

Competitions for singing and dancing, best window displays, best uses of garden space, window boxes, anything that was asked of people was met with a willingness to take part and do their best. People were already frantically busy with war work, shopping, finding food, making do and mending items that years before were fit only for dusters or the scrap heap.

Women turned sheets sides to middle to make then last a while longer. Men were unaware of tails being cut off their shirts to make new collars. Husband's suits were made over to provide costumes for their wives. Flour sacks were bleached and sewn to make tablecloths to sell in aid of the Red Cross. There was no spare time. Everyone was busy from the moment they woke until they put out the light to sleep.

Cecily still spent every working day at Watkins' store with Van, helping her, teaching her the intricacies of the complex business, while a succession of assistants came, learned enough to be useful then left to join the forces. She presumed Van was grateful for her generous help, but never heard her say so. Van spoke to her mother as little as possible, and even when Cecily asked her a direct question she seemed unwilling to reply. Hurt, puzzled, Cecily said nothing. Only to Peter did she talk of her dismay. There was still the continuing mystery of where Van went on her afternoons off. Several people reported seeing her at the railway station and she presumed she was going to Cardiff, but Van

235

said nothing about where she went, or indeed whether Cardiff was her destination. Cecily tried to ignore it all and concentrated on her work, with the fading hope that one day her daughter's attitude towards her would change.

Beside the work at Watkins' there were other things on Cecily's mind. She was bound, out of loyalty, to help Van, while desperately wanting to get back her own business. She was worried about the neglect, which was worsening now, as Phil insisted on closing for the odd hour during the day when he felt Ada needed a rest. How she longed for this war to end, so she could find a manager for Van and return to Owen's where she belonged.

CHAPTER
TEN

Cecily woke one morning early in June 1944 and was aware of a strangeness. Something was different. She listened and realized there was a low murmuring that could only be voices, yet couldn't be. It was too vast a sound to be workmen on their way down the hill to the docks and there was no accompanying clatter of boots. She woke Peter who was snoring gently beside her and he reached out an arm.

"Sleep, love, it's early yet."

"Listen," she whispered. "What's that sound? It isn't people. What can it be?"

He listened, became curious and walked to the front room and looked out. "Good God, help us!" he gasped. "Come and look at this!"

Cecily joined him and stared down in utter disbelief into the street far below them. It was full of soldiers. Helmeted heads like a sea of bobbing, netted globes, stretching as far as they could see.

"It's started," Peter breathed. "God help them all."

"Tea," Cecily decided. She called Ada and Phil, who, sleeping at the back of the house, had not been disturbed. She hurried downstairs, dressed in slacks and a thick jumper. She and Ada handed out cups of tea to those within reach and along the road other doors were opened and similar comfort offered. The men drank gratefully and surreptitiously, hiding their luxury from the sergeants who paraded up and down the narrow gap at the crown of the road.

When Cecily struggled up to Watkins' stores via the back lanes, she saw the NAAFI van pull up and the occupants were handing out tea and a cake or some bread to each man.

Throughout the men waited, conversation desultory and low. Apart from the supply of food handed out at intervals, they didn't move, but sat or stood, waiting for orders to embark on the ships waiting for them in the docks and the lanes beyond.

Van spoke to her mother, a rare occasion. "Paul is out there somewhere," she said. "Frightening when you know they won't all get back."

"Paul Gregory's a survivor, he'll be back." Cecily didn't intend the words to sound so sharp. She didn't like the man but didn't wish him to be among those who wouldn't return. "Don't fret, lovey," she said more softly. "Paul's a trained soldier and stands a better chance than some of these poor boys. You'll see, Paul will be back. Survival is what they're taught."

"Survival is only second to doing what they're told, regardless!"

The long lines of men filling the streets in the small seaside town began to move during the late evening. The efficiency of the enormous undertaking was remarkable. The shuffling feet going past the shop would increase for a while, then stop, the movement repeated throughout the day as more and more were packed into the area. Then, throughout the night, the mass of men gradually depleted and no more came. By morning they would all be gone. Cecily watched from her bedroom with heart-aching sadness, thinking of the thousands of men and boys and the multiplicity of loved ones that would be affected by this night and the horror-filled days to follow it.

She was glad of Peter's presence, of his strong arms around her and the warmth of him as he stood behind her, watching as the last trickle of men and machinery disappeared, leaving only an echo of their quiet voices and shuffling feet. Already ghosts.

"I'm so glad you are here, Peter," she said softly, weeping with the sombreness of what they had witnessed.

News came slowly at first and it was bad, but during the weeks following the mass exodus heading for the invasion beaches of France, it improved. No letters came from either Gareth or Johnny and it had been weeks since they heard news of Edwin, who they believed was still in North Africa. In common with thousands of others, they watched with dread as postboys with their pillbox hats delivered telegrams to the bereaved. Paul did get a letter to Van, in which he told her not to worry, but little else besides.

When Cecily and Van were working in the office of Watkins' one Wednesday morning a few weeks after the mass embarkation, an assistant came in and told them

Miss Van was wanted on the shop floor. "A soldier," she explained, "to see Miss Van."

Van gave a cry of joy and ran out of the office, down the stairs, without even glancing to see who it was through the window overlooking the floor. She stared in surprise and barely disguised disappointment at her visitor.

"Edwin! But where have you come from? I thought you were in North Africa — does your mother know — I mean — Oh, Edwin, it's so lovely to see you safe and well!"

His expression changed then and a scowl replaced the smile. "I'm sound in mind and body and that's more than you are, Myfanwy!"

"What d'you mean? Oh, come on, let's go to the office. Mam's there and she's seen you, look!" She pointed up to where Cecily was waving excitedly. She called one of the girls and asked her for a tray of tea. Taking Edwin's arm, she led him up to the office.

Before they reached the door, he held her back. "What's this rot about you marrying some sergeant called Paul Gregory?"

"You've heard then? Isn't it exciting?"

"It isn't exciting or wonderful and it isn't going to happen." He pulled her to him and glared down at her. Van had forgotten, or had perhaps never really been aware of, how large he was. Broader, taller and, she guessed, very much stronger than Paul. His eyes contained fires of fury; dark and smouldering with rage. "You're mine, Van. You always were and no tinpot little sergeant with a reputation for womanizing is going to change that!"

"Of course he's attractive to women," she defended, trying to struggle free of his powerful arms, to get away from that unblinking stare. She felt her defences weakening as the familiar face moved closer to her own. "I wouldn't want a man who wasn't attractive, would I?" For an answer he reached for her hand and removed Paul's ring. "Edwin, you can't —"

"You are mine, and whether other women find me attractive or not doesn't matter a jot."

A kiss hovered in the air between them and she wanted to get away, to think about how she felt, remind herself of Paul, relive *his* kisses, remember how she wanted *him*.

Edwin wouldn't release her. His lips moved agonizingly closer and he whispered, "Van, you're a fool. I know you did this simply to annoy your mother."

"Don't be ridiculous!"

"Well? Didn't you?" Does she like this Paul Gregory? Did she welcome him with open arms?"

"No, she disliked him, but —"

"So, you were delighted, as usual, at the opportunity of upsetting her and that was that. It wasn't a grand passion that made you encourage him, just your spiteful, childish anger because you're illegitimate. Forget the loving childhood you had, forget how well you've been cared for, just remember the worst of it, the secret. Admit it, Van, you're so mixed up and angry with your mother for keeping her secret about who you really are, you've spent hours dreaming of some revenge. Admit it!"

All the time he was pressing her closer so all she could see were his eyes and the smooth cheek, and the dark brows meeting above the nose in a frown of disapproval. Closer still and there were only the eyes, then the lips of the full mouth, soft, tempting and suddenly so very dear to her. She gave a little squeal as their lips met. Then she was floating, no longer earthbound, but ethereal, a phantom made of gossamer thread, aware of nothing except herself and Edwin, clinging to each other, together as one.

Cecily had run to the door and had her hand on the handle to pull it open and greet Edwin but she stopped on hearing their voices raised in anger. She heard his accusation that Van had encouraged Paul to revenge herself on the mother who had denied her, and she moved away, tears of distress flowing down her cheeks. She opened the side window looking out over the street, leaning out over the sill in an attempt to block out the voices outside the door. She wished the traffic was denser so she couldn't hear the words still coming through the thin door and she covered her ears with her hands to block them.

Why hadn't she handled the situation differently? If only she had told Van she was her mother as soon as she had been old enough to understand. But as for the rest, about how she had turned to Waldo for comfort when she and Danny had parted, how could that have

242

been explained to a child? What could she have done to make the child less resentful?

She removed her hands from her ears and the voices had stopped. When she opened the door, the short passage and stairs were empty. She repaired her make-up and went down to the shop floor. There was no sign of Van or Edwin. She went to the cellars but apart from two young boys packing dried peas, there was no one.

"Where's Miss Van?" she asked an assistant.

"She went out, Mrs Marshall, with that soldier."

Cecily thanked her and returned to the office.

Van was led by Edwin, who held her hand and pulled her along like a reluctant child, through the main road and down the hill parallel to the one on which Owen's shop stood, and along the road past the docks to his parents' house. It had withstood the bombing with only the loss of a few slates. She noticed how bright the gardens were with the huge border of summer flowers behind the inevitable plot of vegetables, which Beryl hated so much. She saw that the door had been newly painted and was stupidly aware of the way the paint had run across the glass in a slipshod way. Passing it several times a day she hadn't noticed how badly it had been painted, yet it was glaringly obvious today, when everything seemed so clear. The distraction calmed her and when Edwin closed the door behind them she took off her coat and hung it in the hall cupboard, instead of putting it on a chair and leaving it for the maid to attend to.

Edwin led her into the lounge and then left her, calling to see that the house was as empty as it seemed. When he returned, she was sitting beside the empty grate in which Beryl usually arranged a display of flowers. He came to her and lifted her up to stand in front of him, then enfolded her in his arms and lowered his head for their kiss. It was slow and loving, warm and so natural that she felt no alarm when he began to undress her.

She was vaguely surprised to see how brown he was, but too enchanted with the thrill of the moment to consider the deserts of North Africa. He loved her, tenderly, all the hurt and fury gone from his deep brown eyes, his gentle fingers and firm body a delight that filled a long awaited need in her that she only just realized was there.

They spent the rest of the day just talking, sitting close to each other on the velvet settee, relaxed and completely content.

Van was conscious of her dishevelled appearance and it was Edwin who combed her hair when they heard his parents at the door. She was flushed and they both looked utterly happy. Possibly Bertie, and certainly Beryl, guessed at least a part of how the young couple had spent their day. They hugged their son and Bertie said, "Edwin, we're so relieved you're safe. We were afraid you might be out there." He pointed vaguely in the direction of France. "Such a relief to know you aren't."

They asked a lot of questions, the first being when do you go back, and that was the only one he was able to answer. Edwin couldn't explain that he was on his way to Scotland for a top-secret meeting, but said, "I have two days only."

Van stood to leave. "I'll get back to the shop."

"I'll go with you, to see Auntie Cecily and Auntie Ada. We'll be out today, Mum, but tomorrow you and Dad and I will have the morning together."

"Van as well?" Beryl smiled at the girl who was as close as a daughter, but her eyes darted to see that the engagement ring belonging to Paul was still on her finger, replaced only moments earlier. "You'll have the morning off, won't you, dear, to see Edwin before he goes back?"

"I'm sure Mam won't mind if I mitch for the morning." She looked at Edwin for agreement.

"Of course Van as well. That needn't be said. Part of our family she is and always will be." He was looking at Van, making sure she understood the message underlying the words.

Beryl had sensed the undercurrent as soon as she stepped into the room. Something was going on and with Van engaged to that sergeant, she was curious and excited to know what it was.

"Dinner at seven, Van, dear," she reminded her. "Don't let Edwin forget."

The shop was locked and silent, of course. Van had forgotten it was half-day closing. Hand in hand they walked. First through the town, pausing for a while to watch the attempts of bomb disposal experts checking the site of an unexploded bomb that had been reported that day, long after the latest raid. Then on, through the lanes towards the old village.

They wandered far from the houses, following the stream out into the fields where children played. They passed the deep craters of a landmine which had missed the docks by more than two miles, perhaps jettisoned by a pilot anxious to get home after narrow escapes from the battery of guns protecting the coast. Rabbits hopped in the fresh raw earth and there were already burrows appearing near the top of the crater where turf overhung like a protective porch for their front door.

Birds sang in the summer air, carefree and unaffected by the nights of destruction. Dippers walked through the shallow but turbulent stream and a heron flew with its lazy flapping flight across their path. It seemed so far away from the war that it was impossible to imagine the harsh sound of the siren disturbing the peace and tranquillity, or the fierce life and death battles taking place in France.

They spoke very little, just walked through the tall grasses, stopping occasionally to admire some of the wild flowers which added a thousand hues to the meadow. Corn was ripening in the fields beyond, adding its own rich colour, the gold patched here and there with the gaudy red of poppies.

They approached the houses of the village and were brought abruptly out of their dream and back to reminders of the war they both wanted to forget. The cottage gardens were full of cabbages and carrots and beans, where there had once been an abundance of flowers, victims of the Dig For Victory campaign. The buildings were in desperate need of repair, many with boarded-up windows and all with the criss-cross tape or net stuck to the glass to prevent broken panes from flying about and causing more damage.

"All the effort is going into the war," Van said, pointing to a house from which the thatch was tumbling in green, rotting disarray. "The women are all at work and their spare time is spent growing food and helping with voluntary services. It'll be years before this is all returned to how it was. When the men come home there will be so few of them."

"If these people hadn't helped, people like your mother and thousands like her, we wouldn't be so close to victory. It had to be an all-out effort and that's what we had."

They sat on a stile and watched as dusk gradually filled in the distant hills. The sea faded into a continuation of the night sky. Trees shushed softly in the offshore breeze that the cooling earth produced and was a lullaby with the birds making soft soothing twittering in the hedges. Van realized that even though their thoughts were melancholy, she had never been so happy.

It was getting dark, although the night was still warm, as they made their way back over the fields and reached the edge of the town. In a dell, where the air was cool, they stopped and made love slowly, taking more time than before to please each other and coming together in perfect culmination of their love.

It seemed so right, the love that had never before been a part of their relationship. No guilt or uneasiness came to spoil it for Van. Passion grew again and it was some time before they moved. They strolled back home, hand in hand, speaking to everyone they met, wishing strangers a peaceful night and having strangers bestow good wishes upon them too.

"I have to go and see Mam, explain about tomorrow," Van said, when they reached the shop porch.

"I won't come in," he said. "I'll go home but don't be long, will you?"

"I'll be there before you know it," Van said as she surrendered to a final kiss. She watched him walk away, tall, confident and very, very dear. Then she took out her key and pushed the door, the cheerful bell warning Cecily and the others of her arrival.

"Hello, lovey." Cecily smiled. "Where have you been, out with Edwin, is it?"

"Yes. He only has two days' leave. I won't be in the shop tomorrow morning. I'll make a few notes for the reps that are due."

"Of course. I'll cope, don't worry. It's a busy day, mind, most people want their rations on Thursday or Friday, but we'll manage. Young Jennifer is a good girl and she works hard. Go you, and enjoy yourself."

Van was aware of the excitement in her mother's eyes. She knew her mother hoped it was Edwin she would marry and not Paul Gregory.

"Here you are, Van." Ada handed her a cup of tea, quickly made with the ever-simmering kettle. "Something to eat, love?"

"No, I'll go straight back. "She went to kiss them all, including Phil, who watched her with a disapproving look on his thin face. She went through the shop, rattled the door to make the old bell jingle but didn't go out. She slipped back to listen to the conversation.

"Well, there's a surprise for you!" she heard her mother say with obvious pleasure. "It seems I mustn't give up hope of her coming to her senses just yet. If she and Edwin go out for the day and Van comes back looking like that, Paul might not be my son-in-law after all!"

"Let's hope not," Ada said. "Edwin's far more suitable. No chance he's a fortune hunter either, mind."

"She's promised to Paul!" Phil objected loudly. "She's accepted him and she's wearing his ring! You don't want her to have the reputation of a tart, do you? Carrying on with a man and engaged to another, and him a serving soldier. Disgusting, that's what it is, disgusting!"

"If it means that Van doesn't marry that Paul Gregory, then it can only be for the best," Cecily retorted. "I'd be so happy if she became Mrs Edwin Richards. He's the right one for her. Sure of it I am."

Van tiptoed across the wooden floor and slid carefully round the door, muffling the bell with her hand to prevent it giving away her late departure. She was laughing as she ran down the street. Tormenting her mother was so easy and the best was still to come.

At the Richards' house they ate a light supper, then she went to bed, insisting that Edwin would want to talk to his parents as his visit was so brief. In the bathroom she washed her body, examining it, expecting it to be different from the morning. Was she different? She certainly felt different. But her resolve to make her mother pay for her ruined childhood, that hadn't changed. Edwin's unexpected revelation of his love hadn't altered her that much.

She slipped into bed with the delicious feeling that he might defy chance and come to her room while his parents slept, but he did not. She woke longing to feel again his loving hands and warm lips, and enjoy his strong brown body against her own.

They ate breakfast together, the four of them, and she was quiet as his parents brought him up to date on local news. They were still talking as she went up to dress. She chose a summer dress of striped blue cotton, its simple lines showing to advantage her slender figure. The colour seemed to match the sky and the blue of her eyes, which sparkled with secret joy. She chose a straw hat with ribbons hanging down to join her long fair hair. Bathed and scented, she went downstairs. Uncle Bertie and Auntie Beryl were going out for an hour and she waited until they were gone, then, while Edwin was dressing, she left the house.

Turning right, she passed the road where Owen's shop was opening its door and through the lane to the main road. She walked past bombed-out houses where children played dangerous games among unsafe walls and broken furniture, past shops with boards instead of windows, where homemade notices declared "Business

As Usual" in bold letters alongside the Welsh dragon and Union Jack flags waving defiance to the enemy.

A fire engine was emptying water from a basement where a water main had burst. The old Merryweather engine had been retired in favour of the new Dennis in 1940 but had come back into service as a reserve.

Cats and dogs prowled everywhere, many homeless and with no one to claim them they wandered in a constant search for food. She saw a rat scuttle across a piece of wasteground and shuddered. The bright sun shone on a perfectly symmetrical spider's web which joined the two sides of a broken window, as if in an attempt to render temporary repairs. Everything was a fascination; seen for the very first time. It was so long since she had wandered without a thought for anything other than the moment.

There were sweet coupons in her handbag and she went into a shop to buy some chocolate. The entrance was through a zig-zag passageway, made to prevent light escaping during the hours of darkness. It was a dark cave-like entrance to the cheerful shop within.

Handing her coupons and pennies to the assistant, she bought a two-ounce bar, her ration for the week, and dropped it into her handbag. The woman recognized her and said, "Miss Owen, isn't it? From Waldo Watkins' store? Got a day off, have you? There's lovely."

"Not really," Van confided with a chuckle. "I'm mitching!"

"Best for you too." The woman laughed. "Does us good to cheat now and then. I wish I could cheat and come with you, indeed I do. Here you are," she added and picked up a small penny bar. "Take this, a treat for me."

Van smiled widely and thanked her. "I knew this was going to be a lovely day."

She went out again through the dark, zig-zag passage, out into the sun and, still smiling, walked on through the back lanes to the old part of the town. Breaking the penny bar into four pieces and sucking them, she relished the rare pleasure of the sweet smoothness. She usually gave her sweet ration to Willie for his children and tried — in vain — to persuade Owen to do the same.

Following the route she and Edwin had taken the previous day, she stopped where they had stopped, paused to admire the views they had admired and relived the hours they had walked with her pale hand in Edwin's suntanned one. Sitting on the same stile, she looked out over the distant sea, so different in colour from the previous evening but giving her the same air of wonder and peace.

She ate her bar of chocolate in the dell where they had made love, lying looking up at the sky, dreaming of how it had been. She didn't wallow in regrets or wish today had been different. Today was for dreaming and remembering. At three o'clock, the time Edwin was catching his train, she stood, combed her hair, adjusted her hat and walked slowly back to the town.

She didn't go straight to Edwin's home where she had lived since Waldo's death, but to Owen's shop. It was only five but the door was closed. She opened it with her key.

"Van, where have you been?" Cecily demanded. "Edwin has spent his precious leave searching the town for you. I had to leave the office and try to help. How could you be so thoughtless?"

"I went for a walk. You don't begrudge me a day off, do you? It's a long time since I had some time to myself."

"But what about Edwin?" Cecily asked, but Van turned and, ribbons swinging, was walking away, calmly preparing her excuses for Beryl and Bertie.

Phil spent more and more time just sitting in the room behind the shop. He seemed to have lost interest in going out with the horse and cart to find food to sell. He would read the morning paper from cover to cover, then just sit, staring into the fire, promising to do the few things Ada asked of him, but eventually succeeding in persuading her that either they didn't want doing or that Willie was a better person to ask.

On the morning following Van's day out, he waited until the shop had a few customers, mainly calling for a chat rather than to buy. With a gossipy customer in full swing, and Ada pinned down for a while, he opened the drawer in which paper and envelopes were kept. He addressed the envelope to Paul and began a letter.

Dear Paul,
I think you ought to know . . .

253

Phil wasn't the only one writing to a member of His Majesty's forces that day. At the bench which Willie used as a temporary office in a corner of the workshop, he was writing to Danny. He had taken the day off from Owen's where there was little to do, to spend time at the workshop where there was plenty.

Behind him were the sounds of wood being worked on an electric lathe, and chisels shaping a length of replacement skirting board. He had employed twin sixteen-year-old boys, who in the past year had become competent at furniture making as well as repairs and restoring. Although, with wood on a rigid and limited quota, it was difficult to keep them both occupied until they began to buy wood from bomb-damaged houses and advertised it as such.

Leonard and Graham Williams paused in their work and Willie went to see how Leonard was getting on with the child's desk and stool he was finishing, following his own design. The work was good and he praised them both.

"How do you feel about joining me in a new venture?" he asked them before finishing the letter to Danny. "I'm only getting my thoughts down on paper as yet, but I'd welcome your views."

"Glad to listen to what you have to say, boss," Leonard said and his brother nodded. Of the two, Leonard was usually the first to speak, although Graham didn't automatically agree with his twin.

"I can't do the work I enjoyed before the war," Willie said, waving the stump of his arm and giving a wry

254

smile. "A carpenter needs two good hands and that's for sure. But I can write, and telephone, and take down orders and do the invoicing and all that sort of thing."

"Ideas are your department too," Leonard said, and once again Graham nodded agreement.

"Well, I've been thinking that it isn't all that convenient now, getting supplies. Some places sell sand and cement and the heavy materials and some sell wood. Others sell plumbing needs and I want to have a yard so large we can stock everything a builder needs."

"What about the workshop?" Leonard asked anxiously.

"That will continue as before and you two will turn out some really first-class stuff. I want the yard as well."

"Seems worth considering," Leonard said. "Plenty of building to be done when this war is finally over."

His brother shook his head. "Only as long as you can get good honest men to work for you, and the cash to start it." His voice trailed off, indicating his doubts.

"Wouldn't it be better to employ builders?" Leonard suggested. "Extend the business you've been doing and what you've a good name for? Damn it all, Graham's right — you've only to look around this area to see all the work that'll be needed once Hitler's been sorted."

"And that won't be long by the sound of things," Graham added. "Giving it to 'em proper our boys are, according to the papers."

Willie looked thoughtful. "That's a good point — it's what we know, after all. We might make more money building and repairing, but will it be easy to find experienced men? So many have lost their lives and those who do come back might not want to go back to what they did before. And," he added, rubbing his damaged arm, "there'll be plenty who can't!"

"There'll be plenty looking for work, man. Plenty. They'll want to start earning as fast as they can. And we can make a start now, get in quick and take the best jobs so we'll be a going concern before the men get home. Have something to offer them then, won't we?"

Willie looked across the road at the shell of the Spencers' once-neat cottage. The walls were damaged and there was no roof. Windows, and even the door, had been taken by those who needed replacements, and the flowers had mostly gone from the garden that had been Mrs Spencer's joy, to fill other plots.

"Perhaps we could start with the Spencers' place," he suggested. "I'll ask Phil if he wants to sell the place and we could rebuild it and sell it. You two could manage most of the carpentry with my guidance and we're sure to find a bricklayer and electricians and the rest. Yes, I'll put that idea in my letter to Danny and tomorrow I'll talk to Phil and Ada." He looked at the boys, almost seventeen and already strong and very capable. "I think we could do well, you two, me and Danny Preston. What d'you think?"

"Damn me, yes," they chorused.

Willie finished the letter to Danny suggesting both the builder's yard and the idea of working on the large-scale rebuilding of the town that must begin soon. He posted the letter and went to talk to Gladys Davies, who still cleaned the workshop for him and helped Annette in the house.

256

She was just leaving, having helped his wife to repaint the walls of their bedroom, painted white, then decorated with a second colour dabbed on with small pieces of sponge. No wallpaper of any quality could be bought. He waved to her then stopped to look at his neat and happy home.

His home. The first house he had bought on the advice of Bertie Richards an age ago. He had come a long way since then but it had all begun with Bertie Richards taking him in hand and telling him to help himself and not spend his life being a cog in someone else's wheel.

"Annette," he called when his plump and beautiful wife ran out to greet him, "If this new baby's a boy, I'd like us to call him Bertie."

"Hush, love, we don't want everyone to know just yet." She linked with his injured arm, aware that he always wanted his strong arm to be free. "What about Roberta if it's a girl? Then you wouldn't be disappointed."

"You've never disappointed me in anything, my dear, sweet, lovely girl."

CHAPTER
ELEVEN

Cecily kept her promise and she went with Peter every week to inspect Gareth's barber shop and also called on Rhonwen, who was living with Gareth's mother, since Mrs Price-Jones had become unwell. One day they found Rhonwen crawling on the floor measuring curtains. She was trying out a pattern for a two-piece suit, checking to make sure there was sufficient sound and unfaded parts of the material to make the design she had chosen. The curtains were in a small floral print. Gareth's mother sat, shaking her head and insisting that Rhonwen was wasting her time.

"Curtains are curtains and frocks are frocks," she intoned. "Where you get these ideas from I don't know."

"Women's magazines," Rhonwen replied, reaching for the pins.

"Is it to welcome Gareth home?" Peter asked, getting down and helping to straighten the paper pattern which he held while Rhonwen pinned.

"Of course. I want something to wear and I haven't any coupons left," Rhonwen said, through a mouthful of pins. "It seems the war will end soon and I'd hate to meet him wearing what he saw me in last."

"I think we'll have to wait a while yet," Peter warned. "There's still a way to go before the mad decorator is beaten."

"Still, it gives me hope, doesn't it, if we start preparing? It's like Christmas. When we were children Mam used to amuse us on wet, boring autumn days by talking about the fun we'd have at Christmas. We'd mark the days off on the calendar and start making lists of people we'd make cards for and it made the waiting a part of the excitement. The trouble is, we don't have a date like 25th December so we can't count the days." She looked at Peter, sober-faced, supporting the curtains and waiting for her pins. "I know he'll come home," she said firmly. "Oh, I know there's still a lot of fighting to do and there are many alive now who, having survived this far, won't make it, but I just know Gareth will come home."

Ironically, it was Rhonwen who didn't survive the war. She was walking home after selling savings stamps to her regular customer and as she passed an empty building, a bomb, lying unnoticed for over a year, was moved slightly as a rat ran over the loose rubble close to it. The delayed explosion killed Rhonwen instantly.

It was old Zachariah Daniels who saw what happened. He was walking back from his early round, getting to the ash bins before the dustmen emptied them, and picking up unwanted items from the tops of bins. He'd been lucky that day, having found three pairs of shoes in fair condition, a filthy old china teapot with only a small chip in the lid, and several pieces of matting. The matting he would keep. He had layers all around his shed, the best inside on the floor and tacked against the walls to keep out draughts. The older pieces he nailed to the roof. He was whistling cheerfully as he prodded the donkey to greater effort, contemplating the cup of tea he would make as soon as he had unloaded his haul.

The explosion happened as he neared the corner of the docks road and the hill leading to his lane. It blew him and the donkey a staggering ten yards, causing the poor animal to bray continuously long after the noise of the bomb had faded.

Zachariah was panting, leaning on the animal who trembled and complained and struggled against his hold on the reins. The cart was still upright and even before the shock had left him, Zachariah studied his load suspiciously as if the bomb had been a device by someone who wanted to rob him. The teapot was still intact and he smiled happily. It was only then he remembered the woman.

He knew who she was, that Mrs-the-barber-shop. That Mrs Owen as was. She must have touched something, but he remembered her just walking along the pavement beside the derelict hotel. Shame that. Only been married a few years, an' all. Tidy little 'oman, often slipped him a bob or two for a meal, she had. Now he'd have to tell someone.

People were running towards the area, and already the wardens were there, blowing whistles and shouting for people to stay away, and the police and the fire brigade had arrived. He wondered how long he had been standing there. It seemed like a couple of seconds but he realized it must have been longer. A policeman was walking towards him. The shock of what he had just witnessed overcame him and he collapsed, his legs slowly dissolving until he sat on the ground, leaning against the still-braying donkey.

"The poor 'oman," he said in little more than a whisper. "Rhonwen she's called. Wife of Gareth-the-barber-shop, you know her, Rhonwen Owen she was."

"Mrs Gareth Price-Jones?"

"That's what I said, didn't I?" Zachariah snapped. "Shame too. Tidy little 'oman. Gave me a bob or two now and then, she did, for me to buy an 'ot meal."

"And that's what you could do with now, old man. Or at least a hot drink. Come on, we'll get your statement and get you fixed up, shall we?"

Zachariah took the offered hand and hauled himself upright. "Shame," he said, then shook his fist at the sky. "Bloody 'itler!" With the donkey walking between them, they moved away from the now busy scene.

From the thick of the fighting, Gareth came home to see Rhonwen buried and the loneliness hit him like a blow. When he saw the new suit hanging in the wardrobe with the simple blouse she had planned to wear under it, he cried like a baby. He and Marged grieved together in the short leave he had been allowed then he went back to where death was commonplace and home was only a dream.

Before he left, Gareth called on Cecily and Peter.

"Thanks for keeping an eye on the business," he said. "That's all there is now for Marged and me. If it went, there'd be nothing for us when I get home for good."

"That's not true," Cecily said at once. "Besides Marged, there's your mother to care for, friends who will welcome you, and the shop will still be here, Peter and I will make sure of that. And remember, we're still here."

Cecily looked at the man who had been her regular dancing partner for years and who had almost been her husband. He had changed. There was no sparkle now in the light brown eyes. He was thinner and his ears, about which she used to tease him, seemed larger against the pale, slender neck. The mouth was still full and sensitive and to her surprise she felt a surge of love and affection that startled in its intensity. She gripped Peter's comforting, familiar arm and drew him close; protection, perhaps, against the ghost of a past love.

Marged stayed with Gareth's mother. It had been her home since Gareth had left, and besides she was afraid to leave her. Mrs Price-Jones was suffering from the loss of a daughter-in-law who had become very dear to her, and was becoming frail, needing help with many of the tasks she had managed before.

Cecily and Ada had offered Marged a home but understood her reasons for staying with Mrs Price-Jones and praised her for them.

Van went to Cardiff to tell her gran the sad news. Between tears of grief over the death of someone so young and the thought of Marged being left alone, Van explained to her that despite the loss of the much-loved

Rhonwen, the widow of Cecily's brother, Nan's son, her mother was still unwilling to forgive Gran and make contact. "Very bitter woman, my mother," Van said with dishonest sadness.

In her grief, Kitty wondered, as she studied the young girl's face, whether there were reasons that she wasn't being told about why Cecily and Ada were adamant in their determination never to forgive her for running away from a marriage in which she was desperately unhappy, to find the happiness she had known since.

Van went down to the Old Village one Wednesday afternoon. She walked along the lanes but this time not retreading the wandering stroll she had taken back in July with Edwin. She walked with a purpose in mind. She wanted to talk to someone, and she chose Annette, her cousin and the wife of the boy she had known for many years as a stable boy, then general assistant to her mother and Auntie Ada.

As she approached the white cottage, where the door stood open to let in the warm, September air, she glanced across to the house where Auntie Ada and Uncle Phil had once lived, which was now a ruin. She saw someone in the garden and, recognizing Willie, she waved.

"Not working today, Willie?"

"Not much to do in the shop these days," he said, coming to join her. "Damn me, your auntie's let things slide good and proper."

"She's doing her best. It isn't easy, you know, with Uncle Phil to watch as well as the shop."

"We don't have a single ration book now, did you know that? People gradually took them from us, preferring the bigger shops, like the Home and Colonial or Lipton's, or shops like yours where there's an occasional treat for registered customers."

"Can't blame them, I suppose. We have an allocation of tinned pears this week and we even managed two eggs per ration book a few weeks ago. Then there's fat bacon. We handle so many sides every week there are often spare, fatty pieces. Rendered down they make a tasty bit of fried bread to fill the kids at breakfast time."

"Phil still goes out very occasionally," Willie told her. "He brought back some duck eggs and even a few goose eggs too. Just one of them fills a dinner plate when it's fried!"

Two boys appeared from the side of the ruined building and Van recognized them as Graham and Leonard Williams. "What are you doing in the Spencers' old place?" she asked.

"Just an exercise at present," Willie explained. "I thought I'd talk to Phil about rebuilding it."

"You?"

He smiled and touched his handless arm. He had fastened a notebook to the sleeve with elastic and had been writing measurements on to it when she had called him.

"Willie! I didn't mean that and you know it!"

"Yes, I shouldn't be so sensitive. You mean my firm, mine and Danny's. Well, we're thinking of expanding.

264

There's a lot of rebuilding to do and we think we ought to get started, be in on the first wave of enthusiasm, like."

"That sounds a good idea. Good luck, Willie. You're a man after my own heart."

She watched him walk across to rejoin the twins. As the boys shouted figures he wrote them down on the pad fixed to his arm. There'll be a lot of people like him, Van thought sadly. She crossed her fingers and hoped both Edwin and Paul were safe.

Annette had seen her coming and had brewed some tea. Small biscuits had been placed on a pretty plate, green and white and trimmed with a thick band of gold. The cups and saucers set out were the same. "Aynsley," Annette said proudly. "My Willie bought them as a belated wedding present. I keep them for special occasions and you call so rarely I decided this was one." Annette was heavily pregnant and Van carried in the tray.

As they drank the tea, Annette could see something was on Van's mind. She tried to coax her to talk. "Is everything all right? Your Paul? Your mother?"

"Yes, so far as I know Paul is safe and sound. Oh, Annette, I think I'm going to have a baby."

Taken aback, Annette took only a few seconds to recover and say, "But that's wonderful news. Paul will be so proud. Men are so thrilled, especially with their first. Does he know yet?" Van seemed unwilling to add anything more and Annette prattled on, but then, seeing the serious expression on her cousin's face, she asked, "There's something else, isn't there? Oh Van, don't worry about gossips. They all had a great time with me and Willie, but they soon forget."

"It isn't Paul's child. He and I never — you know."

"Then whose is it? Or don't you want to tell me?"

"It's Edwin's."

"But I thought you and Paul were engaged to be married?" She glanced at Van's left hand where the diamond ring sparkled in mocking disregard of the announcement. "Have you changed your mind?"

"No. But Edwin and I, we've always loved each other. Paul is — different. If Paul really loves me, he'll still marry me."

"You've told him about this?"

"Not yet. I didn't want to worry him while he's fighting and so far away. This is something I have to tell him, face to face, and only when he's safely home to stay. It shouldn't be long now, the war, I mean." She looked at her empty cup and added, "If I lose the baby he never need know."

"You aren't planning to get rid of it!" Annette was more shocked by the suspicion of an abortion than her cousin's pregnancy.

"No, Annette. I'd never do that. If my mother can face bringing up an illegitimate baby, then I can too."

"I don't know what to say to you. It was so different with me. I've never loved anyone but Willie and it's always been so right between us. I've never even thought of another man in the way I think about Willie." Annette refilled their tea cups, shyly avoiding Van's eyes.

"Lucky you are, to be so happy."

266

"I suppose I am. Happiness isn't something you think about often. I know I wouldn't change a single thing in my life."

"I still don't know where life will take me," Van said thoughtfully. She twisted the ring on her finger and for a moment, her lovely face, with its small features and brilliant blue eyes, looked pensive and a little sad.

"You still want to marry Paul?"

"Yes. But if he doesn't want me when he learns about 'Blodwen'," she said, patting her belly, "then I'll probably marry Edwin."

The coldness, the arbitrary decision making, made the gentle and loving Annette shudder.

"Edwin loves you?"

"There's never been any doubt in my mind about Edwin's love."

"And Paul is special? You hardly know him and Edwin's been there all your life."

"Perhaps that's the trouble. I spent a lot of time with his family when Mam went dancing and since Uncle Waldo died, and I learned that he was my father, I've lived permanently with them. Edwin is too much like a brother."

" 'Blodwen' wouldn't have happened if you thought of him as a brother," Annette said wryly.

"What about another cup of tea?" Van sighed. "It's the usual solution when things are impossible."

She stood up to help with the dishes, inches taller than the plump Annette and probably two stone lighter. We aren't alike, the cousins in the family, Van thought as she watched the efficient way Annette dealt with the preparation of the fresh brew. Annette was a natural homemaker. Owen was lazy, overfed and useless. Marged was woolly, giggling and a lot of fun, Johnny Fowler anxious, skinny and awkward. And me, she wondered, as the kettle spurted boiling water onto the fire, making it hiss. How would someone describe me? She glanced again at Annette and wished, just for a moment, that she had been as easily content as her glowing, serene cousin.

When Van left, she saw that Willie and the twins were still measuring and making notes on the Spencers' place. They waved as she walked up the green lane towards the park, where a view of the sea met her and dazzled her eyes. She pretended the tears were not for envy of the happy woman she had just left, but the sun, doubled by the expanse of blue water. The scene was so bright and cheerful but hiding the image of what was happening beyond, in France and Germany, to Edwin, Paul, Danny, Gareth and Johnny, and thousands of others, fighting for their lives and hers.

Van happened to be staying at Owen's shop late in September when Paul arrived in the early hours of the morning.

"Where's she to? Where's Van?" he demanded. "Come on escort duty I did, fiddled it I did, so I could see her and I'm not moving from here till I do!"

Cecily and Ada were in their dressing gowns and behind them stood Phil, a raised poker in his trembling hand. "Just in case," as he'd put it, before they'd opened the door. And from Paul's expression and obvious rage, he might just need it.

"Where is she?" Paul's voice rose higher and louder as he began to suspect they weren't going to let him see her. "What's this about her expecting a baby, then? I can tell you straight off it isn't mine." He pushed the oddly immobile trio aside and stormed into the living room, filling it with his anger and throwing his rucksack across the room in fury.

"Nice, isn't it, to get a letter from 'a well-wisher' telling me my girl is expecting? Well, there's no knowing whose it is but I do know it isn't *mine*. We never did anything, see, not once!"

He became aware of the silence. He looked at the sisters, who were both standing with hands to their faces, their eyes wide with shock. "Don't pretend you didn't know."

"But we don't, I mean, it isn't true. You've been misinformed. Van is perfectly well and she isn't going to have a baby. How could she if what you say is true?"

"I'll soon find out. Where is she? Tell me or I'll start smashing the place up!"

The door opened. "I'm here, Paul. I didn't expect you home so soon. There's a lovely surprise." She went to him and raised her face for his kiss but instead Paul slapped her so hard she staggered.

Phil, who had not let go of the poker, raised it higher and threatened the soldier. "Leave her alone, boy! Talk you can, talk you must, but don't touch her again or I'll — I'll swing for you!" Brave words but he was clearly terrified.

It seemed to Cecily later that the tableau remained fixed for an age, but it was probably only seconds before Paul sank into a chair and covered his face with his hands.

"How did you find out?" Van asked.

At once his head shot up and he demanded, "Whose is it?"

"None of your business. The father is going to be told by me, not some clecking busybody. The same as I wanted to tell you, privately, next time we met."

Peter came down then and a hurriedly whispered explanation took place between him and Cecily. But it was Phil, braver since Paul's capitulation to his poker, who seemed to take control of the situation. He was visibly shaking but said firmly to Cecily, Ada and Peter, "Come on, we'll go out and let them talk. But," he threatened the much larger man who sat staring at Van, "stay well away from her, right? We'll go into the shop but I'll be watching through the window and if you go nearer than you are now, I'll knock your head from your shoulders, big as you are. Right?"

Cecily and Peter stared in disbelief at the small, obviously terrified man. Ada was tearful with pride.

Paul seemed unable to retaliate. He nodded agreement and waited until the room had emptied and Phil, whom he could have broken without effort, was standing, looking through the window, his weasely face pressed close to the glass.

"Why, Van?" Paul asked, all the fight gone from him. "Why couldn't you wait for me?"

270

"This is nothing to do with you and I," Van told him calmly. "This is my baby. I'll understand if you want to end our engagement — even if you haven't been faithful to me while you've been away." There was an edge to her voice as she spoke the last words.

"It's different for a man," Paul muttered, glancing up at Phil's white face to see if he'd heard. "I hate you for doing this to me," he added with a growl. He went to rise but urgent tapping on the glass stopped him. Phil raised an imperious finger, his lips tight in disapproval. "You've made a fool of me. All that talk about how we'd wait till we were married and all the time you were cheating on me. Damn it all, I've only been gone a couple of months. Shamed I am. Shamed."

"Oh, come on, Paul. You won't be the only one coming back from war to a pregnant wife or girlfriend. The town's full of them. And half of them are Americans. Accept it or go away."

"I hate you for doing this."

"Then go. I'm not frightened at the prospect of being an unmarried mother. My own mother survived it and so will I."

"Tell me who it is."

"No."

"Then I'll tell you! It's Edwin flaming Richards!"

"Who told you?" For the first time Van seemed alarmed.

"Let's say a friend. Although he was hardly that, but that was how he signed his letter. It must be someone you know for him to care enough to write or to know where to send the letter."

"But this wasn't confirmed until a few days ago."

"Women get sick, don't they? And there are other signs," he sneered.

"Then it's someone very close." They both turned to look at the thin, white face still pressed against the window. Van frowned. "But there's no way he could . . ."

Phil jumped up and entered the room. "Finished talking, have you? I'll go and get you a cup of tea. I expect Peter and the girls have got it organized." He went through the passageway to the back kitchen and called back, "Behave yourselves, mind!"

When he returned with Ada, Cecily, Peter and the tray of tea, the tinkling of the shop bell indicated that Paul was gone and Van was alone.

"Why, Van?" Cecily asked. "Please tell me this isn't part of your urge to punish me. At least tell me that."

"Have a baby to get back at you, Cecily?" Phil said. "What importance you place on yourself!"

"Shut up!" Van glared at him. "You've done enough damage."

"Phil?" Ada demanded. "What has Phil to do with any of this?"

"It *was* you who wrote to Paul, wasn't it?" Van accused.

She ran upstairs, leaving them all asking questions and trying to sort out the truth from Phil's denials and his offence at their not understanding the honourable motive of whoever had.

★　★　★

Without stopping to do more than brush her hair, Van dressed and ran through the shop, leaving the door open and up the hill to Watkins'. It was still early but she busied herself until the staff arrived and spent the morning doing the jobs she liked least, every moment expecting to be told there was a soldier to see her. But Paul didn't come, and Cecily failed to come to work.

Beryl and Bertie were away — the reason she was sleeping at the shop — but she decided it was preferable to sleep in the empty house rather than face the barrage of questions waiting for her at home. So when the shop closed she went to the big, empty house overlooking the docks. There, with the post, was a note from Paul: "I'm going back to think about this. We'll talk on my next leave."

It was signed just "Paul".

Back in August, Paris had been liberated and the scenes that followed were repeated through other towns as the Allies marched through, heading for Berlin. A week after Paul returned to his unit, he was among the first to enter a newly liberated town and he walked through the streets and accepted the adulation and kisses of the population, and witnessed the unfurling of hundreds of French and British flags which had been hidden ready for the day the Germans were driven out. A sniper hiding in the ruins of a barn fired only once before being killed by a sharp-eyed British soldier but his bullet had liberated Paul from his decision whether or not to marry Van.

When she went to visit Kitty and was told the unbelievable news of Paul's death, Van didn't cry. She went in cold anger to see Phil and shouted at him, "He needn't have known! If he had to die, then he could at least have died happy and without the worry of this!" She hit her stomach in anguish. "You're evil and insane. Why did you have to interfere?"

She allowed Cecily to take her to her old room and she slid fully dressed under the counterpane and lay there, staring at the walls and wondering why she had allowed "Blodwen" to happen. Had it really been some distorted urge to punish her mother by shaming her and make her watch the same ordeal again, by proxy? Was she so determined to prove how much better she'd deal with the problem?

The simple solution was to go at once to Beryl and Bertie and tell them. They wouldn't be angry; they'd allow her to talk it through, and knowing it was Edwin's child would give them further involvement. They had always supported her, as when she asked them not to tell Edwin about her engagement to Paul. They had understood then her desire to tell Edwin personally, rather than let him hear in a letter. Although, sadly, in that instance, as in this, Phil had frustrated her intention.

She didn't go straightaway to the Richards to tell them. Edwin and "Blodwen" could be dealt with later. Now there was Paul's death to cope with.

Many suspicious people believed that births and death come together in a family, and although Paul was not family, Ada strengthened the myth by joining his death with the birth of Annette's fourth child. It was a boy, and they called him Bertie and asked Bertie and Beryl and Van to be his godparents.

CHAPTER
TWELVE

As 1945 came in, Cecily and Ada remembered all the other New Years which had seemed to herald such an exciting beginning. This one held greater promise than any they could remember. The war seemed truly about to end and even the news that Danny and Gareth were prisoners seemed less frightening than it would have been years or even months ago.

"It won't be for long," Peter consoled them whenever they admitted to being afraid for them. He read the news avidly and reported all the hopeful signs of approaching victory.

"It's wonderful to think they might be home for Easter," Ada said.

"Be murdered before that," Phil muttered. "That Hitler won't allow prisoners to survive. Waste money feeding the enemy? What does he care for a lot of British and Americans and all the others who have helped us to victory? What does he gain by handing them back?"

He glared at Cecily, who told him to hush.

They ignored his comments and instead thought of the friends who they wouldn't see again — poor Jack

Simmons, who had run the shop next door to provide cheap food for the poorest families, and Paul.

As April approached, Cecily asked her daughter, now heavily pregnant, what she wanted for a twenty-first birthday present.

"Nothing."

"You must have a special gift for your twenty-first, Van, lovey, it's such a special date. I thought we could all go out and have a celebratory meal."

"No."

"But why?" Cecily pleaded. "Expecting a baby doesn't alter the fact that you've reached the age of consent and you'll inherit Waldo's shop with all the money and power that will bring. Surely you'll want to mark the day with a party or something?"

"No. I'll mark the day all right, but in my own time. On my birthday I'm going to stay home with Auntie Beryl and Uncle Bertie. Just me," she added firmly when Cecily tried to speak. "Edwin says he'll try to phone me there. That's all I'm doing for the moment. Later, I'll have a very special celebration."

"Will we be invited to that?" Cecily asked sarcastically.

"Oh, yes." Van's eyes shone in suppressed excitement. "You'll be invited to that one all right!"

Cecily wondered what it was about the statement that made her uneasy.

"You're imagining things," Peter said when she told him of her apprehension. "Having a baby, the confusion of her feelings for Edwin and Paul, Paul's death, it's all mixed up in her head and she'll need time to unsnarl it, bit by bit."

Van's birthday was not what she planned at all. She woke early in the morning and the pains began, low in her back. She lay there for a while, trying to remember what Annette had told her, not wanting to rouse anyone or have doctors fussing her too soon. But by seven o'clock she knew she needed help and she called Beryl.

The baby was born, a few weeks prematurely, at three in the afternoon, in the room Beryl and Van had prepared; the room that had once been Edwin's nursery. It was a boy and Van said he would be called Richard.

"But if you marry Edwin, he'll be Richard Richards. Would you want that?"

"And if I don't marry Edwin he'll be Richard Owen," Van replied in a voice that forbade further discussion.

The maid was sent with a message to Cecily written by Van, telling her of the birth of the baby and adding that, in a few days, she would invite her to see him, but at the moment she and Beryl were far too busy to cope with visitors.

Cecily read it and cried.

An hour later, she left the office at Waldo's store and went to Beryl and Bertie's house, banging furiously on the door. A surprised Beryl opened it. "Cecily! I'm so glad you decided to come, Van was upset when you said you were too busy." Luckily Cecily had Van's note and she showed it to Beryl, who read it without a word.

278

They went together to where Van was sitting with the baby in a cot beside her and she looked startled when her mother came in. She said nothing as Cecily looked at the baby then picked him up and held him.

"He's to be called Richard," Beryl told her.

"Richard Richards?"

"We don't know about that," Beryl said, shaking her head as warning to Cecily not to say any more.

The two friends went downstairs and sat for a while talking about the resentment Van felt for her mother. "She seems to be getting worse, but I wonder if having a child of her own might make her soften towards me," Cecily said. But a look at Beryl's face showed her that her friend had as little hope of that as she did herself.

Three weeks later, Van was back at the store, to Cecily's concern and Beryl's disappointment. Jennifer, the young girl who had worked at the store, had agreed to become Richard's nursemaid and Beryl prepared a room for her next to the nursery.

Cecily had grown fonder of Peter as the years passed. He worked long hours at his garage, where he employed a young man on a temporary basis until Johnny Fowler came back from the war. At Johnny and Sharon's wedding, he had promised Johnny a job and he had no intention of letting the man down. With the house, where Sharon and her three girls waited for him, Johnny would have a good start after his years away.

Because of his refusal to get more help, he would leave the shop before six each morning to open the garage. It was often seven in the evening before he returned. Besides servicing the few vans and cars still managing to get petrol, he also repaired bicycles, prams and pushchairs for women without husbands to do the jobs. He sharpened knives and, sometimes with Willie helping, fixed clocks and garden mowers, never refusing any demands on his skills and time.

Milk vans were allowed to work only in specified zones, being given areas of streets in which to deliver, commensurate with the size of their pre-war business. This cut down on petrol and also, to the roundsmen's delight, made it easier to collect payment, as there was no second firm waiting for the business if a customer got into debt. Because Peter was quick and utterly reliable, most of the milkmen took their vans to him, so they wouldn't be without a vehicle longer than the finish of one day and the start of the next.

Cecily saw how tired he was on some days and would fuss over him, spoil him and take great pleasure in finding and cooking his favourite food. She was hurt and irritated when Phil, who occasionally managed to buy a fresh salmon from an illegal source, refused to bring any more once he had learned how much Peter enjoyed it. He made the excuse that he was endangering the farmer who offered them.

"I know that isn't true," Cecily said angrily. "It's knowing I want it for Peter, isn't it?"

Ada hotly denied this but Cecily knew from the way Phil relished any disappointment in her life that for some unimaginable reason his dislike of her was not lessening with the years. That inexplicable dislike had never been more apparent than one day when he was in

280

the stables where he sometimes stabled the horse he still occasionally borrowed. He had been grooming the animal, talking to it in conspiratorial whispers when he saw Cecily and Peter in a close embrace amid the diminished stock and the empty boxes.

"Disgusting," he said in a low, growling voice he used to show disapproval.

"What's that, Phil?" Cecily asked, hugging Peter tight. "What have you heard straight from the horse's mouth then?" She was blatantly rude to him at times, not trying to cover up his strange behaviour, but talking about his long silences and his frowning stare and the way he would sometimes appear to be talking to someone who wasn't there. She didn't believe he was seriously ill, just playing games with her.

"You! That's what!" he said now. "You're disgusting! Carrying on like that at your age. It's forty you are, woman, not sixteen. A fine example you've shown that daughter of yours. No wonder she's a floozy, getting pregnant. Sure it was Edwin, are you? Could have been an American. Handsome they are, and they pay well, don't they? Five pairs of nylons she'd got upstairs. Five pairs!"

"How dare you go through her things?" Cecily shouted, but Peter pulled her away, across the yard and into the living room.

"Don't rouse him more than he is already, love," he warned quietly. "I really think he's going to flip one day. I just hope you aren't the catalyst. Best you leave him be."

"It's an act. And I can't let him say those things about Van," she protested angrily. "He's been putting his grubby hands through her things. How dare he do that!"

"Please love, you must ignore it. Phil is unbalanced, a real danger if things don't go his way. Believe me, he's not a well man. Promise me you'll ignore anything he says. I worry about you being here with him while I'm at the garage."

"Don't worry about Phil. I'm not afraid of him."

"Perhaps you should be."

"I'm at Waldo's all day, it's only the time between me finishing there and you coming home and even then I'm not alone — Ada's here too, remember."

"Please, my darling, be careful, don't upset him. As soon as Johnny gets back I'll spend a lot more time here with you, but until then, promise me you won't antagonize him."

"You really believe he's unbalanced, that this isn't some game he's playing?"

"If I had my way he'd be in a hospital and locked away where he can't cause any harm."

Phil was listening to this at the door and his eyes wore a glassy look as he went swiftly and silently down the passage, through the back kitchen, across the yard and into the air raid shelter below the stables. Insane, was he? He'd show them how insane he was.

An hour later he had calmed his racing heart and wiped the perspiration from his face with a handkerchief and went in to his wife.

"What about a walk?" he said. "We ought to look at the house and think about Willie's proposal to rebuild it. I don't think we should sell. We don't want to stay here much longer, do we?"

Ada was delighted to see him showing an interest in something. She put on a swagger coat and tied a cheerful red scarf around her neck ready to take Phil's arm and walk down to the Old Village. She fussed over dressing him warmly, fastening his overcoat and raising the collar and insisting he wore the brown trilby over his thinning hair.

They caught the bus for part of the way, planning to walk down the green lane from the park, where preparations were being made for an open air concert the following afternoon. They sat in the park for a while, looking first at the distant shimmering sea and then turning to look down on the irregular roofs and gardens and houses that made up the area called the Old Village. Ada pointed to the building near the church where they were married, that had once been their home.

"It will be lovely to be back in a place of our own, won't it, Phil?"

"Let's have some fish and chips on the way back, shall we?" he said. "Just you and me. Not Cecily or Peter. They can get their own treat."

Down the green lane and across the road and they were clambering over the rubble that had once been the neat home of Phil's mother. Phil touched the walls, looked through gaps where windows had once been. He stared at the tangle of wild flowers in his mother's garden which had once attracted admiring glances. When he examined the remnants of his workshop he was smiling, his eyes glowing with an inner excitement that Ada took for joy at the prospect of returning home. But when she talked about it, and remarked at the absence of the mangled machinery, long gone for scrap, he seemed to be smiling at some secret thoughts of his own.

"Wake up, Phil." She shook him gently. "I was saying that the machines went to help the war effort with all the fences and gates." He came back from wherever his mind had taken him. "We'll get it looking just as it was when we lived here with your mam," she said. "Exactly the same. We won't go in for anything fancy, we'll recreate the place where we were so happy."

"Prisoners they are, locked up for the duration," Phil said.

Ada sighed and tried again. "The walls are all skewiff and there's no wood left. Pinched for firewood I bet. Doors, windows and even the wooden troughing, all gone."

"Locked up," he said.

"Don't worry. Willie will sort it all out for us, we'll just leave it to him."

"I want to do the planning myself, mind!" He startled her with his sudden return to the subject. "I want to be the one who makes it grow again."

"You shall, love. Come on now, it's getting cold. We'll get the fish and chips we promised ourselves, shall we?"

"Fish and chips? That'll be nice."

They walked back up the green lane without calling on Annette and Willie. With four children to get ready for bed, they were bound to be busy. The sea was dark now and the village behind them was dissolving into the mist of the evening. When they reached home with their parcel of fish and chips, they ate, with Ada apologizing for not bringing them any.

Phil left them discussing the plan to rebuild his home and he went once more into the cold cellar-cum-air raid shelter. He took out some playing cards, halved the pack and with the top half began turning them over one at a time on to the top of the cupboard. "Cecily, Peter, Cecily, Peter, Cecily, Peter," he chanted, until the pack ran out.

He removed the electric light bulb from the wire-protected holder and smashed it, then replaced it. He took the blankets from the cupboard where they had been placed when the air raids had begun and hid them behind some empty boxes in the stable loft. Then he went back to the house.

"Peter," he said, when he managed to get him on his own, "there's something funny down in the cellar. Don't tell them in there, don't want to worry them. It's probably only a rat but you never know, do you? An escaped prisoner perhaps, or a runaway soldier. I'll meet you outside and we'll have a look see, shall we? Don't tell the women, they'll only panic."

Peter went in and picked up two letters Cecily had written, one each to Johnny and Gareth. Taking a couple of two and a half pence stamps from the drawer, he said he needed a breath of air and would post them.

"Want me to come, love?" Cecily asked.

"No need. It's looking miserable out there. I won't be more than a few seconds."

Going out through the passage, he picked up his overcoat. It was misty and quite chilly. Following Phil into the darkness of the yard, he reached for the torch that usually stood on the window sill but his fingers failed to locate it. He didn't worry; Phil would certainly have it. The darkness of the yard was unbroken and the mist had thickened into an all-concealing fog. He felt with slippered feet for the steps, no longer familiar in the dense foggy night which had obliterated even the stars.

The stable door was open and he stepped inside, calling for Phil to show a light. There was no reply and he walked to the top of the steps leading down to the shelter which Danny and Willie had built.

"Down there, look." Phil appeared at his side momentarily and shone the thin beam of the torch down the steps. As Peter bent slightly and asked him to shine the torch again, he was pushed viciously and in such a way that he completely lost his balance and fell with no possibility of grasping the handrail and saving himself. The door was closed, cutting off his cry of alarm and the shout of pain as he landed awkwardly across the bottom step.

Phil appeared in the living room moments later wearing pyjamas and dressing gown, having gone up to change and give the impression he hadn't left the house. He joined in the women's conversation and frowned with them when Peter failed to return. As the

286

minutes passed, he offered to go and look for him, going back upstairs to get dressed.

He came in shivering. "It's freezing cold, the fog's like a wet blanket. No sign of him, though it's hard to see anything. The back lane door's open but he isn't there. I walked as far as the postbox."

At midnight Cecily called the police, who assured her there hadn't been a road accident reported in the vicinity. "Met someone and got talking, I bet," the policeman said, although that seemed a very unlikely explanation. "It's happened to me and I've felt the rough edge of my wife's tongue more than once."

"Peter isn't like that," Cecily said. "He's lying somewhere hurt, I know it. Go and search for him, please. This isn't the weather for being outside and helpless."

A constable arrived and Phil offered to help him search. "You go along the lane and I'll look in the stable in case he's stumbled. I'll even look down the shelter again, although how he could have fallen down there I can't think."

"If, as you say, the door is closed, that's unlikely," the constable said.

"We have to be thorough," Phil insisted.

They sat up all night waiting for news but none came. Cecily was white and her eyes abnormally large and she walked up and down, listening for the slightest sound at the door. Dawn broke and she went out through the stables and into the lane, looking up and down foolishly, hoping to see him walk around the corner as if nothing untoward had happened. She handed the constable the key of the next door shop without any hope of finding him there; he didn't have a key and apart from a window that refused to close properly there was no way he could get in there.

Two more constables arrived to begin a new shift but the first one refused to go home, promising another couple of hours to search. He went into the shop next door using the key at half past six and woke Horse and his wife, who were wrapped in blankets and coats and surrounded with the remnants of a fish and chip meal and a half-empty flagon of beer.

"Let them stay," Cecily said when she was told. "I wouldn't want to see anyone without a roof over their head today." Horse rolled himself back into the blankets and went back to sleep.

"Get that window fixed or they'll invite all their friends," she was warned.

Peter called. Quietly at first, then with more and more abuse, convinced that Phil was outside the door listening to him. He had slipped into unconsciousness when he fell and had not realized how much time had passed. When he woke and tried to rise, the pain was enough to want him to scream and he had lain there panting with the shock of it, knowing his leg was broken.

Coldness rose from the concrete floor and made every inch of him ache. If he had been able to move, there was nothing to help him. There was a first aid box but the cupboard where the blankets were stored was too far away and it was warmth he needed. Warmth and a hot drink. Fully aware of what had happened to him, he swore that he'd live long enough to make Phil face his evil act and convince Ada to accept it. To do that he must survive. Surely Phil wouldn't leave him much longer? It can't be his intention for me to die here? A chill of fear spread through him as he thought that, yes, that could be Phil's intention.

He reached in as wide a circle as he was able but pain restricted it and he could find nothing that would help him. He tried to visualize the cellar contents. A brush had stood in a corner just inside the door, near the top of the steps. If he could only reach it, he might be able to make himself a splint and succeed in moving. But it might as well be on the moon as there was no chance of moving up the steps to reach it.

It was a blackness he had never before experienced. There wasn't even a crack of light around the cellar door, situated as it was, well inside the stable. Was it night? Nearly morning? How long had he been there? Where was Cecily? Hunger would have been a guide if it hadn't been blunted by shock and the pain in his leg, which he knew was lying at a peculiar angle. That, plus the cold which drained away any other sensation. There was pressure on his back but he was afraid to move and try to ease it, although he knew he must.

If only he could have a drink. The thought of a hot, sweet cup of tea hovered before him like a tormenting nightmare. He drifted into a doze in which he saw Cecily walking towards him, smiling and carrying a bowl of soup and a warm blanket. Momentarily the dream gave him the sensation that he had in fact received these things. His thirst eased and the blanket and warm soup revived his energy. He woke with a shout of agony as he moved in his dream, to stand and walk towards Cecily, the movement reminding him of his injured leg.

The pressure of the bottom step on his spine was worse. He looked up and thought he saw a thin slit of light around the bottom of the door. Morning? Midday? Where was Cecily? He concentrated on listening but there was no sound of feet above, encouraging him to shout, but he shouted anyway. He had to move. He tried, shouted in agony and knew that without a splint of some sort he would never succeed.

Why didn't someone come? Where was Cecily?

The search which had centred around the shop and the back lanes was extended. No one went near the stables any more. The police and friends went over to the beach, in case he had wandered over there with some kind of memory loss, but although they approached the stall and the cafe owners who knew him, there was no information to cheer Cecily during that long and terrible day. They called on Sharon in case he had called at his house where he had lived until he and Cecily were married. She had seen nothing of him, but offered to help search.

Ada served in the shop where curiosity brought a larger than usual number of customers and Phil followed her around, never leaving her, frequently glancing back to where Cecily sat huddled near the phone, with his strange, nervous smile but not speaking to her.

Peter knew that unless he did something soon, hypothermia would gradually weaken him and he would lose the strength to try. The dream, in which he imagined he was warm and fed, was dangerous. The first aid box was his only hope, as long as Phil hadn't moved it. He called for a while but there was no response. He tried to move, reach for the first aid box, but the movement caused so much pain he fainted.

The policemen had gone to be replaced by others, who went over the same ground as the others had done several times before. One actually looked into the stable, saw it was empty and didn't go to the cellar door. It was locked from the outside so there couldn't be anyone down there. He called softly but Peter was unaware.

A while later, while the search went on through the stables and sheds alongside the lanes, Peter decided he had to make an effort to support the injured leg. He removed his braces and tie and, using the good leg as a splint for the broken one, he tensed himself to tackle the steps.

He slowly, painfully moved, inch by inch, to the edge of the step on which he was half lying and lowered himself down to the floor. He rested a while, then moved again, slipping in and out of consciousness, each time taking longer to recover sufficiently to go on. He reached for the first aid box and pulled it down, scattering bandages which he used to add to the support for his leg, winding them around to strengthen the bonds. Then he tensed himself to get up the steps to the door.

It seemed to take hours but he slowly managed to rise backwards, step by painful step, towards the door at the top, thankful that the steps were shallow. When he reached the top he pushed the door and called but his voice was alarmingly weak. He sobbed. He would never get out of this prison created by Phil.

The latch was on the door and as he couldn't possibly stand he was unable to reach it. To have freedom so close but denied him was even worse than lying helpless at the bottom of the steps, to have reached the door and be found dead here so near success was a cruel fate. He was so tired but, determined to resist death, he felt around him in the dark. Less dark than when he had been entombed below but dark all the same, a different kind of darkness. He couldn't see it but knew there was a yard brush, which they used to lift the loft door and swing it back on its hinges. He found it with a gasp of satisfaction and dragged it into position. Steadying it was extremely difficult, his arms were so weak. It rattled against the door as he tried to position it under the latch and lift it. It was then he realized that the door had been locked on the outside.

Cecily knew she wouldn't sleep. She went out and stood at the back door staring across at the stables as if somehow the building held the secret of Peter's disappearance. Where could he have gone? Why had he left her? He went out to post two letters and the postbox was only on the corner at the bottom of the lane. What could have happened between here and there? She gave a big shuddering sigh. If he were ill, surely he wouldn't go away from her? Where else was there for him to go?

Something in the darkness made her stop and listen. Something was moving, and there was the slightest of sounds at the stable door, which was closed. She heard the sound again, a door rattling. Someone was in there. Picking up the torch from the window sill, she walked up the yard, afraid to hope. She opened the stable door and called, "Anyone there?" The cellar door rattled and she heard the sound of the broom falling and clattering down the steps inside.

"Peter!" She opened the cellar door and saw Peter lying on the top step.

She knelt beside him and took in the white face and the film of sweat, the legs tied together and heard him say weakly, "Phil. Phil threw me down the cellar — locked me in — my leg, it's —" He once again slipped into unconsciousness.

Running, shouting, she told Ada to call the ambulance and the police. She paused only long enough to see these things done then, grabbing some coats, ran back to stay with her arms around Peter until help arrived.

They knew Peter's story was true. It all added up so neatly; the way Phil had been the one to search and re-search the stable, the way he had prayed aloud that there shouldn't be an air raid although there hadn't been one for many months. The way he had encouraged the searchers to go further afield. He didn't even deny it when the police came, but boasted about his skill in organizing it.

The constables were reprimanded for not undertaking the proper searches when they admitted leaving it to Phil, and argued that they had no reason to suspect him of involvement. He played the part of a concerned relative too well.

Phil was taken away, and with Peter in hospital, the two sisters were thrown back to the time after their father's death. They were alone in the house without even Van to comfort them. Van, whose twenty-first birthday had been marked with the birth of her own son, who they were rarely allowed to see.

The temptation to hurl abuse was strongly felt by Cecily, but she desisted, superstitiously believing her tolerance would be rewarded by Peter's full recovery.

Silently they sat, hour by hour, waiting for the time of their next visit to the hospital. Cecily wondered bitterly why Ada had ignored Phil's growing strangeness but was honest enough to admit that if it had been Peter she would have acted the same way. She would have protected him, tried to ease him out of the cocoon of confusion he had woven around himself, convinced that with her love she could help him without involving the experts.

Peter was her life. Her strength and happiness were tied up in him. She couldn't imagine a world without him and prayed silently for his health to return. She needed him and his love and his unfailing support. He had fitted into her life so perfectly and completely that "being made for each other" no longer sounded like a romantic fantasy.

Days and nights passed in a blur of anxiety. Cecily and Ada visited their husbands every hour that it was allowed, and between times, Ada opened the almost empty shop and Cecily went up the hill to Waldo's.

Peter developed pneumonia and seemed likely to be in hospital for a while. For Ada, there was little hope of Phil ever returning home.

As Peter gradually regained strength, sympathy grew in Cecily for both Ada and the confused and unhappy man who was her brother-in-law. She occasionally found time to go with Ada to the hospital where Phil, looking smaller and older, seemed likely to remain.

The sisters heard the news of the Allied victories from customers and friends, but their reaction to them was less enthusiastic than it would have been weeks before. They smiled when it was announced on 23 April that Berlin was surrounded. They cheered with the rest when told that Mussolini and his mistress had been shot, but they rarely read a newspaper or listened to the wireless. All their thoughts were close at home on Peter and Phil and on worries for the future if one or the other didn't come home again. But they did actually hear the announcement: "This is London calling. German radio has announced that Hitler is dead. I repeat, German radio has announced that Hitler is dead."

"At last," Cecily sobbed. "Now it must end soon."

★ ★ ★

When Peter came out of hospital, a field marshall was in a tent a long way off, signing a document of surrender with a two-penny pen. Montgomery made an error and had to cross out 5 May and alter it to 4 May. But this did not affect the validity of the surrender. War in Europe was ended.

It seemed to Cecily that the town was celebrating Peter's recovery with her. Bells rang from churches, boats and ships of all sizes sounded hooters and sirens. The streetlights allowed since the previous November after years of darkness seemed brighter than normal. Many cars that travelled along the streets sounded V for victory on their horns.

People filed out of their houses and walked the streets in pairs or in long lines, or singly, just wanting to be out there, a part of the nationwide celebration. Bonfires were planned and hurriedly built — blackout material among the first items to be donated. Children made "guys" to be placed on bonfires, all effigies not of Guy Fawkes but of the little man with the little moustache, who'd caused such havoc in the world.

In the area around Owen's shop, women quickly organized street parties, and bunting grew like exotic climbers from some distant forest, up and over walls and across the road from one bedroom window to another opposite and repeated every few yards so the places were transformed from the drabness of wartime to a colourful, magical place that had children walking around staring in disbelief and wonder, eyes huge in the thin faces.

From church halls, mothers and grandmothers dragged trestle tables to make a line of even greater splendour down the centre of each road, where they were covered with white cloths and red, white and blue decorations. Cecily and Ada and many other shopkeepers and householders raided their depleted stores and managed to find jars of meat paste, tins of luncheon meat, pots of jam, stored for this wonderful time. These were gratefully taken to swell the feast.

Cecily revelled in every aspect of the celebration. It was going to be all right. Peter was recovering, Johnny Fowler and Edwin were safe. And with Gareth, Danny and unknown others on their way home from prison camps from where already hundreds had been released, there was nothing but good times ahead.

"Best of all, Peter, love," she said, tucking an unnecessary blanket around his knees as he sat by the fire, "the very best of all, you are here to share it with me." She put her head close to his and said, almost shyly, "I've been so glad to have you here with me during these awful years."

"And I couldn't have been more content, darling Cecily." He kissed her affectionately. "I love you, very, very much."

"Just think," she said happily, "the Pleasure Beach will be filled with families again. Not just women and children pretending to enjoy themselves, but families: dads, brothers, uncles, and no more partings. No more fear. No more bombs."

But her biggest bombshell arrived the following morning.

CHAPTER
THIRTEEN

Leaving Ada prepared to serve any customer who might bother to try them for the few items they still stocked, and having settled Peter near the fire with a copy of *Rebecca* to keep him entertained until she came home, Cecily set off cheerfully to her daily work at Waldo's store with Van. The shop was busy in contrast to the one she had just left and she waved to the staff as she walked through the chattering customers, to the stairs leading to Van's office.

She heard voices raised as she climbed the stairs, her daughter's low and firm, the more petulant, whining voice of Owen-Owen in counterpoint. Owen constantly received the worst of Van's temper.

She opened the door and went in. Van was standing behind her desk and Owen was standing near the window, his face ashen, his eyes staring in disbelief at the papers Van had thrust into his hands.

"How many times do you want me to say it, Owen? You're sacked. And you can be thankful I haven't done it before. Soft I've been for not getting rid of you sooner. But now I have full authority, it's one of the pleasures, long delayed, that I can relish."

"Van?" Cecily asked. Her daughter ignored her.

"Well?" Van said to the shaken young man. "What are you waiting for? More home truths? I'd have thought you'd heard enough!"

Owen seemed not to have noticed Cecily as he stumbled from the office.

"Van, lovey? What's this all about?" Cecily reached for a chair and gently pushed her daughter into it. "Sit and calm yourself. You mustn't get into a state like this."

Van's voice was calm and she smiled as she said, "In a state? I haven't enjoyed myself so much for years. Now, we come to you!"

"Me?" Cecily laughed. "Is it my turn to be told off by the boss? Come on, then, tell me, what have I done wrong?"

"You are sacked, Mam. Sacked!"

Cecily's laughter broke out again but it suddenly painfully died when she saw the expression on Van's face.

"All right, lovey, you've had your little joke. Now let's get on, shall we? I have to go at twelve to see to Peter's lunch, Auntie Ada's visiting Uncle Phil today and there's a lot to do here this morning."

"There is precisely nothing for you to do here." Van reached into a drawer and handed her an envelope similar to the one carried by Owen. "Here are your wages up to the end of the month."

"What?"

"This store is mine now and I want you out of it."

"But, Van —"

"Mam. I'm twenty-one and from now on I'll live my life not as the bastard daughter of a rundown shopkeeper but as the proprietor of Waldo Watkins' store." She walked out, leaving Cecily holding the envelope in a shaking hand.

"But I've lost everything. I've given it up to help you!" she shouted after her daughter's retreating figure. "And what about my contracts? I want them back immediately!"

"*Your* contracts, Mam? They all belong here. You handed them over without any coercion on my part."

They all tried in turn to persuade Van to change her mind and return the contracts to Owen's but she was adamant. The contracts, she insisted, were better served by the large Watkins' store, as agreed by Cecily and Ada a long time ago. She laughed as she looked around the almost empty shelves of the once-successful shop.

"How could you hope to service them?" she said in her cold, calm voice. "With such strict restrictions how could you possibly get the stock to satisfy the local people, let alone the shipping orders and the cafes and tea rooms over at the Pleasure Beach. There's really no point discussing this, is there?"

Cecily cried a lot and was comforted by Peter.

"She's been trying to punish you for what she sees as your guilt for years," he said. "Let her have her day. The less you show her how hurt you are, the quicker she'll come back to being the sensible young woman she really is, underneath this built-up hatred."

"Hatred?" Cecily was shocked by the terrible word.

300

"Not hatred of you, but of the person she thinks she is, a dark secret no one was allowed to speak of. She'll realize one day how wrong she is to think of herself that way, and that no forgiveness is needed for the way you coped with her birth."

"But hatred?"

"Don't let the word frighten you, my dear. It's only very rarely that hatred is a true intent to harm. Look at Phil. He hates you but wouldn't harm you. In some strange way he almost loves you."

"I find the thought of being loved by Phil more frightening than being hated!"

"Phil has never actually harmed you, only those around you." He didn't know that the card game on the terrible night of his imprisonment had been to decide which of the two of them to push down the cellar steps.

"It's all too complicated for me."

There were a great many phone calls from a very angry Bertie and Beryl wanting to help but not knowing how. A very distressed Melanie called, insisting this was not what Waldo would have wanted and she was furiously angry, imagining his dismay and disappointment at the behaviour of a daughter he had denied but whom he had loved. She tried to bring peace between mother and daughter and persuade Van to start arrangements to return some of the business to Owen's.

Cecily told her not to distress herself by trying. "Peter's right," she explained. "Van has been planning this for years, the ruination of the shop, after encouraging me to put so much of our business in her hands, humiliating me by sacking me at the same time as Owen. I'll just have to wait for her to work it out of her system." If she ever does, she thought with dread.

Van's baby was christened in June but Cecily and Ada were not told by Van. It was Beryl who telephoned them with the date, time and venue.

"She told me not to tell you," Beryl said angrily. "I don't know what's the matter with her. She isn't the little girl we thought we knew. Bertie and I won't go, knowing you and Ada aren't invited, so you *are* invited, by me! I know how difficult it is for you, but please come, all of you, for the sake of appearances if nothing else."

Cecily, Peter and Ada ordered a taxi and went to sit at the back of the church. The sun streamed past the thick wooden door and shone on the dusty footprints on the ancient tiled floor.

The church wasn't full. Annette and Willie were there with their four children. Bertie and Beryl were godparents, as was Melanie. Van stood at the front of the pews beside the font, holding her baby. But apart from a few local people standing outside to see them arrive and depart, it was going to be a quiet affair.

Cecily turned to see who was the first to arrive. It was Edwin and he walked in alone. That his appearance was a shock to Van was apparent. Cecily saw her turn and ask a question of Beryl, who shook her head, which appeared to Cecily to be stating that no, she hadn't invited or expected her son to be there.

Edwin walked through the church and went to stand beside Van. He looked down at the baby she was holding, then took the child into his arms and nodded at the vicar for him to commence the service. He hadn't looked at Van, yet seemed to belong there, his tightly clenched jaw the only sign of unease.

Cecily held Peter's hand tightly, watching the tableau, hardly able to draw breath. Then she realized that Peter was unwell. His breathing became laboured quite suddenly and as soon as the service ended, Bertie came and helped Cecily get him outside and into the car. Half an hour later, a doctor told them it was pneumonia again.

Ada had, on Cecily's insistence, stayed with the others and reported to her sister later on what had happened.

"Van insisted on not naming Edwin as the baby's father, or giving him the surname Richards. She seems hell-bent on her own destruction. Beryl and Bertie have been wonderful to her yet she denies them the grandchild they want so much to love and enjoy. Having the little boy named Richard Owen instead of Richard Richards is so cruel. Does she want her son to go through all the things she was supposed to have suffered because of your lack of a husband? Van is cruel, Cecily, there's no other word for it. But why is she like this? What have we done between us to make her like this?"

Cecily explained to Peter all that had happened. He was in hospital and making slow progress.

"Where will she live? She can't stay with Beryl and Bertie after this," Peter said. "Specially with Edwin coming home soon."

"She isn't," Ada told them. "She's bought a house up near the park and she'll live there with Jennifer to take care of the baby while she works."

It was difficult to respond to the questions and good wishes of people and have to pretend that she knew, and understood, Van's intentions, but Cecily found that concentrating on caring for Peter helped. He recovered more quickly from the pneumonia than before but still looked unwell when the doctor allowed him to return home. He went back to work at the garage, mainly overseeing the work done by others. He also spent some time trying to persuade other stall holders to return their regular orders to Cecily and Ada, without saying too much about the deceit of Van in taking them. His days were short, on Cecily's insistence, and as the shop was still abysmally quiet she often closed when he came home at 4.30.

Apart from what Peter achieved, they didn't do much to recoup their lost customers at the beach. For one thing it was impossible for Cecily to go to them and admit that her daughter had stolen their business. Pride, she decided, was costly. The other reason was Peter's health. Although he didn't have another reoccurrence of the pneumonia, he remained a constant worry.

With little to do in the shop, Ada and Cecily spent a couple of days sorting through accumulated rubbish in the shop next door. Unused, it had become a dumping ground for boxes, discarded stock and newspapers once needed for recycling. They discussed possibilities for its use, businesses they might start, coming up with several suggestions but none of the ideas came to fruition.

Cecily continued to write to Gareth and Johnny, who had not yet come home. They were still far away in the theatre of war not ended, the Far East. She listened to the news more avidly than ever, wanting the last of her close friends to be returned safely to the town.

When the atom bomb fell on Hiroshima on 6 August and was followed by the Nagasaki bomb on 9 August, people cried openly for the thousands of innocent people destroyed in those cities. Even when the Japanese prisoners were released and men little more than walking skeletons began to appear, the compassion for the ordinary Japanese people only lessened slightly, knowing it was the few and not the majority who were the evil ones.

The war finally ended in September but Gareth and Johnny still didn't come home. Cecily learned that many of the men serving in the Far East were held back and rested in hospitals before they could travel. As October came, she feared for them.

"At least Gareth will have a business to come back to," Peter consoled her, "and so will Johnny. I gave him a promise that I intend to keep."

"Poor Gareth has to face the loss of Rhonwen. From his letters it's easy to see how he dreads coming back to the shop, with evenings spent with his mother. Thank goodness there's Marged to cheer him up." She smiled at Peter, affection clear in her eyes. "I'm so lucky to have you."

"Gareth is young, there's time for him to start again."

"He's forty, like me!"

"That's young." He laughed. "When you're my age, that's young!"

Prisoners were slowly released and the town was filled with wounded or pale, thin men, including many who seemed bemused by their sudden freedom. Some went back to jobs waiting for them, women dismissed to allow for their promised return. Others were escorted around the town on the arm of a wife or mother, too weak and ill. Even those who were strong seemed unable to suddenly slot themselves back into lives they had been forced to abandon. In new and often ill-fitting suits, they walked the roads in groups, or sat outside their front doors wondering how to recapture the pre-war existence they barely remembered, and watched their children — some as young as four, whom they had never seen before — who stared at them like the strangers they were.

Johnny was one of the lucky ones. He went straight to the disordered but welcoming house he could now call home. He brought Sharon and the three girls down to see the sisters and Peter as soon as he had found himself some decent civilian clothes.

"I've learned a lot working on army vehicles, adding to my knowledge in a way that was better than any mechanic's course I've done. I was trusted to make sure the lorries and trucks, and even tanks for a time, were in good order. Did you mean it, about giving me a job in the garage, Peter?" he asked.

"Of course. I've been waiting for you. I could do with some reliable help, so when would you like to start?"

"Tomorrow morning?"

"It's only now you're home! Don't you want a holiday first?"

"Working and not having to follow shouted orders, that's a holiday!" Grinning, he asked, "You won't shout orders at me, will you?"

"I'll ask you very nicely," Peter promised.

"Thank goodness you'll be able to take things easy now," Cecily remarked, but Peter smiled and said, "Not yet. We must give the lad a chance."

Sharon, like Rhonwen months before, had been busy making clothes to welcome her husband home. She wore a two-piece suit cut from brocade curtains bought at a jumble sale. The buttons were not a good match, coming from an old coat. Her high-heeled shoes were too large but had been a bargain at a second-hand shop. A substitute for stockings, made with powder mixed with water and painted on with a sponge, made her legs a bright orange. She had drawn the seams with an eyebrow pencil, but unfortunately they were crooked. Pancake make-up stopped visibly at the neck of the suit and her hair was frizzy with a bad perm. But somehow, Cecily thought later, her appearance didn't matter. You remembered the warmth of her and the affection she showered on Johnny and the girls and everyone who came near.

"There's something very special about your Sharon," she whispered to Johnny. "She makes you feel happy for having met her. She appears to be fluffy, helpless, hopeless and lovely but she has the rare gift of spreading happiness. You are very lucky to have her."

Johnny laughed. "She's helpless all right. You should see the cake she made to welcome me home. Burnt to a crisp, but I'll eat it if it kills me! I adore her and the girls. They make me feel important and clever and all the other things I am not."

Danny came back but didn't call straightaway. Cecily knew of his return from Willie, who told her Danny was going back to his job delivering the Royal Mail for a while, but was excited by the ideas Willie had expressed for extending their business.

"I wonder if Zachariah Daniels will lend us his donkey and cart?" Willie said one morning. "There's a lot of second-hand timber for sale and if we buy it, we'll need something to bring it home."

With a laugh, Cecily reminded him that the elderly donkey was hardly reliable. She gave him the address of the man from whom Phil used to borrow a horse and cart. "You can use the stable to store it if you want to," she offered. "There's little enough stock we've got to put in it!"

She heard them later, talking in the stable and, curious to see Danny, who had been the love of her life for so many years, she opened the door and called, "Tea, anyone?"

Danny was thinner than when she had seen him last, his dark eyes set deeper in the lean face. He was still without his earring and somehow that was a disappointment, the lack of the piratical air, something she had hoped to see returned. His curling hair was short and streaked with grey and she realized with a shock that he was no longer a boy she had been visualizing in her memory but a man of forty-two, two years older than herself. It reminded her of how life was passing and how little time she had to revive the business and give them an income on which they could comfortably live. Sadly, she began to doubt it was possible. Van had ruined everything for her. If that had been her intention, she had succeeded remarkably well. Again she wondered why and was startled out of her reverie to hear Danny ask if the tea was for today or tomorrow.

As she handed out the cups, she looked at Danny, who was enquiring about Phil, his face showing animation and interest. He hadn't really changed but he'd lost the magic that had separated him from all the other eligible men so many years ago. Now, he was just Danny Preston, Willie's partner and a past love.

Her musings saddened her and she was even more thankful than usual when Peter returned, thoughtful, reliable and utterly dear. Whatever happened to her she would never regret the years she had spent with him. She told him of Danny's visit with Willie.

"That was nice. Did you see any changes in him?"

No sign of jealousy. Wise as well as wonderful Peter.

"He's changed but so have we all, except you, my lovely Peter. You are as constant as the dawn and as welcome."

There was one more surprise that summer. Jack Simmons walked into the shop. Jack, who had sold cheap vegetables on the corner and whom they had believed was dead, was safe and sound, having been released from a prisoner-of-war camp. He turned up one morning when Cecily and Ada were filling the shop window with apples and a few spotty pears brought to them by a farmer.

"Jack?" Cecily stared at him in disbelief. "Jack Simmons? Is that really you? Or are you a younger brother?"

"I likes the younger bit, that I do!" Jack laughed, delighted at her surprise. "Yes, it's me. Thought you'd seen the last of me, did you? Seems the few letters I wrote after I'd been reported killed didn't get through, so everyone thought I was a goner. My wife and kids too. They were bombed out, see. Gone off they have and I can't find them nowhere. They'd have given up hope of me coming back this ages. I've searched and searched but I can't find 'em. I've tried the Citizens Advice Bureau and the War Department, they can't trace them, either. I haven't given up, mind."

"I'm sorry, Jack. We didn't know or we'd have helped, kept in touch with them, but they just went, after the bombing and we had no way of tracing them. I'm so sorry."

"I've come about the shop next door. Want to rent it, do you? Got an idea for making a bit of money, like.

Need it for living in and for a base while I'm searching for the wife and kids."

He was invited in for the inevitable cup of tea and told them of his plans to start selling second-hand items.

"Just as long as you aren't setting up in competition with us again," Ada teased.

"No, it's clothes, furniture, old brass and kitchen utensils, anything people don't want any more. I'll get a horse and cart or perhaps a van and I'll go 'Totting'. That's what they calls it in some parts. Can I have the shop, then? It's empty and you don't seem to have need of it. What's happened to all the stock you used to carry? Surely more than rationing is the reason for the shop being this empty?"

Cecily glanced at Ada then said, "It's a long story. Maybe we'll tell you one day."

They agreed a rent and Jack began filling the place rather untidily with odds and ends of furniture and rails of clothes and he put out notices inviting people to step inside and browse. Cecily and Ada gave him some of their old dance dresses that were too small for their now fuller figures, and in material unsuitable for Sharon's nimble fingers to make into dresses for Victoria, Debora and Leonora.

With some men's suits, he arranged a window display of a couple dancing, which made passers-by stop, smile and with more and more frequency go inside. He bought a horse called Whizzer and an old cart, both of which he kept in the Owen's stable. He went around calling for unwanted junk. He also brought back books on antiques and began studying with great interest.

On Sundays, the sisters learned, he went to Swansea on the train and wandered about following the faintest of leads, looking for his family, who had moved after their house had been destroyed, without leaving an address with anyone they had known. He didn't blame them. He mentally prepared himself not to blame his wife — if — when he found her and she had a new husband. He had been reported killed.

Week after week he searched but found no trace of her. He wondered whether her name was no longer Simmons and that was why she was so hard to find. Meanwhile, the business grew and he felt assured that at least he would be able to offer her a home and a wage once she had returned to him.

Cecily was sitting by the fire in the room behind the shop when Beryl told her the latest news of Van. Cecily jumped up and stared out of the window, through the shop to the street. It was raining, and the chill and the dark gloom of the day seemed apposite. What Beryl told her was so wrong, a defiant disregard for her feelings and yet more contempt for convention. Peter left his chair and stood beside her, his arm on her shoulders.

"Van is getting married in November?" she repeated. "With bridesmaids and everything? How can she?"

"That's what she's telling us." Beryl and Bertie sat on the edge of their chairs, looking very unhappy.

312

Of all the things Van had done to her, Cecily thought, this was the worst. That two dear friends like Beryl and Bertie should be sitting on the edge of their seats feeling ill at ease with her. She went to them and put a hand on theirs.

"We're all thrilled, of course, that she's marrying Edwin. It's what Peter and I have dreamed of, but how can they have such a wedding? How can Edwin agree to such a mockery? Dressed in white? And in church? What vicar will perform the ceremony? Is she going to carry baby Richard down the aisle wrapped in tulle?"

"She wants me to carry him," Beryl whispered.

"And Peter and me? Does she want us there?"

"Of course," Beryl said quickly — too quickly.

"No 'of course' about it! I'm only her mother," she said sadly. "She wouldn't have invited me to see my grandson christened if you two dear friends hadn't insisted." She gripped their hands tighter. "And this invitation, I suspect that too is yours and not Van's idea." She was shaking her head in dismay.

"Apparently there are quite a few unusual weddings these days," Bertie said. "Men coming home to find an unexplained child has been added to the family."

"The others aren't my concern. This is Van, my daughter, and I cannot support her in this blatant, arrogant farce."

Ada sat listening to the exchanges and she spoke now, quietly but with a firmness that surprised Cecily. "No matter who the invitation comes from, Cecily, you are going. Even if Peter and I have to drag you there."

"I don't think I can."

"You are going! There'll be plenty of talk. A gift this'll be for the gossips but it will be far worse for her if you aren't there. And, when the gossip dies down, as it will, it will still be better for people to remember you there, giving her your support. Showing a strong line is what families do best and we are a family, don't forget that."

"Ada's right, my dear," Peter said in his quiet way.

"I think so too, Cecily, love," Beryl agreed.

"All right, I — we'll all go. But only to the church. I'm not sitting through the reception like an unwanted skeleton at the feast!"

"The reception is at the hotel and the meal will be perfect," Bertie said. But on that, no one could change Cecily's mind.

When Beryl and Bertie had gone, Peter fell asleep, as he often did these days, tired by the worry of Van's latest defiance. Cecily carried the tea cups to the back kitchen and Ada followed.

Cecily opened the back door and looked out through the sweeping rain, across the dark yard to the stables, where Peter's illness had begun after Phil's insane attack on him. When Ada spoke to her she was afraid to turn around to answer her for fear the raw hurt would show. Although it had not been Ada who had harmed Peter, it was her knowing Phil was unbalanced and refusing to do anything about it that lingered in Cecily's mind. Ada spoke to her again and this time she turned but still didn't look at her. "Sorry, love, what did you say?" She closed the door and looked out through the rain-washed window, misted with the warmth within and the chill without.

"I said we'd better look in our depleted wardrobes to find something we can have altered to wear at the wedding."

"One of our old dance dresses, if we haven't given all the most suitable to Jack Simmons. Dress up and paint on the smiles, eh?"

The November weather was typical. Sea mists or heavy fog seemed to be the only variation. The cold, dank air affected Peter badly and when the day of Van and Edwin's wedding drew near, it seemed unlikely he would be well enough to go.

"You and Ada must go," he urged when, on the day, Cecily refused to go without him. "I'll sit here by the fire and hear all about it when you come back."

"I'll miss having you beside me, love."

"I won't have Phil either," Ada reminded her, unaware of the spark in her sister's eyes and the shake of Peter's grey head to stop Cecily retorting with anger. She went on, "We'll have a taxi there and back. It won't seem so bad then. Better than us waiting like lost souls for someone to remember to send a car for us."

The wedding was to be held not in the little church where both Cecily and Ada were married but at the imposing building, high above the town, with its view over the streets and beyond, to the wide expanse of the sea. They arrived early and went into the church, sitting at the back and turning occasionally to watch for the arrival of the various guests.

Both sisters had dressed in blue. Cecily's dress was of mid-blue lace over a darker blue satin. Her hat was full-brimmed with a band of the same material made into a bow with the ends hanging down her back. Her handbag and shoes were old but had been dyed to match the dress and decorated by the addition of some diamante earrings fixed to the sides. She carried a coat over her arm, determined to freeze solid before she would put it on.

Ada's dress was a simple style over which she wore an edge-to-edge coat. Unlike Cecily, she would not defy the cold damp weather although there were many, like Cecily, who did. It was easier, in a time of clothes rationing, to buy a dress than to buy a new coat plus all that went with it. A shabby coat could not be worn for a wedding as important as this one.

Cecily saw Edwin was already there and he raised a hand and blew her a kiss. Then he walked up the aisle, his footsteps hollow in the almost empty place.

"Come, Auntie Cecily and Auntie Ada, you can't sit back here among the stragglers." His tall, heavily built figure stood waiting for them to rise, refusing to accept their protests that they were happiest where they were, and he led them to a place in the second row.

He had changed, Cecily thought. Still big and rather fleshy like his father, especially around the jaw, but there was a greater confidence in him, a purposeful thrust of the jaw. The uniform he wore altered his appearance too, making him no longer the quiet boy who had been Van's constant companion, but a man of importance. She saw from the insignia that he was now a colonel.

Ada wriggled in her seat and turned to look through the rapidly filling pews towards the door. "It's full," she told Cecily. "Look, every seat taken. I've never seen so many people!"

"Some to cheer, most to gossip," Cecily remarked. She didn't turn around.

The procession was breathtakingly beautiful. First the vicar in his traditional robes and carrying a prayer book, then Van. She was dressed in a billowing white gown which floated about her like a sweet-scented cloud, giving Cecily the impression it was all a dream. Her veil reached her chin but was delicate enough to reveal her face in secret loveliness.

Her train spread out behind her and was watched over by no fewer than eight bridesmaids. Two were in differing shades of blue, two in greens, two in creamy yellows and the smallest, being Claire, Willie and Annette's daughter, and one of Johnny Fowler's stepdaughters, in pink.

"A rainbow wedding! Oh, Cecily, how beautiful." Ada was already wiping tears from her eyes and Cecily fought not to do the same.

"It's amazing what can be done with some old muslin," they heard someone murmur.

Another whispered, "It wasn't new, mind, that dress of Myfanwy's. Cut down from Beryl Richards' own it was."

None of the practical investigations about how the difficulties of rationing had been overcome could prevent Cecily from being entranced at the sight. Even when she heard another guest wonder how Van had persuaded the church to marry her, an unmarried mother, in such style, and the remark that the service was a mockery, she could only marvel at her daughter's audacity and style.

She hardly heard a word of the service. She just stared at the beautiful woman who was her daughter, and marvelled at it all. The choir sang while the bride and groom went into the vestry to sign the register and Cecily was called to join them, still feeling that the whole thing was a dream. It was unbelievable, entrancing. The colourful spectacle was a tonic, not only for her but for the people who watched either inside the church or standing in groups around the sombre tombstones and on the street. For them all it was a promise that austerity was over, that ahead lay only joy.

If only Peter were here to see it. That thought kept running through her mind at every new wonder: as the children smiled, as they posed for photographs, as the happy couple kissed to a chorus of giggles from the youngsters.

Walking out of the church, she was sure she spoke to many but she saw none. It was just a sea of faces and her eyes took in only the stunningly beautiful bride and her tall, handsome husband, and the procession of bridesmaids in their fairy-like dresses. Beryl came and handed her the baby and she stood looking down at his round little face, long lashes like fans on his cheeks as he slept through it all.

"If only Peter were here." This time she said the words aloud and it was Gareth who answered her, gaunt, grey-faced and looking much older but with a sparkle in his eyes as he leaned forward and kissed her cheek. "Is Peter ill again?"

"Gareth! When did you come home?"

"I heard about the wedding and I thought I'd make the effort to come."

"But how are you? How is Marged? We thought she'd be here."

"Marged and her new husband are fine."

"What?"

"Yes, Marged married an engineer she met a year ago. They were married in France. Nothing but weddings these days, just like at the beginning of the war."

"Oh, Gareth, it's lovely to have you back. You're the last. Even Jack Simmons turned up although we thought he'd been killed. Now everything's perfect."

He hugged her and the baby, who stirred and opened his dark blue eyes in reproach at the disturbance like an old man, then settled back to sleep.

"He's wonderful, isn't he, Gareth?"

"Takes after his grandmother."

"Now there's a thought, me a grandmother!"

Jennifer came and took the baby and Cecily walked back with Gareth to find Marged and her husband, and Ada, and Gareth's mother.

"About Peter, is it the same trouble you wrote to me about?" Gareth asked.

"Yes. He thought it best to stay at home, but I'm sorry he missed all this." She waved an arm, encompassing all the smartly dressed men and women. The clothes varied from the very out of date to the new, the blatantly altered and ill-fitting to the immaculate and fashionable.

The rainbow colours of the wedding group had separated and spread their brightness among the crowd. Uncle Ben was there in a greasy waistcoat with his wife. Maggie's hat had a hint of mildew around the brim. Johnny Fowler's wife was overdressed but making friends wherever she went, her suit conspicuously like a man's suit, cut and refashioned.

"It's exactly what was needed to show that war is really done and we can go back to enjoying ourselves," Cecily said. "Gareth, love, you know how sorry we are about Rhonwen. But we're so glad you survived to come home safe and sound."

As the wedding party returned to the cars to be transported to Bertie's hotel for the wedding breakfast, Cecily and Ada held back. Gareth tried to usher them into one of the waiting cars but Cecily shook her head.

"No, I won't be going. I have to get back to Peter. I'm never happy leaving him when he's like this."

"We'll all come back with you and show him our finery." Marged appeared at Gareth's side with a young man she introduced as "Martin, my husband".

In the bustle of hurried introductions, Cecily saw only a pair of laughing eyes in a bearded face before being pulled away.

"Come on, let's walk," Gareth said. "They'll catch up with us later. You all right to walk, Mam?" he asked.

320

So they stood and watched as the guests departed in the procession of cars and the well-wishers, the gossips and the downright nosy had moved away, until they were the only ones left. Then they began to walk down the steep hill towards the town centre.

"We should have ordered a taxi," Cecily said, looking back at Mrs Price-Jones in her ancient fur and the black dress beneath it. She looked cold.

"Not for me," the old lady insisted. "I needed some fresh air. God help us, the smell of mothballs nearly did for me! Everyone must have dressed from trunks in their attics!" The laughter was needed and the small group strolled on home.

"Will you come in and see Peter, and stay for a bite to eat?" Ada suggested. "We've got a small tin of salmon we've been hoarding this ages."

The chattering party pushed through the shop door, the bell tinkling its welcome, and Cecily called to Peter. She stopped while they put their coats over the counters and was surprised when Peter didn't appear in the doorway to greet them. She called again. "Peter, my love, we're back and it was beautiful. You should have . . ." She stopped, hands to her face as she saw Peter on the floor. He was unconscious, his face red and shiny, his breathing shallow, hardly visible.

Gareth ran in and knelt beside Cecily briefly, then shouted, "Ambulance! Quickly!"

Cecily lay beside her husband telling him how much she loved him while they waited for the ambulance to arrive.

He didn't regain consciousness in the ambulance or the hospital. He died with Cecily whispering to him, holding his hand, at four the following morning.

There were lights showing at the shop when she stepped out of the taxi and, to her surprise, Gareth and his mother were still there with Ada. Mrs Price-Jones it was who handed her a cup of tea to which brandy had been added, and she drank gratefully. Then, for the rest of that terrible day, she talked.

She talked about how she shouldn't have gone to the wedding, how it seemed that Van had ill-wished her, from the moment she had learned about her illegitimacy, of how it was Ada's fault for not having her crazy husband taken away sooner.

They all let her talk, accepting the accusations, and when she fell asleep it was Gareth who carried her upstairs and put her fully dressed into bed. It was Gareth who took away Peter's pyjamas, which had been placed, waiting for him, on his pillow.

Gareth's mother's reaction was a revelation. She had always been such a difficult lady, keeping her son close and refusing to allow him to make decisions or friends of his own, but today she had been concerned, helpful and filled with pity for Cecily in her grief. Ada wondered whether it was the gentle persuasions of their cousin, Rhonwen, who for a while had been her daughter-in-law that had changed her into the kinder person she now was.

Grief hit Cecily anew when she woke and memory returned. The realization of what had happened slowly filled her mind. She relived the previous day, seeing herself walking away from Peter, laughing and joking, to face the embarrassment of seeing her daughter married, and knowing Van hadn't invited her, didn't want her there. The beautiful wedding, the walk home, no haste. Then the moment when she walked in to tell Peter all about it, and all that had followed.

She stayed in bed, not moving, just staring at the ceiling and trying to pretend it hadn't happened. Her hand strayed across the cold sheets to search for his warmth and when he was not there she began to cry, a wailing cry, calling his name, pleading for him to come back to her.

The day was a nightmare, with people calling to offer their condolences from all parts of the town. The people who worked at the beach came and dozens of customers from his garage and workshop. People for whom he had done work and refused payment came for a final farewell. Uncle Ben and Auntie Maggie called briefly, quoted what they hoped were comforting words from hymns, sang a line or two and departed after promising to sing at the funeral.

Other members of the family came too including Johnny Fowler and his family, and finally, in the middle of the afternoon, when Cecily had given up hope of them appearing, Van and Edwin, who had cancelled their honeymoon to stay for the funeral. Van was pale and subdued and said little as she stood beside Edwin. They didn't stay long and Cecily could see that Van was anxious to leave.

Later that day Van managed to slip away from Edwin to catch the Cardiff train. Gran had to be told.

Edwin saw her leave, wondering, not for the first time, where his wife went on such occasions. This time he determined to find out. What or who could be so important that on the day following their wedding and the death of her stepfather she had to leave the family and go?

She made no attempt to check she was not being followed and as she stepped onto the train, she didn't see Edwin get into the final carriage. The corridor led no further so he felt it unlikely she would see him. Keeping her in sight as she walked swiftly out of the station was no problem either. She led him along bomb-damaged streets to the poorer area where, at a house shored up on one side where a landmine had demolished the rest of the row, she stopped. It wasn't until Kitty Owen answered the door that he stepped forward and confronted her.

"Van! How long have you known where Auntie Kitty lives?" he demanded. He was unaware of the startled shout from the lady he had called Auntie all his life.

"You'd better come inside," Van replied quietly.

Edwin's anger frightened her. She had rarely heard him raise his voice and now he was marching up and down the small room, threatening to crack the weakened walls with his rage.

"How *could* you, Van? What has she been telling you?" he demanded of Kitty, who sat as far into an armchair as she could squeeze, wondering how the quiet boy she remembered had turned into this outraged man.

"Only what I'd guessed," she said, "that Cecily and Ada haven't forgiven me and wouldn't welcome me back into their lives."

Edwin turned again to Van, bending his powerful body in an arch so he could stare into her face and allow the full vent of his anger to show. "I see. *You* decided that for them, did you? Well I can tell you, Auntie Kitty, that Van was the one to invent such unforgiveness. Van's mother is not the sort to harbour grudges and resentment against anyone for years on end. Only her daughter is capable of that!"

Kitty scuttled out to the dilapidated back kitchen to make tea and allow Edwin's anger to subside. She was confused. What if Van had exaggerated Cecily and Ada's resentment? Did it mean she might see them again? Her hands shook as she filled the kettle from the solitary tap on a stand pipe against the outside wall. When she went back into the room, Edwin was still glowering at Van, who sat, shaking, on a chair.

"I've made Van promise to end this disgraceful situation, Auntie Kitty, and face up to her lies before the year is out."

"Thank you, Edwin," Kitty said tearfully. The inadequate remark was all she could manage.

"You've lived here all alone since Paul and his father died?"

"I manage all right," she said, as he looked around the damaged walls and the cracked window pane.

Before they left, Edwin promised to start enquiries about getting the dangerously weakened house repaired or for Kitty to be rehoused. "Something Van should have done," he reminded his still-shocked wife.

"Thank you, Edwin," Kitty said again.

He was silent on the return journey but before he went into the house he held her firmly and told her she had to tell her mother what she had been doing. "You have to face your devils, Van, or you'll never be free of them."

"I can't."

"You have to," was his final word.

Peter's funeral had been almost as large as Waldo's. It had held up the traffic, for it seemed half the town was there to pay their respects to the quiet, kindly man. A number of people came back after the service and crowded into the room above the shop for refreshments. When all but the interested parties had gone, Mr Grainger, now in his eighties, began to explain the bequests in Peter's will.

He began by telling them that the money in his account, after everything was settled, was for his darling wife who had made him so very happy. Next was the house, which he had rented to Johnny and Sharon. "The house is to go to Cecily, but with the hope that she will allow the Fowlers to remain there for as long as they wish."

"Of course," Cecily agreed at once. She smiled at Johnny, who showed his relief by returning her smile.

"The garage is to be shared ownership," Mr Grainger went on. "Peter wishes that you, Cecily, and Johnny Fowler share that responsibility. He believes that

Johnny's enthusiasm and your sound business sense will be a perfect partnership."

Cecily blew a kiss at Johnny. "I'm so glad Peter thought of that. It's what I'd want anyway."

"The cafe at the Pleasure Beach is for Cecily in the hope she will keep it and spend a few afternoons there during the summer and enjoy being a part of the happy season."

The rest of the will contained little of interest, except a sum of money for Willie and Annette. His gold watch was also for Willie, to replace the one he had "lost" during Phil's house-breaking period.

"For young Victor after your time," Cecily suggested.

"He'll treasure it as much as I will."

"Clever Peter," Ada commented when the others had all gone.

"Clever?"

"You've enough money to live on comfortably without bothering with the shop, or anything else for that matter. But he tied you up learning to run a garage and taking over the cafe at the beach."

"He certainly didn't intend me to be idle."

"He knew how much you relish a challenge. You could never settle down to doing 'good works' and living an aimless life. No, he knew you really well, your Peter."

CHAPTER
FOURTEEN

During the weeks following Peter's death, Cecily was kept very busy, as Peter had intended. She spent a lot of time with Johnny at the garage and examining the books of the small, seasonal cafe that had been Peter's hobby rather than a real part of his income. As always, she quickly grasped the main points of each business and was able to pick out areas where improvements could be made. She called on cafe owners and listened to them, absorbing everything of value while appearing to chat aimlessly about the seasonal occupation.

Between visits to her new businesses, she cleaned the shop. It was therapy rather than necessity but she scrubbed the shelves and cleaned out cupboards using a large bar of Sunlight soap and some scouring powder to bleach the wooden boards. She washed walls and polished windows and treated the marble slabs until they looked new. She even whitewashed the stables, where Jack Simmons still kept his horse, Whizzer, and the brightly painted cart.

Jack's shop was thriving. As men returned from the forces and wives began to improve homes in which there had been few changes over the war years, furniture was sold to Jack and replaced by utility furniture as it became available, although it was rationed like so many other commodities. The discarded pieces were eagerly taken by young couples starting out. Tables, chairs, benches and stools as well as buckets and bowls and galvanized washing baths, were taken by Jack for a few pence, cleaned up and sold to new and grateful owners.

With his horse and cart, Jack went out each morning and returned to open his shop in the afternoons but soon found it worthwhile to take on a young boy to help, and it was David — the red-headed boy who had worked for Cecily and Ada until told to leave when Danny's divorce was being discussed — who turned up one Monday morning, full of enthusiasm for the fascinating trade. At times the shop was crammed full of assorted stock, then it would gradually empty. Then Jack would extend his rounds to refill it, buying anything on which he could turn a profit, not resting until it was barely possible to find a path through the clutter to the rooms above, where he lived.

Every afternoon at four, he came in and had a cup of tea with the sisters. He put a notice in his window which read "Dave is here but I'm next door having a cuppa" which made his customers smile as they searched among his eclectic displays for a bargain.

One afternoon, he invited Cecily to see what he had done with the rooms above the shop. He pushed back chairs and sofas and tall bookcases, boxes of saucepans and kitchen paraphernalia to make a path for her through the shop and led her up the stairs, now boasting a thick, only slightly worn carpet, and into his living room.

Cecily was surprised. The room was attractively furnished in good quality items. Not too much, and with every piece set to show to advantage. The windows were draped with velvet, deep red like the carpet and a perfect setting for the seven-piece suite. This consisted of four dining chairs, two armchairs and a chaise longue, all upholstered in rich dark leather.

The room looked out over the docks, the view enhanced by the demolition of several buildings that had blocked the shop in. The dining table was standing near the large window so diners could look out and catch a glimpse of the distant sea.

The bedroom had curtains of green, and a deep fluffy eiderdown and bedspread adorned the double bed. Here too there was an air of opulence Cecily hadn't expected from the man whom she had once refused to employ as an errand boy after he'd been in a fight with Willie.

She praised him fulsomely and admired his excellent taste.

"It's for the wife and my kids, when I find them," he said. "Poor we was, see. But Sally, she always loved a bit of 'posh' she did."

"You haven't had any luck tracing her?"

"Not really — only a few false trails that led nowhere. There's a possibility that she remarried, see, her not knowing I was still alive, so I don't even know her name. Can't blame her, like. She won't be the only one caught in a mess like that. But the Citizens Advice

330

Bureau and the Salvation Army are looking. I know she'll come back to me, her proper husband, when I finds her."

He shook off the serious discussion and went into the small kitchen where a rather old gas stove had been installed, and turned up the jet under a hand-painted, enamel kettle. There was a teapot to match and he set cups and saucers on the table and asked, "You'll stay for a cuppa and a *cwlff*?" He cut a thick slice from the loaf and offered a two pound jar of damson jam, telling her to "dig in". The furnishings were elegant but there was no false image of grandeur about Jack.

"You've done marvellously well here," she began but gave up politeness to concentrate on the food. She spread jam thickly on the *cwlff* and ate with lack of etiquette, biting into the huge, overloaded slice as he did, without cutting it, the jam sliding off and being licked into shape with their tongues, like hungry children.

She and Ada sorted out a number of unwanted items and gave them to Jack, insisting they were gifts, and refusing payment. The treadle sewing machine Ada offered to Sharon who accepted it with delight. They also gave a number of ornaments and cushions and books to a fund collecting to give the little extras to people who had been bombed out and needed the smaller items to help make their houses into homes.

They were sorting out a few things their mother had left behind, when Van called.

"I still miss Mam," Cecily said, fingering one of her dresses that should have been discarded years before.

"So do I," Ada agreed. "When something worries me, I long for her to come, talk to me, promise everything will be all right."

"She'd have helped when Phil was ill, and when Peter died," Cecily added.

"Rubbish, you never need anyone. Too self-contained you are, everyone knows that."

Startled by the vehemence in Van's voice, they stared at her. "You won't remember her," Ada said. "She was someone we could talk to about anything and everything and she always understood."

"She'd make problems go away."

"Stop pretending!" Van stormed out, slamming the shop door and making the bell jangle angrily. Do they know? she wondered. Are they trying to make me feel guilty?

But if they had found out about her visits to Nan they would tell her straightaway, not play games. She hoped that was so, she still needed the secret, she needed to be able to smile and tell herself she had Nan for herself.

The shop was still very quiet. With the stocks having been allowed to run down, it was very difficult to find things to sell, but slowly the customers came back.

"Once summer comes bringing visitors to the town, then we'll see a difference," Ada said, but Cecily didn't expect it to be that easy.

Although customers were few, the stream of visitors to Owen's shop didn't lessen. Bertie and Beryl called often, bringing news of the baby and descriptions of the house which Van had bought and to which neither

Cecily nor Ada had been invited. Johnny brought his family over to tea one Sunday and this became a regular event. With Uncle Ben and Auntie Maggie, Gareth and his mother, and even Dorothy also appearing from time to time for a meal of sandwiches and homemade cake, there was little time to grieve.

The sisters mused over how people had changed. Uncle Ben, white haired, less large and important-looking but still with the booming voice of old. He called with his small but less disapproving wife and offered any assistance in "matters you girls can't manage". He had returned to his easygoing self, always too willing to burst into song or thump out a melody on the piano. Dorothy too found nothing to complain about in the sister's behaviour, and took opportunities to be kind whenever one offered. Gareth's mother seemed to have found a fondness for Cecily that no one would have imagined. War had harmed so many, had touched almost every life with tragedy, but perhaps it made some more content, remembering how much had been lost and how thankful they should be for what they still had.

With Christmas approaching, Cecily sometimes went over to the beach and just wandered, reviving memories of days spent with Peter, and already planning ways of coaxing the stall holders to become customers of Owen's shop again. This Christmas was something to ignore. Without Peter, and with Phil in a hospital for the mentally ill, how could they decorate the house and pretend everything was fine? Then she stopped her tearful thoughts and hurried home to Ada.

"Ada, love. This is the first Christmas of peace, we can't let it slide by as if it isn't important. Whether you are aware of the religious meaning or not, it's still a family celebration. This house has always welcomed family and friends and this year won't be any different. Right?"

"If only Mam would come back."

"If only." Cecily sighed. "It's obvious she doesn't want to or she'd have come for Dadda's funeral, or our weddings, or the birth of Van's baby. No, she cast us aside all those years ago and her coming back to us is a dream we might as well forget."

Whatever the weather during the early days of December 1945, Ada went to see Phil in hospital and Cecily went to the beach where she walked from one end of the promenade to the other. The biting cold winds of early winter helped to blow away the frowns. The buffeting gusts made her laugh, releasing some of the fun that had been locked away since Peter's death. She would smile, remembering other days, other gusting winds and other rainstorms she had shared with him.

One cold, damp Wednesday, she had just reached the bus stop, preferring to be a passenger, the others on the bus making her feel less alone, when the door of the barber's shop opened and Gareth stepped out with his trainee. He was locking the shop when she called to him.

"Where are you off to on your afternoon off? Feel like a blow over the beach?"

"The beach? In this weather? You must be mad, Cecily Owen."

"Why not?"

He grinned and agreed, "Why not?" He called to his apprentice and asked him to take a message to his mother, then stood with her waiting for the bus. They walked together over the deserted promenade, laughing at the wind's attempts to bowl them along with a few discarded pieces of paper. They ate at a cafe at the far end of town but on the following Sunday they met again and this time Cecily took pasties made with potato, onion and a scrap of cheese, and they found a spot sheltered from the wind and ate their simple picnic. They sat and reminisced, looking out to sea and along the sad, empty sands, remembering all that had happened to them since the days when they had danced together.

Ada was on her way back from seeing Phil and began talking to someone sitting beside her on the bus, and by chance she mentioned Jack Simmons and his search for his family.

"Thought he was dead, she did, and married again. At least, she took the man's name. I don't remember any ceremony," she was told.

Excitedly, Ada asked for the name. "Jack wants to find them and understands that, like many others, Sally might have a new husband. They'll sort it out if only he could find her."

"Let me think." The woman was irritatingly slow and Ada was convinced she would reach her stop before the woman remembered. She would stay on, travel to the next town if necessary. "Robbins, yes, I think he was called Bertie Robbins," the woman said at last. Although she knew she wouldn't forget something so important, Ada wrote it down. "You don't know where they lived, do you?"

"Somewhere near a railway station, but I don't know which one. I just remember her saying that the children used to enjoy watching the trains passing."

Ada ran into Jack's shop and called excitedly, "Jack, I think I've found a couple of clues!"

Jack left Dave in charge and went for the bus, intending to start at one station and work his way through them all, as far as Cardiff. He needed a car. Whizzer and the cart wasn't any use for all this wandering. He tried not to get excited, but spent the journey working out the best way of approaching her if he found her. Sally would still believe he had been killed. He was sure of that. She'd have come back to him if she knew he had survived. For him to suddenly appear could be a shock, but how could he approach her without her thinking he was a ghost?

For two days he searched the area around the small railway stations through the town and the smaller places, spending hours knocking on doors, asking passers-by, but no one had heard of a Mrs Robbins who had three children including twins.

"Could you have misheard the name?" he asked Ada, who shook her head.

"I wrote it down." She showed him. "But she might have been mistaken — she did take a long time before coming up with the name. Robbins. Could it have been Robinson?"

"There's a pub called the Railway Inn. Closed now and abandoned, but that used to be nicknamed the Station. Could she have been mistaken about that too?" Jack wondered.

Jack set off again and two days later he found her. The area was very run down and he almost didn't bother to ask, but someone pointed out a place not far from where the railway line ran. A pair of small cottages were near the old public house. Curtains were at the windows, the door stood open and they looked occupied.

He stood at a distance and watched. A small, thin, poorly dressed woman came out and began hanging out washing. It wasn't Sally. Dejected he began to approach her and ask if she knew where he could find his wife, then the young woman called, "Dolly, love, will you bring some more pegs?" And he recognized her voice. Then a child ran out, a young child, too young. Not his.

"Sally?" He almost whispered the name and she looked up and stared, before bursting into tears.

He went into the sad little home, sparsely furnished but surprisingly clean. Clothes hung over a wood fire and there was the smell of something cooking in the oven. He took all this in in seconds, then opened his arms for his wife.

It took a while before they could relax and talk to each other, both unsure what the other would want, but Jack quickly asked the most important question and learned that, yes, there had been someone else but, no, he wasn't there now.

He left, promising to come the following day and talk again. A week later, he went with Whizzer and the cart and brought his family home.

Cecily pestered the warehouses and wholesalers for anything she could sell to encourage lost customers to come in. The shop windows were filled with whatever vegetables she could buy, some tins of fruit were decorated with tinsel tarnished with age and some silver stars cut from the lining of cigarette packets to add some cheer and hide their emptiness.

Jack came in with his wife Sally and their children, Sam, who was eight, and the twins Jennie and Susan, who were seven, and Amy, his little surprise, as he called her, who was two. He proudly introduced them all.

Sally spoke honestly about the man she had lived with and who had left her once he learned about the baby. To their surprise, Jack, who had once had a reputation for fighting, seemed unfazed by the life his wife had led after being bombed out of her home and he showed no difference between his children and his "little surprise".

"There seems to be so much to celebrate this Christmas," Cecily said as the little family trooped out carrying gifts the sisters had found for them. Ada agreed and they began planning how they would fill the two days of that special time.

338

"It will seem like a week off, with Sunday, followed by Christmas Eve, then the two days of Christmas. We'd better get the food planned," Ada said practically, "or we'll have people knocking on the door and nothing to feed them on."

They were woken late that evening by loud banging on the door. On opening it they were surprised to see two policemen there. "Can we speak to Mrs Spencer?" one of them asked.

"Is it Phil?" Ada asked, already looking frightened of what they were going to tell her. "What's happened to him?"

"He's all right as far as we know, but he left the hospital, slipped out when no one was about and we think he might be heading back here."

They were invited in, the two men assuring her that they had no reason to think he'd come to any harm. "He talked about coming home and as you know, Mrs Spencer, he isn't well enough yet, so he must have made up his mind not to wait for the doctors to decide and to come anyway."

It seemed like an echo of what happened when Peter was missing, but this time Cecily made certain that the cellar was properly searched by more than one person. Yet, deeply wrapped in hay, near the horse which he had been so thrilled to see, Phil sat and watched as the search was carried out. As the door closed behind the searchers, Phil crept out and fondled the horse's soft coat and talked to it, telling him all about his journey from the hospital and the places he had stopped to admire the trees and the river and all the things he had missed.

Cecily feared for her safety. He had always disliked her and locking Peter in the cellar was, she believed, a way of hurting her, rather than anger against Peter. She said nothing of her anxiety to Ada and tried to share her sister's concerns for Phil out in the cold darkness. She and Ada sat all night in the small room behind the shop, neither able to consider going to bed to try to sleep.

Morning came and they stood in the shop, looking out at the people hurrying past on their search for something extra to add to Christmas. It seemed like a world to which they didn't belong.

Jack was told and he promised to lock up securely after feeding Whizzer. "I won't be taking the cart out today," he told Ada and Cecily. "I intend to spend the time introducing the children to the shops, buy them clothes and some decent presents."

"How are they, Jack, are they settling in?"

"Slowly. They're surprised at the home I had waiting for them. I'll have to decorate a couple more rooms, though. Sally is very happy to be back with me, although it will take time before she feels she belongs. Plenty of time for all that. I'm just grateful to have them all back, and with Amy, our little surprise. Aren't I the lucky one?"

He wished them luck with their search and hoped Phil was safe, then went to the stable and fed the horse, unaware he was watched by Phil.

340

When Jack had gone, Phil harnessed the horse, his hands delighting in the well-remembered routine. Opening the large sliding doors, he walked the animal out and closed the doors after him, then set off up the lane, walking beside the horse, smiling happily, holding the reins and talking to the patient animal.

They had no reason to check the stable again but Ada went to get some fresh wood for the fire and noticed that neither the horse nor cart were there.

"I thought Jack said he wasn't going out with the cart today?" she said when she returned to the shop.

"He isn't, he's taking the family shopping."

"Well, the cart isn't there and neither is Whizzer."

They told the policeman who was nearby and at once he sent out a message for people to search. "Something as big as a horse and cart can't be hidden for long," he said. "Don't worry, Mrs Spencer, he's obviously all right and we'll catch up with him in no time."

It was Willie who found him. He was sitting near his old home, watching the twins rebuilding the ancient walls, measuring for new windows, chatting to each other about their work. Willie sent one of the twins to tell Ada and went inside to telephone the police. Then he sat and talked to him.

Phil seemed calm and all he talked about was the horse, how much he had loved working with his, before the delivery van had made him redundant. When the police came closely followed by Ada, he smiled, shook hands and asked Ada how she was managing without him. Then, when Ada began to hope that he was well again, he went on to say, "I have to go now, dear, my mother will have dinner ready and you know how anxious she gets if I don't get there on time. Goodbye, Ada, I'll see you tomorrow."

Ada watched as Phil was led away. He was talking to the policemen as though they were friends, and when the ambulance came, he shook hands with them and thanked them for arranging the lift. She went with him but he seemed to be unaware of her presence. Willie followed in her car, to bring her back. Jack collected Whizzer.

She talked a lot when she got back home later that day and Cecily just listened as she reminisced about their marriage, and the fun Phil had been, and gradually seemed to accept that the man she had loved and who had made her so happy was gone from her.

"I'll still visit as often as before and talk about the old days, which is all he seems to remember, but I'll no longer hope for some magical recovery."

"Come on, then, there's still a lot to do before Christmas is upon us," Cecily said brightly. "We still haven't decided how we'll spend Christmas Day."

Edwin walked in two days before the day and invited them to share Christmas dinner with himself and Van and baby Richard. "We've been promised a goose," he said to persuade Cecily, who was hesitating to reply. "Lovely crackly goose. Do come, both of you. Van will be so pleased to have you at our first Christmas."

"Sorry, love," Cecily said. "We'd love to come, but we've made arrangements now." She looked at Ada for support. "Jack Simmons, he's coming for dinner with all his family. And there's Uncle Ben and Auntie Maggie. She isn't up to cooking a big meal any more, and —"

"And we're going to Annette's and Willie's for tea," Ada finished.

So Edwin, out of uniform and dressed in a smart new suit and overcoat, kissed them and wished them both a Happy Christmas. He handed them three parcels, one being for Phil, and left, with disappointment showing in his dark eyes.

"Why didn't you say yes?" Ada asked when he had left the shop. "You should have taken the olive branch when it was offered."

"Not unless the olive branch was offered by Van. Now, we'd better get some invitations out. We don't want to look like Tom Peppers, do we?"

Ada smiled at the expression for liars their mother used.

Van still visited her grandmother but insisted that she was still trying to persuade Cecily and Ada to forgive her and were not yet prepared to meet. Edwin warned her that if she didn't put things right before the end of the year, he would tell Kitty exactly who was to blame. Van didn't know how to end her deceit without admitting her dishonesty, so during each visit she talked about the baby and the shop and said very little about her mother and her Aunt Ada.

Christmas Day passed happily for Cecily and Ada. A fire was lit in the large room above the shop and it was there they set a festive table. Jack and Sally and their children enjoyed the unexpected invitation and tormented Uncle Ben with renderings of Christmas carols sung off-key and with the wrong words. Uncle Ben thumped out his revenge on the piano, playing melodies they hadn't heard for years, bringing poignant memories of childhood. By volume alone, Ben tried to convince Jack he was wrong.

They had a taxi to Annette's and Willie's for a late tea, which Annette served on her beautiful Aynsley china. They came home after midnight, if not happy then content that their day had been spent among people who cared.

On Boxing Day they went to see Sharon and Johnny, their daughters, their three cats, the dog and a goldfish called Gloop. The place was chaos with Sharon trying to dry dishes so she could offer them tea, and watching potatoes boiling over the stove, tripping over the cats and laughing at the attempts of Leonora to dress the dog in pyjamas.

They stayed to admire the children's presents and drink tea made by Ada, during which time she had managed to restore some kind of order to the kitchen, to Sharon's delight. The three girls had made them each a present: a doll each from Victoria made from a dish mop, a handkerchief from Debora and from Leonora a sweet each which she assured them had only been sucked once.

The visit to Peter's old home should have made Cecily sad but it didn't. The chenille cloth was still on the table and the place still lit by gas. The few ornaments he had left were there but carelessly placed as if they had been moved during one of Sharon's infrequent and frantic dusting bouts and left where they happened to be at the end of the onslaught-by-duster!

That they were happy there was no doubt. Laughter rang from the walls and in the middle of Sharon trying to cope, contentment was on every face. Cecily swallowed the lump in her throat and smiled across at Ada, who was separating a kitten from Sharon's knitting.

"Your Peter was so right making it theirs, wasn't he?" Ada whispered.

"He was right about so many things. I miss him very much. But I'm so grateful for the time we did have."

"As I am for the years with Phil." She spoke with a hint of defiance, as if expecting her sister to argue or repeat her accusations about Phil causing Peter's death, but Cecily smiled and nodded. "At least you still have Phil."

"Not really. The Phil I married, the cheerful, cheeky, double-dealing printer, who cheated while he laughed and dared you to prove his dishonesty, he died in that prison. Since they locked him up he hasn't been the same man. He knew he was taking risks when he stole and cheated to buy things for me that I didn't want or need, but he wasn't prepared for the punishment. Taking risks was the 'fun' part for Phil. Being ready for the consequences is another side of it and Phil hadn't reached that level of maturity."

They left the Fowlers to walk home. It was a clear night, chilly, but they were well wrapped against the night air. They passed the house where Danny still lived with Jessie. Cecily didn't even glance at the house but voices reached them clearly and she recognized the now-strident shouts of Jessie arguing with the lower, pacifying tones of Danny, who, it seemed, was neglectful of her. They were both human enough to slow down and listen.

"Willie and Annette! They're your family, Danny Preston! They always have been. Never us, me and your daughter! Hours you spend with them. Apart from sleeping here you're never with us!"

"And why do I stay away? Ask yourself that," Danny retorted. "Damn me, what a Christmas this has been. Dread coming home I do, all this nagging. It's peace I go to Willie's for, Jessie. And you damn well know it!"

The sisters looked at each other and they crouched down and tiptoed past for fear of being seen.

"We've been luckier than some," Ada said. They linked arms and walked on.

When they opened the door, the telephone was ringing in unison with the shop bell. It was Gareth. "Cecily, there's a dance on New Year's Eve, want to come? Ada too, of course."

"Gareth, I'd love to." She discussed it briefly with Ada, who declined, having decided to spend the occasion with Waldo's widow, Melanie.

It was with almost girlish excitement that Cecily dressed in her one reasonably smart dress and sat waiting for Gareth to call for her.

That first Christmas since the end of the war was frenzied in its celebrations. The dance hall was full. The conversations, the greetings between friends, filled the air with the feeling of a new beginning. Many old friends were taking the opportunity to see the New Year in with music, laughter and gaiety. The company was cheerful and full of optimism.

Dancing was not easy. Apart from the slow foxtrot and the waltz it was next to impossible as the floor was crowded and so many were determined to jitterbug their way through the livelier tunes. People filled the balcony looking down on those brave enough to try and dance, feet tapping to the rhythms that visiting Americans had made so popular.

Gareth and Cecily ignored the crush, laughed at the collisions, and stayed on the floor for every dance, improvising where they were met with strange new steps. She thought with momentary sadness that this was one occasion when Phil Spencer couldn't be accused of selling extra tickets to fill his own pocket. He was locked away and would never again see a litho printer or a letter press. At twenty minutes to twelve, Gareth suggested they leave. "Let's make our way to the town hall square and join the crowds there to listen for the chimes," he said.

"I should go back to Ada, she might be on her own. I don't think she'd have spent the whole evening with Melanie."

"We'll go to see her as soon as the chimes end." Gareth promised, then persuaded her to leave the crowded hall. She managed to get to the cloakroom and collect her winter coat and matching hat. She had difficulty finding Gareth again but he was standing at the door, calling, waving. He took her hand and they walked with an increasing trickle of people heading towards the town centre and the big clock.

"I think this coming year could be a special one for many reasons," Gareth said as they strolled along the well-lit streets to where a huge crowd had gathered to watch the clock signal the end of 1945. "For us, I mean," he said. "We've been through a lot since the time our wedding was cancelled. Perhaps now, being older and a great deal wiser and on my part a lot more understanding, we could start again. Who knows, we could reach a time when a wedding wouldn't be unthinkable."

"It's too soon," Cecily protested.

"Oh, I'm not thinking of now, or next month. But perhaps this New Year will be the last we celebrate as two separate people, eh?"

She tightened her grip on his hand, her only reply, but he smiled and bent down to lightly touch her lips with his own.

"Happy New Year, love," he whispered.

The promise, half made, half agreed, lightened their mood further and they began to dance along the pavement with Gareth singing. Soon others joined in and the crowd swayed to the tunes they sang with enthusiasm.

Over the heads of the crowd, Gareth saw the tall figure of Edwin standing beside Van under the brightly decorated Christmas tree.

348

Gareth danced Cecily over to join them, making a path for them without complaints.

"Fancy spotting you two in all this crush," Gareth said, as he and Edwin shared a conspiratorial wink.

Cecily looked at her daughter and said brightly, "A very happy 1946, lovey," as though there had been nothing more than a momentary disagreement between them.

She moved to kiss Van's cheek and was relieved when Van didn't move away. Then as the chimes rang out and the crowd cheered, she was brought to tears as Van kissed her lips and hugged her. Then, disobeying her husband's wishes by only a minute, she said in a tight voice, "Mam, I'm sorry. Revenge doesn't mean anything in the end, only regret and guilt. A Happy New Year."

She hugged her mother again then moved to stand beside Edwin as he said, "There's someone else here waiting for a hug." From behind him a small, nervous woman stepped out. "Come on, Auntie Kitty, give 'em both a hug."

"Mam!" Cecily held her mother's small body against one side, Van against the other. Over their shoulders, Gareth and Edwin nodded approval and they winked to each other again, before wrapping their loving arms around the three sobbing women.

Also available in ISIS Large Print:

Emily Dennistoun

D. E. Stevenson

Emily Dennistoun lives alone with her elderly tyrannical father at Borriston Hall on the Scottish coast. Her mother died many years before, and her younger brother is at Oxford, presented with opportunities that Emily can only dream of. She has few friends and lives through her writing. Then she meets Francis, and despite vicissitudes of fortune, despite uncertainties, loneliness and unhappiness, Emily holds steadfast to a love she knows is true.

Originally entitled *Truth is the Strong Thing*, this has never before been published.

ISBN 978-0-7531-8950-4 (hb)
ISBN 978-0-7531-8951-1 (pb)

Love or Duty

Roberta Grieve

Louise Charlton sees herself as plain and uninteresting beside her vibrant sister Sarah, a talented singer. When she falls in love with young Doctor Andrew Tate she is convinced he is not interested in her. While Sarah sails to America to pursue her musical career, Louise stays at home, duty-bound to care for her selfish manipulative stepmother. Tricked into marrying James, the son of her father's business partner, she tries to forget Andrew and make the best of things. When James reveals his true nature, Louise throws herself into war work to take her mind off her situation. Her life becomes constrained by duty. Then she meets the young doctor again . . . will love win out over duty for Louise?

ISBN 978-0-7531-8940-5 (hb)
ISBN 978-0-7531-8941-2 (pb)

Goodbye to Dreams

Grace Thompson

In a small seaside town popular with summer visitors, Cecily and Ada run their father's grocery shop. Since their mother left them, they have lived above the shop with Myfanwy, a six-year-old they adopted when her parents died. The business is successful with the assistance of friends and Willie, their hardworking stable boy, and their deliveries extend to the stalls and cafes on the beach, where one stall handler, Peter, becomes a close friend. Love for the sisters brings only heartache. Cecily's wedding is cancelled and a secret revealed changes her life forever. Ada is happily married to Phil until disappointment touches her too. Is the growing business the only part of their life to offer them happiness?

ISBN 978-0-7531-8906-1 (hb)
ISBN 978-0-7531-8907-8 (pb)

Gull Island

Grace Thompson

The year is 1917, and Barbara Jones is shocked to be told that she is carrying a child. Her boyfriend is a soldier and there is no one to whom she can turn for support. Indeed, her horrified father sends her away in disgrace when he learns of her condition. Fortunately, the generous Carey family give Barbara a home in a derelict house on a beach near Gull Island, and it is there that her daughter Rosita is born. Gull Island traces the lives of Barbara, Rosita and the Carey family over many years — through wars, hurt, hope and betrayal. When Rosita grows up, she must cope with more than her share of deceit and disappointment — but when she faces danger on Gull Island, those around her find that they are stronger than they ever imagined.

ISBN 978-0-7531-8786-9 (hb)
ISBN 978-0-7531-8787-6 (pb)

Facing the World

Grace Thompson

Sally Travis appeared to have been badly let down by Rhys Martin, who had gone away when under suspicion of burglary. Sally knew he was at college and secretly supported him. She had faced the gossips alone when their baby was born and ignored the worrying rumours about him.

Rhys's father, Gwilym Martin, had lost a leg in an accident but whereas Sally held her head high under difficulties, Gwilym, who had been a popular sportsman and athlete, hid away, unable to face being seen in a wheelchair. But Sally ignored unkind remarks and helped others, especially Jimmy, a young boy put in danger by his parents' neglect during their marital difficulties.

But doubts about Rhys begin to grow. When Rhys finally returned, would she still be waiting? Or had too much happened for things to be the same?

ISBN 978-0-7531-8586-5 (hb)
ISBN 978-0-7531-8587-2 (pb)

ISIS publish a wide range of books in large print, from fiction to biography. Any suggestions for books you would like to see in large print or audio are always welcome. Please send to the Editorial Department at:

ISIS Publishing Limited
7 Centremead
Osney Mead
Oxford OX2 0ES

A full list of titles is available free of charge from:

Ulverscroft Large Print Books Limited

(UK)
The Green
Bradgate Road, Anstey
Leicester LE7 7FU
Tel: (0116) 236 4325

(Australia)
P.O. Box 314
St Leonards
NSW 1590
Tel: (02) 9436 2622

(USA)
P.O. Box 1230
West Seneca
N.Y. 14224-1230
Tel: (716) 674 4270

(Canada)
P.O. Box 80038
Burlington
Ontario L7L 6B1
Tel: (905) 637 8734

(New Zealand)
P.O. Box 456
Feilding
Tel: (06) 323 6828

Details of **ISIS** complete and unabridged audio books are also available from these offices. Alternatively, contact your local library for details of their collection of **ISIS** large print and unabridged audio books.